"You do realize this marriage is just one of convenience for both of us, don't you, Arabella?"

"Of course I do," she shot back, her voice rising. "I don't want to be engaged to anyone, least of all you, and I certainly don't want to be married. Yes, this suits us both. As you said, it saves you from a beating and it saves me from my father's incessant matchmaking."

"And we'll both be free to pursue our interests, free from the other's interference?"

Arabella nodded, and looked around the room at all the beautiful women. Her stomach clenched at the thought of Oliver pursuing his interests with all his *very good friends*. There would be other women in his life, women who he would take in his arms and kiss the way he had kissed her in the dressing room.

She lightly touched her lips, remembering that kiss. After such a kiss she could see why so many women fell under his spell. It had been a kiss that had caused her to forget herself, to abandon all reserve, to want more, so much more.

Author Note

Awakening the Duchess features Arabella van Haven, an American heiress who is an aspiring actress determined to succeed on the London stage.

Her father has other ideas and wants to see her married off to a member of the aristocracy. He wants to acquire connections to the nobility through his daughter and sees acting as a disreputable profession for a woman.

Mr. van Haven was not alone in his attitude to actresses, who were often looked down upon by members of "polite" society.

This negative attitude to actresses has a long history. In Shakespeare's time the idea of a woman appearing on stage was deemed so offensive that female roles were played by young men. It wasn't until King Charles II decreed that it was acceptable for women to act that women could legally perform on stage, but the stigma against actresses continued for many years.

These days it is hard to imagine why the Victorians objected to a woman becoming an actress. It would also be interesting to know what those disapproving Victorians would think if they knew that a member of the royal family would one day marry an actress, and an American one no less.

EVA
SHEPHERD

Awakening the Duchess

Recycling programs for this product may not exist in your area.

ISBN-13: 978-1-335-50543-9

Awakening the Duchess

This edition published by arrangement with Harlequin Books S.A.

For questions and comments about the quality of this book, please contact us at CustomerService@Harlequin.com.

Harlequin Enterprises ULC
22 Adelaide St. West, 40th Floor
Toronto, Ontario M5H 4E3, Canada
www.Harlequin.com

Printed in U.S.A.

After graduating with degrees in history and political science, **Eva Shepherd** worked in journalism and as an advertising copywriter. She began writing historical romances because it combined her love of a happy ending with her passion for history. She lives in Christchurch, New Zealand, but spends her days immersed in the world of late Victorian England.

You can find her on evashepherd.com and Facebook.com/evashepherdromancewriter.

Books by Eva Shepherd

Harlequin Historical

Beguiling the Duke
Awakening the Duchess

Visit the Author Profile page
at Harlequin.com.

To Jacqui for starting me on this journey, and for your continued support and encouragement, and, of course, to Linda Fildew, Bryony Green and the talented editorial team at Harlequin.

Chapter One

London—1893

Oliver Huntsbury, the Fifth Duke of Somerfeld, was not usually a man to run from a fight.

But when faced with five armed assailants, all hell-bent on causing him as much harm as possible, and when one of those assailants was brandishing a knife and threatening to part him from his manhood, there was only one sensible course of action. Run.

So run he did down the backstage corridors of the Limelight Theatre.

He vaulted over props left carelessly lying in his path, dodged past stagehands moving scenery and flew past preening showgirls, their perfume wafting out like a floral cloud, masking the musky smell of the damp building. He ignored the temptation to stop and admire the scantily clad beauties. For once he had something more important on his mind: self-preservation.

'Come here, you guttersnipe, and take your punishment like a man,' Lord Bufford bellowed behind him. The irate peer of the realm raised his knife above his head, causing the corridor to clear immediately of showgirls and stagehands, as if a conjurer had waved his magic wand.

That left Lord Bufford, backed by his four burly henchmen, armed with an assortment of chains, knuckledusters and coshes, at one end of the corridor and Oliver at the other.

So once again he turned and ran. Somewhere in this labyrinth of corridors was Lucy's dressing room. He had to find it before the thugs caught him and stripped him of his most prized possession.

Oliver was loath to hide behind a woman's skirts, but Lucy would provide him with the necessary alibi to prove to these murderous marauders that he could not possibly be Lady Bufford's lover. Not when he had spent every night in the inviting arms of Lucy Baker. At least that's what he hoped the renowned actress would say. He had indeed spent many a night in her lovely arms, with her even lovelier legs wrapped around his waist, but he had also spent the occasional night sampling the abundant charms of Lady Bufford. And, yes, he had been known, on occasion, to have more than one woman at a time in his bed. But even he was not capable of servicing one woman in London while at the same time tupping another woman at her Essex estate.

As long as Lucy vouched for him and said he had spent every night with her, then his beloved body part would be safe. As would Lady Bufford's reputation. While the lady had never been reticent about taking a lover to her bed, she most definitely did not want that fact made public.

And having your lover dismembered by your irate husband would certainly get the tongues wagging. Not to mention putting a damper on your lover's ardour.

Lady Bufford had long ago lost interest in her boorish husband, but she had never lost interest in his money, or the comfortable life and position in society that their marriage provided. If Lord Bufford took the drastic action of petitioning for divorce on the grounds of adultery, it would be the ruin of her and such public shaming was not a fate Oliver wanted for any of his mistresses.

No, he had no choice but to keep running. He increased his speed as he rounded another corner. Where was Lucy's dressing room? He was sure he knew the way. Was he running down the same corridor he had just speeded down? Was he going in circles?

He overturned a rail of brightly coloured costumes, sending it crashing behind him. Hopefully that would slow down his assailants and give him time to think.

Hadn't Lucy mentioned something about taking up another position last time they had been together? He'd assumed she wanted him to get even more adventurous in their lovemaking, but perhaps he'd misunderstood and she'd secured another acting position in a different theatre. He really should pay more attention to what women were saying. He hadn't noticed her on stage during tonight's performance, but his attention had been taken by a new actress, one he hadn't seen before. She certainly had been a delight, with her midnight-black hair, ivory skin and that stunning body. But he should not be thinking of that now. He had to find Lucy. He had to keep running.

'It's blackmail, it's extortion, it's…it's…it's just plain wrong.' Arabella glared at her father, her hands placed firmly on her hips to emphasise her point.

'Call it what you will, my dear, but it's the best offer you're going to get.' Her father stared back at her, his stony face implacable. It was the look Arabella imagined he wore when he stared down any business rival foolish enough to try to get the better of Mr van Haven. Her father hadn't dragged himself up from poverty to become one of America's richest men by being faint-hearted. And now Arabella was on the receiving end of his merciless deal making.

But she shouldn't be so surprised. Hadn't she learnt from bitter experience that her father would do anything to get what he wanted, regardless of who got hurt and that included his only daughter?

'I'm being more than fair. Most men who discovered their daughter had defied them and become a professional actress would not be as forgiving as I'm being. All I'm saying is, you've had your fun and now you're going to have to do what I sent you to England to do: marry a man with a title. And to sweeten the deal, and to make sure you do nothing to undermine my plans, I'll save your precious theatre. It's as simple as that.'

Simple. There was nothing simple about this outlandish proposal. 'Basically, you're going to pay me to get married, or rather, you're going to pay the theatre if I marry.'

Arabella had hoped to shame him. Surely he could

see that blackmailing his daughter into marriage because he wanted the status that came with being related to a member of the British aristocracy was something any decent man would be thoroughly ashamed of.

But his expression showed no shame—instead he sent her a self-satisfied smile. 'Good. Finally you understand what's expected of you.'

Arabella shook her head rapidly, her bottom lip trembling. What was she thinking? Of course he would feel no shame. When it came to financial transactions nothing mattered to him except winning the deal. And in this instance, his daughter's marriage was nothing more than another financial deal to be won.

'I won't do it. I just won't.'

'Oh, yes, you will,' her father said, his voice a calm contrast. 'You can pout all you want. You can even throw a temper tantrum if you must, but you will marry into the aristocracy. And I won't be returning to America until you do. You've let me down once and it won't happen again.'

He drew in a deep breath and exhaled loudly. 'But I suppose I have only myself to blame. I should have known better than to let you come to England with my sister rather than accompanying you myself. All Prudence had to do was chaperon you when you met the man I had arranged for you to marry. But even that was beyond her.' He shook his head. 'And how the Duke of Knightsbrook ended up married to my ward instead of you I'll never know. But now I'm here, so there will be no more of your tricks. You *will* be getting married to a titled man.'

Arabella blinked away tears of anger and frustration. 'How can you possibly do this? It's…it's…'

'It's all for your own good. Left to your own devices you know you'll make the wrong choice—haven't you already proven that? So now you will do as you're told and I will generously inject the necessary money into this theatre. And if you're not convinced by that offer, I believe you should consider the alternative. You will have to come back to America with me on the next ship. You will never act again, even in amateur productions, and this theatre you inexplicably love so much might struggle on for a few weeks more at its present dismal level, before sinking without trace and all your new friends will be without a job. And unlike you, I doubt if any of them has a rich father to support them. Would you really see them thrown out on the streets, without money, without a job?'

'It's despicable, simply despicable,' Arabella muttered under her breath, sorrow clenching her heart. She could not stop acting, it was the one thing she lived for. Nor could she deny the theatre the chance of survival. It desperately needed more funds for advertising, for better props and scenery. Tonight's house had been less than half-full and, now that their leading lady, Lucy Baker, had left them for brighter prospects, they had also lost their main drawcard. The theatre desperately needed more money if it was to survive.

But this? Marriage? And to a man of her father's choosing. It was too much to ask.

'I can see you're upset, my dear, so I'll make you one concession.'

Arabella's tense shoulders eased slightly and she waited for him to throw her a lifeline.

'It can be any sort of title. I'm not that fussy. Duke, earl, viscount, even a baron will do, as long as you become Lady Something.'

Arabella's mouth almost dropped open and she stared at him in disbelief. It was hardly a concession. No matter how you looked at it, she was expected to sell herself in marriage to any man with a title to satisfy her father's need for self-aggrandisement. Being one of the richest men in America was not enough for him. Now he was going to use his daughter to get the social status that he'd always felt he lacked because he had been born poor. She was going to be sacrificed on the wedding altar just so that her father could feel superior in status as well as financially to those snobs back in New York. It was unconscionable.

'Oh, stop sulking, Arabella,' he barked at her. 'It's the first thing I've ever asked of you after a lifetime of indulging your every whim. Haven't I always given you everything you've ever wanted?'

Arabella continue to stare back at him, too shocked to answer. Yes, he had given her everything she could ever want in terms of material goods—fine clothes, expensive jewellery, music lessons, singing lessons and more—but as for affection, attention, they were areas which he'd severely neglected.

'I even forgave you when you acted in those little amateur shows back in New York, but I never thought you'd be so simpleminded as to do it professionally. Hopefully the substantial amount of money you'll bring to any marriage will counter the damage you've already done to your reputation. But now that I'm here in England we can put all this nonsense behind us. Once you're married you'll be a lady, living the life of luxury on your country estate, and all this acting nonsense will be forgotten.'

The ground wobbled under Arabella's feet. She wouldn't do it. She would not give up the life she loved and she'd find some other way to save the theatre that didn't involve her being sold off like a piece of chattel. She had worked so hard to get this acting job. It hadn't just taken skill as an actress, but had also involved scheming and planning so she could attend rehearsals without Aunt Prudence knowing. Her subterfuge had become more complicated when her father had arrived in England to attend his ward's wedding to the Duke of Knightsbrook. But she had succeeded. That is, until tonight.

'I mean you were born for better things than this,' he continued, looking around her tiny dressing room with distaste. He scraped a piece of flaking cream paint off the wall with his thumbnail, further exposing the rough grey plaster underneath, then glared at the dressing table with its split timber and tarnished mirror, and the racks of costumes and props cluttering up the corners.

It might be small and, yes, perhaps a little shabby, and it was unfortunate that it doubled as a storeroom, but Arabella was pleased to have a real dressing room in a professional theatre, to have her first part on the London stage, even if it was a minor role.

And she'd much rather be in this shabby dressing room than being bored to death at the tedious balls and social events that a woman of her class was expected to attend. Thanks to her father's constant absences she had been able to avoid most of the events hosted by New York society. And since her arrival in London, she had been given almost free rein. Her hypochondriac Aunt Prudence took to her bed most days with one imagined illness after another, and Nellie, her lady's maid, was more a friend than a servant and would do anything she could to help Arabella achieve her dream.

It had been her dream since she was a child to make her own way in the world as an actress. And now that she was on the cusp of achieving that dream, she would not have it snapped away from her by her father. She just had to find a way to do what countless businessmen and politicians had failed to do and get the better of her father, the notoriously ruthless New York banker, Mr van Haven.

The door flew open and Arabella's attention was drawn to a tall, blond-haired man barging into the room. Every inch the dashing leading man, he was staring straight at her with those deep brown eyes and heading in her direction, fast.

'There you are, my darling,' he said, sending her a roguish smile.

Before she could register who he was or what was happening he grabbed her firmly around the waist, tipped her backwards until one leg was off the ground and kissed her.

A gasp escaped Arabella's lips and she clung on to the stranger to stop herself from falling backwards. Although with him holding her so tightly falling was the least of her worries.

This was an outrage. She should stop this. Immediately.

So why didn't she? Was it because it felt strangely comforting to be held in his strong arms? Or was it because his fresh masculine scent, all musk and leather with the hint of a citrus shaving soap, was somewhat enticing?

She melted into his arms, her body moulding against his in a perfect fit. It was as if this was where she was meant to be.

No. That was ridiculous. This was not where she was meant to be. This had to stop. Right now. Especially as his tongue was running temptingly along her bottom lip, causing her to part her lips so she could fully appreciate the experience.

No. This was outrageous. She had to put a halt to this before he deepened the kiss. Stop it before she started kissing him back. She ran her hands through his tousled hair, telling herself it didn't matter how good his lips felt on hers. It didn't matter how nice it was to be held so closely. No, it didn't matter at all.

He pulled her in even closer, causing her to dissolve against his body. His strong body. How could she not fail to register the muscles of his chest? Hard, firm, powerful muscles.

Oh, yes, this was wrong. So wrong. But it felt so right to be kissed in such a manner. When that double-crossing Arnold Emerson had kissed her, it had been nothing like this. This time she was in the arms of an expert. Opening her mouth wider, she relished the masculine taste of him, loving the feel of his skin rasping against her cheek. She had no intention of stopping this pleasure. Not when she was enjoying herself so much.

But he had other ideas. He lifted her upright, back

on to two feet, and sent her a quick wink and the most devilish smile she had ever seen. She stared back at him as if in a daze. Blinked to clear the fog, then looked over at her father and waited for his outburst.

Her father would now do what she should have already done. He would reprimand this man in no uncertain terms for taking such a liberty with a woman's virtue.

But her father said nothing. Instead he took his time to scrutinise the stranger. Arabella watched expectantly as his gaze moved over the man's well-tailored three-piece black evening suit. He smiled as he looked at the solid gold chain of his fob watch suspended between his pockets, the mother-of-pearl cufflinks. His smile widened. Arabella could see he was staring at the large gold signet ring on the man's index finger, etched with a coat of arms. He then turned to the ruffians loitering at the door and his smile grew so wide he was baring his teeth, like a wolf who has spotted a tethered lamb.

'I'm Mr van Haven,' he said, extending his hand to the stranger. 'And after a kiss like that I can only assume that you are my daughter Arabella's fiancé.'

The stranger looked at her father, then over his shoulder at the ruffians, then back at the extended hand. 'Indeed, I am, sir. And I'm very pleased to finally make your acquaintance,' he said, giving her father's hand a brisk shake.

Chapter Two

The phrase out of the frying pan and into the fire seemed disastrously apt, as Oliver continued to shake the smiling American's hand while glancing back at the scowling Lord Bufford.

And it was a fire he was going to have to extinguish as quickly as possible. Being engaged was not for him and marriage was most definitely out of the question. Like his father before him, he was not a one-woman man. But unlike his father he would never subject any woman to the pain of being married to an unfaithful husband. He had vowed never to hurt a woman the way his father had hurt his mother and had sworn off marriage many years ago. That was why he only got involved with women like Lady Bufford and Lucy Baker, women who played by the same rules as him. Keep it fun, keep it casual and never expect commitment.

He looked over at the young woman he was now supposedly engaged to. She was certainly beautiful, the sort of woman many men would be happy to call their wife. But right now, his supposedly future wife was looking as disorientated as he felt.

Her long, slim fingers were gently touching her full red lips, her face was flushed a delightful shade of pink and those big blue eyes were quickly flicking from him to the older man and back again.

It was the same actress he had admired during this evening's performance. The one whose acquaintance he was hoping to eventually make, although most definitely not under these conditions.

It was obvious they were father and daughter. Both had jet-black hair, although the father was greying at the temples, and both had those blue eyes, although on the daughter they gave her a soft, gentle appearance, while on him the eyes were icy blue, accentuating his shrewd, calculating demeanour.

It was also obvious the father was up to something, but whatever it was, for now, it seemed, the plans of Mr van Haven would serve Oliver's needs as well.

He sent the young beauty a silent apology for what he was about to do and hoped that she would not just forgive him, but would also play along.

'Arabella has probably already told you all about me, but allow me to formally introduce myself,' he said, still clasping the American's hand. 'I'm Oliver Huntsbury, the Duke of Somerfeld.'

'A duke? Well, well, a duke,' Mr van Haven purred, his piercing eyes boring into Oliver's. 'My daughter really has made a good catch. We'd better be careful to make sure you don't get off the hook. So, are you going to introduce us to your friends?'

They both looked towards the menacing presence looming at the door.

Friends? That was an exaggeration if ever Oliver had heard one. 'Yes, of course. May I introduce Lord Bufford and his associates: Joe Butcher, Frank Thugger, Arthur Scarmaker, and Fred Killerman.'

Mr van Haven nodded a greeting, but got a line of scowling black looks in response. Perhaps Lord Bufford's associates didn't like the names he had assigned them, but at least they had the decency to hide their weapons behind their backs.

'Lord Bufford is Lady Bufford's husband,' Oliver continued, looking in Arabella's direction and giving her his most beseeching smile. She might not be Lucy Baker, but he could only hope she was as equally good an actress and would indulge in a bit of improvisation.

'Lady Bufford and Arabella are the best of friends,' he continued, turning to Lord Bufford. 'The two of them have spent many an evening together, gossiping the night away. I've felt quite neglected, I must say.'

'We have?' the American beauty asked. He sent her another pleading look and tilted his head in the direction of the door.

'Oh, yes, we have. Your wife is quite a delightful companion,' she added, giving Lord Bufford a tentative smile.

Oliver smiled with relief. He had his alibi. Hopefully now that would mean the departure of Lord Bufford and his murderous entourage. And his own departure. As much as he would like to get better acquainted with the young, black-haired actress, and as much as he'd like a repeat performance of that kiss, it was a pleasure he would have to forgo. This situation was complicated enough already. It was time to simplify things by exiting, stage right.

'As we're all such good friends I'm sure Lord Bufford and his associates would like to join us for a late supper so we can celebrate my daughter's engagement to the Duke of Somerfeld,' Mr van Haven said smoothly.

Oliver's smile faded. It seemed his departure was going to have to be delayed a while longer.

All three turned to look at Lord Bufford, whose lips curled back in a menacing sneer.

'We'd be delighted,' he growled, staring straight at Oliver.

Mr van Haven patted Oliver on the back. 'Right, Lord Bufford, you and I will go and find a couple of carriages to take us all to the Savoy, and while we're doing that you can tell me all about my future son-in-law.'

The four thugs turned to follow Lord Bufford and Oliver could see an opportunity to escape opening up. A quick apology and maybe a goodbye kiss to the young actress and he'd be off.

Mr van Haven held up his hand to halt the thugs' progress. 'Oh, no. You four can wait here. We won't be long.' He sent what could only be called a triumphant smirk in Oliver's direction. 'You can chaperon my daughter and the Duke while we're gone.'

Chaperons? More like prison wardens.

With a sinking heart Oliver saw his opportunity to escape close off. It seemed only an unwise man would underestimate Mr van Haven—the man was a veritable mind reader. And he had made sure that

Oliver would continue to be engaged to be married to his daughter, at least for a while longer.

Arabella stared at the stranger, this Duke of Somerfeld, her fiancé. He sent her an apologetic smile, a smile that was difficult not to warm to. It lit up his face and drew her eyes to his full, sculptured lips.

She was determined to be angry with him. This man who was obviously trouble with a capital T. But it was hard to maintain that anger while gazing into tawny-brown eyes that sparked with mischief, and a face so handsome that he should be on the stage. Arabella's appraising gaze took in the small crinkles round his eyes, lines that showed he laughed a lot. She moved to his strong jawline with the hint of stubble, then back up to his lips, those lips that had kissed her into a state of oblivion.

At the time, it had felt as though he was kissing her as if his life depended on it. Now it was apparent that was not far from the truth, if the murderous looks of the four burly brutes still looming at the door were anything to go by.

Arabella gave herself a small shake. There was no point thinking of that kiss now. This was an impossible situation and they had to find a way out of it.

She stepped towards him and his smile changed from apologetic to appreciative. Arabella ignored both that look and the way her heart was beating harder now that she was so close to him. So close she could feel the warmth of his body. So close that his masculine scent was once again filling her senses.

'So, who are you really and what are you doing in

my dressing room?' she whispered so the ruffians at the door wouldn't hear.

He raised an amused eyebrow. 'I really am Oliver Huntsbury, the Duke of Somerfeld, and I apologise for my somewhat unconventional entrance. I was looking for Lucy Baker.'

Arabella's spine straightened and she tilted up her chin. 'Oh, I'm sorry to disappoint you.' She heard the offended note in her voice and mentally kicked herself. Who cared if it was Lucy Baker he had meant to kiss? He just shouldn't have kissed her. He shouldn't be in her dressing room and he most certainly should not have agreed to be her fiancé.

'Believe me, I am not disappointed, anything but.' He smiled at her again, that heart-stopping, devilish smile that made his eyes dance with amusement. 'But you do deserve an explanation.' He nodded in the direction of the door. 'Lord Bufford and his associates have taken exception to my friendship with Lady Bufford. They were threatening to commit extreme acts of violence on my various body parts, so I was looking for Lucy, who is also a good friend, hoping she would provide me with an alibi to prove my innocence.'

Arabella's posture became more rigid, her lips more pinched. 'I take it Lady Bufford and Lucy Baker are actually more than just your *good friends*.' She hadn't meant to sound quite so judgemental. After all, this man meant nothing to her, so why should she care who he was or wasn't good friends with?

He ran his hand along the back of his neck. 'Well, yes, you could say that.'

Arabella huffed her disapproval. One of her questions had been answered. When he kissed her, she had suspected she was in the arms of an experienced man, a man who knew how to please a woman. And that was quite obviously the case. It explained why she had reacted to him the way she had. It was not her fault. It was simply his technique and experience that had caused her uncharacteristic response.

It also explained the high opinion he appeared to have of himself. His confident countenance was definitely that of a man who knew he could easily seduce any woman he chose. But she wasn't so easily impressed by a handsome face and a strong, masculine body. Nor would she swoon just because she had been kissed until she almost lost all ability to reason. No, none of those things would deter her from thinking he was just a rake, a man of no substance, to whom no sensible woman would give a second thought.

She placed her hands firmly on her hips and tilted her head to emphasise just how much he was not affecting her. 'Well, Lucy no longer performs at the Limelight Theatre. But that doesn't mean you can just burst into the dressing room of any woman you choose and…and…' She waved her hand in the direction of the place where he had taken her in his arms.

'And kiss her.' He sent her another devilish smile. 'You're right, that was a terrible affront to your virtue and I apologise if I upset you.'

Good, at least he had the decency to apologise, but that charming smile seemed to make a lie to any claim of regret.

'Just because I'm an actress doesn't mean you can treat me disrespectfully. People make all sorts of assumptions about actresses and they're just plain wrong. Most of us are respectable women who take our art form seriously.' It was an argument she had also had with her father, but it had fallen on deaf ears.

He nodded his agreement. 'Yes, I know, and I can see that you are a talented actress. I saw your performance tonight, very impressive.'

Arabella's hands left her hips. Her body relaxed and she couldn't help but beam with pleasure as warmth rushed through her. 'You saw my performance tonight? Really? And you enjoyed it? It's only a small part, but I do appear in every scene and have lines in most of them.' She was burbling, but couldn't stop herself, it was so delightful that he had noticed her on stage.

'You're a natural. And you certainly gave a stunning performance here in the dressing room, too. I've never been kissed with such conviction by a total stranger.'

The warmth engulfing her turned to a fiery blush, exploding on her cheeks. 'Well, you…you…caught me off guard. I was still in character. I was still acting. I was continuing to act as if I was still on stage. That was all.'

He gave a mock frown. 'Didn't you play a vestal virgin in tonight's play?'

Arabella shrugged, her cheeks still burning. 'Anyway, that doesn't explain why you pretended to be my fiancé,' she said sharply, hoping to move the conversation away from her overly enthusiastic response to his kiss.

He rubbed the back of his neck again. 'I'm sorry about that as well. At the time my choices were, become engaged or become the victim of a violent

crime. And engagement seemed the less painful option.' He grimaced slightly. 'Forgive me, but I have
no intention of marrying anyone.'

Arabella flicked her hand to dismiss his excuses.
'I'm not stupid. I realise that. And I have no interest in getting engaged either and even less interest
in being married. It's all my father's idea. He wants
me off the stage and married before he returns to
America. It doesn't matter who my husband-to-be is,
or what he's like, as long as he's got a title. It seems
you fit the bill.'

He stared at her, his brow furrowed, concern in
his eyes. 'And what of your mother? What does she
have to say about this?'

Arabella gave a little shrug and ignored the hard
lump that had formed in her chest. 'My mother is
dead.'

'Oh, I'm so sorry.' He placed his hand lightly on
her arm.

She shrugged again. 'It was a long time ago.
Twenty-one years.'

He gave her an intense look and she could see him
gauging her age and doing the calculations. Yes, she
was twenty-one and, yes, her mother had died mere
months after she was born, leaving her in the care
of a man who had little interest in his daughter. And
that lack of interest had continued throughout her life.
It was only now that he could see how much use a
daughter would be for advancing his position in both
English and New York society that she had suddenly
become something worth having.

'That must have been very hard for you,' he said.

Arabella shook her head. 'Well, I'm sure if she was

alive, she wouldn't want her daughter married off to just any man. But my father doesn't care who I marry and he's not going to relent until I've got a title. But that doesn't have to be your problem.'

He raised his eyebrows and looked towards the door, then back at Arabella and exhaled loudly. His look appeared to be saying that, for now, it was his problem as well.

'When does your father intend to return to America?'

'As soon as he gets me married off, which he's going to want to do as quickly as possible. He's already been away from his precious bank for over a month. I doubt if he'll be able to bear to stay away much longer. He's already starting to pine for the smell of freshly minted dollar bills.'

He tapped a thoughtful finger against his sensual lips. 'Then leave this to me. I think I can save both of us from an unwanted marriage, while getting your father off your back for the foreseeable future and saving my valuable body parts from dismemberment, all at the same time.'

Chapter Three

The four thugs were starting to look bored. One thug was absentmindedly running his hand back and forth along his knuckleduster, another was tapping his cosh rhythmically against the door jamb. The third was repeatedly cracking the knuckles in his gnarled hands and, perhaps most surprisingly of all, the fourth one had wrapped a feather boa around his thick neck and was running his hands over the satin and silk fabric on the racks of brightly coloured costumes.

Oliver was unsure whether a bored thug was more dangerous than an angry one, but he didn't appreciate being in the company of either.

He knew that at some stage he could make an escape from Lord Bufford's henchmen, but that wouldn't solve the problem of the delightful Arabella van Haven. What her father was planning to do to this talented young actress was inexcusable. It was reprehensible to sell her off in marriage to any passing man, just because he had a title. And now it appeared he was in a position to save this rather enchanting damsel in distress, as well as saving his own skin and preserving Lady Bufford's reputation. In anyone's estimation that had to count as a good night's work.

As long as the thugs didn't get so bored that they needed a bit of entertainment, in the form of carrying out Lord Bufford's threat to his precious body part, he would be safe.

The four thugs all looked in his direction, as if reading his thoughts. The rhythm of the cosh thumping against the door jamb increased, accompanied by the sound of a knuckleduster being smacked into a fist and knuckles being cracked. This thumping beat of their weapons was not reassuring. When the fourth thug unwound the feather boa and tugged on it hard, as if testing its use as a garrotte, Oliver knew he was in trouble.

Mr van Haven and Lord Bufford entered the room and he released a surreptitious sigh of relief. He had never been happier to see the husband of one of his mistresses.

'All right,' the American said, rubbing his hands together. 'The cabs are ready and waiting so let's all depart for the Savoy and a spot of supper.'

Whatever Lord Bufford and Mr van Haven had been discussing during their absence it had obviously pleased the American banker. His wolfish smile had grown even more predatory. Presumably Mr van Haven was now even more certain he had Oliver right where he wanted him. That was heading up the aisle and tying the matrimonial knot with his daughter.

Marriage or a beating by four thugs and the loss of a vital body part—what a choice. Oliver suspected marriage would be the greater torture and both would be a threat to his manhood. But if his plan worked, he would have to suffer neither fate.

He looked around the room. Everyone was staring at him, waiting for his response, and none of the expressions was friendly. Five people wanted to tear him limb from limb and one wanted to use him for his own purposes. Only Arabella meant him no harm. She was the only completely innocent person in the room. He could not see her suffer. No matter what happened tonight, he would make sure he saved her from her father's outrageous plan of marrying her off to him.

'Excellent,' Oliver replied. 'Supper at the Savoy to celebrate our engagement sounds like a splendid idea. And I couldn't wish for better company.' He gave a small bow to the assembled party and received matching scowls of murderous intent from Lord Bufford and his henchmen, a resigned sigh from Arabella and a smug look of satisfaction from Mr van Haven.

He turned to Arabella. 'Let me help you into your coat, my dear.' Oliver lifted a jacket from the coat stand and held it open for her, but got a suspicious, narrow-eyed glare in return. 'Trust me,' he whispered in her ear. 'Before tonight I will have saved us both from the unwanted state of matrimony.'

She gave him another distrusting look, but turned her back to him and allowed him to slip the coat up her arms and over her slim shoulders.

He paused for a moment before he let her go so he could take a second to reacquaint himself with the scent of jasmine. It was the perfume he had inhaled when he had kissed her, fresh and youthful, just like the wearer.

Disappointment jolted through him as she broke away and picked up her reticule. After tonight he would not be holding her in his arms again, would not be kissing her, would not inhale her wonderful scent. But it had to be that way. It was the right thing to do.

He offered her his arm. 'Right, lead the way, Mr van Haven,' he said in his most cheerful voice as if he hadn't a care in the world.

The motley group left the dressing room and headed out the back door of the Limelight Theatre, where two carriages were waiting. Oliver helped Arabella into one and Lord Bufford and his angry mob entered the other.

Some jostling ensued between Mr van Haven and Oliver, until it became apparent to Oliver that he was expected to sit in the middle rather than Arabella, as manners would normally dictate. Presumably Mr van Haven was determined to stop Oliver from throwing himself out of the moving carriage and making his escape.

With a tap on the roof from Mr van Haven's silver-handled walking stick, they were off, winding their way through London's dark streets. The cab rattled over the broken cobbles, juddering the three occupants, something Oliver could hardly complain about as it caused Miss van Haven's legs to rub against his in a rather pleasant manner.

The ride became somewhat smoother as they approached the more affluent city centre. Under the modern electric street lights, fashionable men and women were climbing in and out of carriages and cabs, and some couples were walking along the West

End streets, taking advantage of the mild summer night-time air.

The Savoy appeared before them, the golden glow of its newly installed electric lighting illuminating the surrounding street, drawing them towards its promise of luxury.

The carriages stopped inside the courtyard and the ill-matched party disembarked and headed towards the doors of the hotel. The thugs for once were looking more ill at ease than Oliver as they adjusted their rough clothing with anxious fingers, straightened their spines and followed Mr van Haven and Lord Bufford inside the foyer.

The maître d' recognised Mr van Haven and immediately ushered them to an alcove, where they seated themselves on the plush sofas. 'Champagne all round and keep it flowing,' the American called, causing the maître d' to click his fingers at the nearest waiters.

As if by magic, silver champagne buckets arrived and with a flourish the maître d' poured the wine. When he departed, with much backward bowing, Mr van Haven raised his champagne flute and offered a victorious toast. 'To the Duke of Somerfeld and the future Duchess of Somerfeld.'

A quiet, unenthusiastic murmur went around the table. It seemed the assembled guests cared as little about the engagement as Oliver and Arabella did.

The four thugs quickly emptied their glasses. A waiter rushed forward and refilled them, which were downed in equal haste. The waiter lifted the bottle out of the ice bucket and almost dropped it when one thug growled for him to leave it.

At least the thugs were making the most of the occasion, Oliver smiled to himself as he sipped his drink.

'We should make the announcement as soon as possible and hold the engagement party next weekend,' Mr van Haven said, frowning slightly as the thugs continued to swill his expensive champagne as if it was cheap cider. 'I'm sure you will be available to host the engagement,' he added, turning his attention to Oliver. 'It will give me the opportunity to meet your family and to see your estate.'

His new fiancée rolled her eyes. 'That's a bit short notice, isn't it, Father? One week.'

'Nonsense. That's all right with you, isn't it, Son?'

Oliver smiled at the American's presumption. He presumably wanted it hosted at his estate so he could make sure that Oliver actually turned up for his own engagement party. 'Of course it's all right. Nothing would please me more.'

'And you are cordially invited, Lord Bufford,' the American added with a pointed look at Oliver.

Lord Bufford bared his teeth in what was presumably a smile. 'Nothing will stop me from attending Somerfeld's engagement party. And I will of course be bringing my wife. I can't wait to tell her that he's about to be married.'

He clicked his fingers at the now slightly tipsy thugs and they rose unsteadily to their feet. 'Thank you for your hospitality, Mr van Haven,' Lord Bufford growled. 'But if you'll excuse me I'm anxious to return to my wife and tell her the good news.' With that he bowed to Arabella, sent another angry glare in Oliver's direction and left the table. The four thugs staggered behind him, but not before one had grabbed a dripping bottle of champagne from the ice bucket.

'What charming fellows,' Oliver remarked. 'It's a shame they had to leave so early.'

'And I think we should start organising the wedding immediately, so it can be held as soon as possible,' Mr van Haven said, grabbing another wine bottle and refilling their glasses.

Oliver adopted his most concerned expression. 'Oh, no. I'm afraid that won't be possible. Won't be possible at all.'

The American paused, the bottle suspended in mid-air, Oliver's glass only half-full. 'And why not?' he barked and looked towards the door, as if intending to call back the tipsy thugs.

'There's the codicil on my title to consider.'

'The what?'

'Yes, the codicil,' Oliver said, taking the bottle from Mr van Haven's hand and filling up his glass. 'It's a clause in a will that...'

'I know what a codicil is, man,' he snapped. 'But why should it stop you from marrying my daughter?'

Oliver took a sip of his champagne while the older man's face turned a shade that could only be described as beetroot red. 'If I get married before I'm thirty-five, I lose my title, the estates, everything. That means, unfortunately, if your daughter is to become my Duchess, she will have to wait for seven years. But at that time I'd be honoured to make your beautiful daughter the Duchess of Somerfeld.' He raised his glass towards Arabella, smiled and drank it all.

She sent him a delightful, appreciative smile in return and turned to face her father.

Her father glared at her across the linen-covered table, his mouth twitching with anger, a dark flush moving up his face, from his neck to his hairline.

Arabella knew it would be wise to not react so obviously to this victory over her father, but she couldn't stop her smile from growing larger and larger.

Her so-called fiancé had done what business tycoons, bankers and politicians on both sides of the Atlantic had been unable to do. He had got the better of the ruthless Mr van Haven. And the pleasure of watching someone finally succeed where so many had failed was infinitely satisfying, especially after what had happened with Arnold Emerson back in New York.

In both cases the result had been Arabella not getting married. But this time it was her fiancé who had saved her rather than abandoned her. Oh, yes, this was a victory to celebrate and she raised her glass to Oliver and took a jubilant sip.

Her father continued to scowl. 'You can't marry before you're thirty-five?' His usual barking voice had taken on an uncharacteristically high pitch.

'Of course, I can marry at any time I want,' Oliver said, refilling everyone's champagne glasses. 'But if I marry before I'm thirty-five I lose my title, as will my wife, and of course we'll have no money. And, as I've never actually had to work for a living, I'm not sure how I'd make any more.' He looked over at Arabella and gave a mock frown. 'What do people actually do when they have to work for a living?'

She smiled as if he had asked a delightfully absurd question, raised her shoulders and shook her head. 'I'm sure it won't come to that,' she said, 'because my father can see now that there's no point us getting married after all. Can't you, Father?'

She glanced at her father, who was looking from one to the other, his brow deeply furrowed. He slowly flicked the side of his champagne glass as he silently contemplated this development for a moment. 'I suppose an engagement to a duke isn't to be sneered at,' he said quietly. 'It's still an engagement to a member of the aristocracy. Even if it does last seven years.'

He looked up at the pair of them. His wolf-like smile returned and Arabella's stomach fluttered with unease.

'Right, that's settled,' he announced decisively. 'We'll hold the engagement party next weekend. We'll announce your engagement in all the relevant newspapers, both here and in New York, and in seven years you'll be married, and my daughter will be the Duchess of Somerfeld.'

Arabella's smile died and her shoulders slumped. She wasn't going to get her victory after all. Her father still expected her to get married, eventually.

But what had she expected?

The last time she had fought her father about a man it had been over that treacherous Arnold Emerson. Her father had insisted that Arnold was just after her money, but Arabella was certain that the charming, handsome actor was in love with her, just as she was in love with him.

But she had been so wrong.

All it had taken for her father to prove his point

was for him to offer Arnold a substantial amount of money to take his amorous attentions elsewhere. He had immediately disappeared, out of Arabella's life, without even saying goodbye.

It had been devastating and humiliating and had shaken her faith in men and her own judgement.

But this time it was different.

She might know little about men, and she might have got it so wrong with Arnold Emerson, but even she could see that Oliver Huntsbury was not the man for her. Yes, he was stunningly good looking, with a devilish smile that could turn a woman to jelly, but he was an obvious womaniser. Not the sort of man any right-thinking woman would ever consider marrying.

But then he didn't want to marry her just as much as she didn't want to marry him. This time she had an ally in her fight against her father.

She looked down at her champagne glass and chewed the edge of her bottom lip. Perhaps this wasn't so bad. She was going to have to get engaged, yes. But a seven-year engagement was better than a marriage. And seven years was a long time. Her father would not want to stay in England that long. And with her father safely back in America and out of her life she would have seven years to dedicate to furthering her acting career. Seven years of glorious freedom, with only the easily duped Aunt Prudence as chaperon. And seven years for her and the Duke to think of a way out of this marriage.

No, it wasn't a complete victory, but they had won a decisive first battle.

Arabella raised her head, smiled and reached out her hand towards her father. 'All right, Father. The

Duke and I will become engaged, we'll marry in seven years, and in exchange you'll follow through on your promise and save the Limelight Theatre. And that is the best deal you're going to get.'

Her father eyed her for a second, then took her hand and gave it a firm shake. And with that handshake Arabella sealed her fate as a woman engaged to be married.

Chapter Four

His mission accomplished, Arabella's father spotted a business acquaintance across the room and departed, but not before reminding her new fiancé about the stiff penalties and the social disgrace imposed on men guilty of breach of promise. Her father was making sure the Duke knew that if he tried to get out of this engagement, he would suffer dire consequences.

But at least the theatre would be saved. When it came to business transactions, her father had a reputation for always keeping his word. And that was exactly what her marriage was, a business transaction.

She looked over at Oliver and sent him a doleful smile. Her new fiancé was as equally opposed to the sham engagement as she was. That had to be some consolation to being sold off by her father. Didn't it?

He refilled their champagne glasses just as the supper her father had ordered for eight people arrived. The waiters lay tray after tray on the table, until it was laden with silver trays overflowing with oysters, cheeses, thinly cut cold meats, truffles and *foie gras*.

Arabella looked at the feast and sighed. Her fellow

actors were staying in a boarding house close to the theatre and would be dining on thin soup and rough bread. Despite such humble fare and their dingy living quarters, she would much rather be with them, enjoying the camaraderie and excitement that always ensued after a night's performance, than sitting in this grand restaurant surrounded by London's most fashionable society.

'Don't worry, Arabella, it's an engagement in name only,' he said, misinterpreting her sigh.

She shook her head and sighed again. 'I know. I know. My father won't be able to stay away from his bank for much longer. He'll return to America and then you'll be free.'

He waved his hand in dismissal. 'It might not be ideal, but I think a long engagement of convenience is going to suit us both very well. So, drink up, eat up, we might as well celebrate. Even if all we're celebrating is freeing you from your father's matchmaking for the next seven years and saving me from being hanged, drawn and quartered by Lord Buffoon and his band of baboons.'

Arabella smiled at his deliberate mispronunciation. 'In that case, here's to long engagements.' They clinked glasses and she sipped her champagne, the bubbles tickling her nose.

Lowering her glass, she gave him a considered glance. 'I take it you don't really have to wait until you're thirty-five before you can marry?'

He gave her a conspiratorial wink, forcing Arabella to use all her acting skills to stop her heart from fluttering and cheeks from burning.

'I became the Duke of Somerfeld two years ago

on the death of my father and nothing can take that away from me. I'm the Duke until I die, but we don't need to tell your father that.'

'No, if he did find out your death would be the least of your problems. He can be somewhat ruthless when he's crossed.'

They both looked across the busy restaurant to where her father was sitting, now deeply engrossed in conversation, presumably making yet another deal. His daughter's future marriage settled, he had swiftly moved on to further business.

'Don't worry, Arabella, with both of us against him, your father doesn't stand a chance.'

His words held a note of reassurance. He might be going along with the engagement to save his own hide, but it was nice to have an ally, someone who also wanted to defeat her father.

Arabella raised her glass again in toast. 'To victory over my father.'

'To us.' He clinked his crystal champagne flute against hers.

'So, if we're going to be engaged for the next seven years, perhaps we need to know a bit more about each other,' Arabella said. 'All I know about you is your name and that Lord Bufford wants to tear you limb from limb.'

He rubbed his hand slowly around the back of his neck. 'You obviously haven't been in England very long if you haven't heard the scandals associated with the Huntsbury family and the Duke of Somerfeld. And I suspect if your father knew he wouldn't be quite so enthusiastic to be joined to our family.'

'Huntsbury? Yes, I have heard something about

them.' Arabella furrowed her brow and tried to re-call where she had heard that name before. Hadn't the other actresses been gossiping about someone called Huntsbury? Their conversation suddenly jumped into her mind and her hands shot to her mouth as she re-called all the sordid details.

'I take it you know after all,' he said.

Arabella gulped and nodded. The actresses had de-scribed in explicit detail how Marcus Huntsbury, the former Duke of Somerfeld, had died in the arms of his mistress. And not just one mistress. The rumours were that he'd had a heart attack while he was at-tempting a particularly strenuous sexual pose involv-ing himself and four women, in a large four-poster bed. A bed that had reportedly been designed spe-cially so he could conduct his own personal orgies.

The actresses had found it particularly amusing as both of them had taken part in the Duke's bedroom athletics in the past. They were just surprised he'd only had four women in his bed that night, as the bed had been designed for eight.

Arabella took another sip of her champagne to try to drive that image out of her mind.

'I don't think...' she coughed again '... I don't think even that would deter my father. He doesn't care who I marry, or what scandals surround the family, as long as I get a title.'

'It seems we both have fathers who care only for getting what they want and don't consider who suf-fers as a result.'

Arabella nodded her agreement and they each sank into their own thoughts.

The restaurant started to fill up with more diners,

many of whom were in high spirits, talking loudly and laughing boisterously. The Savoy was a popular venue for a late supper and many of the revellers would have come from the opera, the various playhouses and the array of illicit gambling houses in the neighbouring areas.

She spotted W.S. Gilbert and Arthur Sullivan enter, surrounded by a group of actors. The famous theatrical duo's comic operettas were performed in the adjoining theatre and they could often be seen in the restaurant. It was one of Arabella's most cherished dreams that she might one day appear in a Gilbert and Sullivan production. Certainly a more cherished dream than being married would ever be.

The group included numerous attractive young actresses and Arabella couldn't help but notice that several looked in Oliver's direction as they passed their table. Nor could she ignore the number of women throughout the restaurant who were smiling, nodding and even winking at her new fiancé.

Lady Bufford and Lucy Baker quite plainly weren't the only *very good friends* of the Duke of Somerfeld. But why should Arabella care? She had no illusions about the sort of man he was. He was most decidedly a lady's man, just like his father. But wasn't that all for the good? He would be less likely to interfere in Arabella's life if he was off chasing other women and she could get on with doing what she wanted to do, which was pursue her acting career.

Yes, it was definitely all for the best.

Another attractive woman passed the table and smiled suggestively at Oliver. Despite her resolve to not care, Arabella couldn't stop herself from frowning at the woman and she received a little, knowing laugh in return.

'Another one of your good friends, I take it,' she said, annoyed at the prissy sound of her own voice.

He shrugged apologetically. 'Yes, I suppose you could say that.'

'So how many of these good friends have you actually had and how many have you got at the moment?'

He turned in his seat to face her. 'Is that going to be a problem, Arabella?'

Heat shot to her cheeks. 'No, no, of course not,' she stammered. 'I'm merely making conversation. It's got nothing to do with me. You can have hundreds of good friends if you like. I don't care.'

He continued to stare at her, his brows drawn together, and despite her attempt to act nonchalantly her cheeks burned hotter under his questioning gaze. It shouldn't matter. It didn't matter. So why did a little stabbing pain strike her in the middle of her chest every time a woman smiled in Oliver's direction?

'You do realise this engagement is just one of convenience for both of us, don't you, Arabella?'

'Of course I do,' she shot back, her voice rising. 'I don't want to be engaged to anyone, least of all you, and I certainly don't want to be married. Yes, this suits us both. As you said, it saves you from a beating and it saves me from my father's incessant matchmaking.'

'And we'll both be free to pursue our interests, free from the other's interference?'

Arabella nodded and looked around the room at all the beautiful women. Her stomach clenched at the thought of Oliver pursuing his interests with his numerous *very good friends*. There would be other women in his life, women who he would take in his arms and kiss the way he had kissed her in the dressing room. Women with whom he presumably did more than just kiss, if the reaction of Lord Bufford was anything to go by.

She lightly touched her lips, remembering that kiss. After such a kiss she could see why so many women fell under his spell. It had been a kiss that had caused her to forget herself, to abandon all reserve, to want more, so much more.

She gazed back at him and he smiled. Even that wicked smile was enough to make her go all weak inside. When he smiled all she could see were those sparkling brown eyes, eyes that reminded her of rich brown chocolate, warm, inviting and satisfying, and those smiling lips, soft lips that had felt so good on hers, that had tasted so delicious.

A stray blond curl had fallen over his forehead and Arabella had to resist the temptation to sweep it back, and then, perhaps, to linger, her hands running through his thick hair, just the way they had when he had kissed her.

Yes, she could see why so many women fell for him.

She sat up straighter in her chair and looked back out at the crowded room. But she was not like most women. She had ambitions that did not include a man. And she had been badly burnt once. She wasn't about to be burnt again.

No, it did not matter to her, one jot, if other women were vying for his attention. They might be engaged, but she had only just met this man. He meant nothing to her. Nothing at all.

And she was determined to let him know that this was the case. 'So if I don't give a fig about you and all your *friends*, which I don't, can I also assume you won't do anything to interfere with my career on the stage?'

'That goes without saying,' he replied.

Arabella didn't know whether to be pleased or disappointed. Did that mean he didn't care one way or another what she did? That he didn't care about her at all? Again, that was a good thing, wasn't it? Of course it was. 'Right, that's settled.'

Another pretty woman passed the table and this one had the audacity to slip Oliver a note. It was outrageous. He was sitting at a table with another woman. Surely that should mean something. Surely other women should keep their distance, even if just for this one night.

But it was apparent that there were so many women in Oliver's life that none was accorded any special treatment. They presumably all knew very well what he was like and accepted him that way. It seemed a title was not the only thing he had inherited from the previous Duke of Somerfeld.

Oliver stared down at the note as if it were an unpleasant stain on the otherwise pristine white tablecloth. Normally a note from Lady Ambrose would be most welcome. It was presumably a reminder that he been invited to one of her notorious parties. Parties that never failed to provide him with an enjoyable diversion. Parties full of women who had no objection to the way he lived his life, who actively encouraged his more libertine ways.

But tonight, he was strangely embarrassed by its arrival.

He slipped the note into his pocket in what he hoped was a surreptitious manner. Out of sight, out of mind. But the disapproving look on Arabella's face showed clearly that it was not out of her mind.

For the first time in his life he almost felt the need to apologise for the way he lived. He was tempted to try to explain to Arabella that no one was ever hurt by his behaviour, at least no women. How their husbands felt was their own concern.

Most of those husbands had married women for their dowries, or for their social connections, and as long as they were discreet, they didn't care what their wives got up to and with whom. And, once freed of the constraints of society and marriage, his mistresses certainly liked to get up to a lot.

Even Lord Bufford was only annoyed because his wife's behaviour had been openly discussed at his club. He felt no jealousy about his wife having a lover, only rage that others had found out about it.

But why did Oliver feel the need to explain his lifestyle now? He had never felt the need to do that before.

Perhaps it was that kiss, which was still lingering on his lips, or the memory of the warmth of Arabella's body so close to his? Perhaps it was her enticing smile, or was it simply that she was not the sort of woman he usually associated with? Whatever it was, something was causing him a degree of discomfort.

It must be simply that she *was* so different from the women he usually associated with.

He fingered the note in his pocket, reminding himself of why he did not get involved with women like Arabella van Haven, no matter how enticing their kisses.

Oliver's father might not have cared about the damage he did in his headlong pursuit of hedonistic pleasure, but in one regard Oliver knew they were different. His father had seduced every pretty woman who came his way. He cared little if he broke hearts or ruined reputations, as long as he was getting what he wanted.

Oliver had definitely inherited his father's love of women, the more the merrier, but he ensured he only got involved with women who were as equally carefree as him. And that was obviously not Arabella.

She was sweet and innocent. She deserved to be with a decent man, not a man like him who shunned commitment with every fibre of his being. She might claim to not want to marry, and that was possibly true, but it was obvious from the way Arabella had scowled every time another woman tried to catch his eye, that she couldn't cope with a man she had to share. And he had never been a one-woman man. Never would be. That was why he only associated with women like Lady Bufford, Lucy Baker, Lady Ambrose, and all the other women who wanted to have fun with no strings attached.

But he would honour his promise to be engaged to her for the foreseeable future. While there were probably easier ways of getting out of a beating from Lord Bufford's baboons, and better ways of saving

Lady Bufford's reputation, what was done was done and he would stand by it.

If nothing else, it would save this lovely young woman from being pushed around by her odious father, a man who obviously saw her as nothing more than a pawn in his power game. It would free her up to be an actress, and a fine actress she was, indeed, if tonight's performance was anything to go by.

He smiled in memory of how she looked on stage. 'What is it you love so much about acting?' He wanted to know, but also wanted to move on to safer ground than his own reprobate behaviour.

Her pouting lips instantly turned into a smile and her blue eyes sparkled with enthusiasm. He gazed into those eyes, trying to determine what colour they really were. Blue didn't do them justice. Sapphire, perhaps, or aquamarine, or the blue of the sky on a warm summer's day. He wished he had the soul of a poet so he could describe them properly and not see them simply as beautiful blue eyes.

But whatever colour they were, they had him captivated.

'Oh, everything. I love absolutely everything about acting and the theatre. I love the smell of the greasepaint when we put on our make-up. I love the sound of the audience laughing or gasping at what they've seen on stage. I love the camaraderie of the cast. And most of all I love the applause at the end. There's nothing like it. It's like being wrapped in loving arms, being told how much all your hard work is appreciated. It's just wonderful.'

She continued to beam and he couldn't help but wonder if there wasn't sadness behind that smile. He looked over at her father, now writing out some plan on the linen tablecloth as the man next to him looked on with undivided interest. It was unlikely she had received much love from that mercenary man, a man who treated her like another commodity to be bought and sold. And she had said her mother had died when she was young. It was no wonder she craved the love and adoration that she would get from an audience.

He placed his hand over hers and lightly patted it as an unfamiliar emotion engulfed him. What was it? Was it the need to protect her from men like her father, to comfort her for the pain she had suffered, or even to provide her with the love she had missed out on?

He quickly withdrew his hand from hers as if it were on fire. Whatever strange emotion he was feeling, he should not be feeling it for a woman like Arabella. There was nothing he could offer her.

He poured himself another glass of champagne. Despite that kiss, she was an innocent and he needed to keep that foremost in his mind at all times. She did not need a man like him in her life.

He cursed himself for remembering their kiss. The scorching intensity of it had been so unexpected. She had been kissing a stranger, but had responded as if they were passionate lovers, desperate for each other. She might be an innocent, but it had definitely ignited a fire inside her, one that had almost engulfed both of them.

It was only the knowledge that they were in a room full of people that had stopped him from fanning the flame and seeing just how hot it would burn.

There could be no doubting that there was a passionate side to this young woman just waiting to be set loose, a passionate nature ripe for exploration.

He knocked back the glass of champagne in one quaff, horrified that he had allowed his mind to stray in that direction. Wasn't that just the sort of thing his father would think? Didn't his father look at every woman and see her as yet more prey waiting to be seduced? But he was not like that. He would never be like that. And he would not be like that with Arabella.

The sooner their engagement was signed, sealed and delivered and they could go their separate ways, the better. Only then would he be safe from these inappropriate desires and only then would Arabella be safe from him.

Chapter Five

Arabella was under no illusions. It was only because of her father's manoeuvring that Oliver was still sitting at this table with her and not off pursuing one of the other women in the restaurant. He had not chosen to be with her, he had been forced to be with her against his will.

And he had made it clear to her that he expected to be free to pursue any woman he wanted, even though they were to be engaged to be married.

She shrugged and took another sip of her cold champagne. He had every right to chase any woman he wanted to and she had no right to try to stop him. And she would *not* try to stop him. She would abide by their agreement. It was the very least she could do. After all, she should be grateful to him. He did not have to agree to become engaged to her. He could have made his escape and left her to her fate. She knew her father well. Her fate was sealed. He would move heaven and earth to ensure she married a man with a title. She had much to thank Oliver for. It was also down to his quick thinking that she would not have to face the prospect of a forced marriage for seven more years.

Thanks to him, she now had a long-term engagement of convenience. It was more than she could have hoped for when her father gave her the ultimatum of getting married or returning to America with him. And if it meant she was engaged to a man who had countless other women in his life, well, so be it. It was not as if they meant anything to each other. They had only just met. And surely, if she really was grateful to him, she would put no obstacle in his way when it came to pursuing other women.

Yes, she owed him his freedom. And that was exactly what she would give him. There would be no more pouting when a woman gave him *that* look. No more snide comments about his *good friends*. No, he could behave in any way he wanted, with whomever he wanted, and he would get no objections from her.

She smiled at him as if to underline this firm resolve. 'I hope you've got some enjoyable entertainment arranged for the rest of the evening. I'd hate to think my father interrupted your plans.'

Despite her determination to feign nonchalance, she couldn't stop her eyes from straying to his pocket, where he had stored the note from that particularly attractive brunette.

He smiled back at her; a smile that was this time more sheepish than devilish. 'It was a particularly pleasant interruption and I have no regrets about how I'm spending this evening.'

He found her company pleasant. He had no regrets about spending his evening with her instead of all those other women vying for his attention.

She returned his smile and his became wickedly tempting, drawing her gaze to his sensual lips. Arabella imagined touching her finger to those enticingly smiling lips, gently stroking the line where they met his olive skin, before she kissed him again. Running her tongue along…

Where on earth had that image come from?

Shocked at where her thoughts had led her, she closed her eyes and shook her head to drive it out.

Yes, he had kissed her once, but it had been for one reason, and one reason only: because he was being pursued by the husband of one of his mistresses and he'd needed an alibi. And it wasn't her he'd intended to kiss, but Lucy Baker. And even if he ever did want to kiss her again, which she was sure he didn't, she could not let it happen. She had made a fool of herself over one man before and she was not about to let history repeat itself. No, if Arnold Emerson had taught her anything, it was to not trust herself when it came to men. And if she couldn't trust herself with Arnold Emerson, then she most certainly could not trust herself with this seductive, charming rake. Their kiss was proof of that.

Opening her eyes, she saw he was still staring at her, his eyebrows drawn together, questioning her unusual behaviour. How long had her eyes been closed while she tried to drive out that image of him kissing her?

Heat tinging her cheeks, she picked up her napkin and dabbed the edge of her eye. 'I think I might have something in my eye,' she said, her embarrassment rising with every word as she tried to explain her discomposure and odd reaction to his attention.

'Here, allow me.' He took the napkin from her hand and began dabbing at the edge of her eye himself. This was worse than Arabella could have imagined. He was now so close she could feel the warmth radiating from his body, smell his intoxicating masculine scent, picture the hard muscles under his crisp white shirt. She tried not to breathe, not to feel, not to think.

'Open your eyes wider so I can see what the obstruction is.'

She did as he commanded, but stared up towards the ceiling so she would not have to look at his handsome face. This situation was uncomfortable enough. She did not need the extra discomfort of looking at that strong, chiselled jawline, or those full, inviting lips.

'I can't see anything. Perhaps when you closed your eyes you dislodged it.'

He lowered the napkin and Arabella lowered her gaze. That was a mistake. Now she was staring straight into his velvet-brown eyes and a delicious sensation of rich chocolate slowly melting on her tongue engulfed her.

She swallowed the sigh of pleasure that was threatening to escape and quickly looked down at her lap in a desperate attempt to still her fevered imaginings.

Why did he have to be so handsome? This whole encounter would be so much easier if he didn't make her turn to jelly every time she looked at him.

There was absolutely no denying he was charming, but he wouldn't have much success as a womaniser if he wasn't charming, would he? And the one thing she did not want was to be charmed by a man who was well experienced in the art of seduction.

She drew in a deep breath. No, it did not matter how charming he was, or how handsome, or how captivating that mischievous smile, she would not succumb. She would keep firmly in her mind at all times the type of man he was. He was a rake, a reprobate, a debaucher. Not the sort of man she wanted in her life.

He handed her the napkin, which she tentatively took from his outstretched hand, taking every precaution to avoid contact with his skin.

If she couldn't trust her body to act as sensibly as her mind, it was time to put some distance between herself and the Duke of Somerfeld. 'Well, I think I'll call it a night and let you get on with enjoying the rest of your evening.'

'I'm in no hurry and you've eaten nothing of the supper.'

She looked at the array of dishes. The last thing she felt like was eating. 'I'm not hungry, but please, don't let me stop you.'

He waved his hand in dismissal, so she signalled to the waiter. 'Would you please parcel up all this food and have it delivered to this address.'

She took a blank white card out of her beaded purse, wrote the address of the boarding house where her fellow cast members were staying and handed it to the waiter. They would appreciate the feast that would otherwise go to waste.

'But as I said, I'm tired and I think it is time I went to bed.' Heat exploded on her cheeks at the mere mention of beds and she was reminded of how his father had died. Had Oliver inherited that bed, the one made to take eight women? Was that where he would be spending this evening? And which of the women in this room would be joining him?

She threw the napkin on the table and stood quickly, anxious to get away from him and away from such disturbing images. 'Yes, I really must be going,' she said and looked around the room as if suddenly unsure of where she was.

'Then allow me to escort you home,' he said, rising, a teasing quirk to his lips.

He knew what she was thinking. That was why he was smiling at her like that.

Arabella's embarrassment intensified. How could she be so transparent? She was an actress, for goodness sake. Surely she should be able to keep her feelings hidden from view. And surely she shouldn't start blushing just because the word bed had been mentioned.

'There's no need to accompany me home. I'm staying here at the Savoy. I'd much rather be staying with the other actors, but Father would be horrified if I did. He sent me over to England a few months ago to marry an aristocrat, not to become an actress. He had one duke lined up for me, but my father's ward, Rosie, married him instead. That's why he is so determined to not let another aristocrat get away.' Her words had tumbled out in a rush, but she seemed incapable of stopping herself from talking.

He smiled at her. 'So you eluded one duke and got a job as an actress, now you're trying to escape from another one. I can see you're an enterprising young lady if you're able to keep your plans secret from your father.'

'Fortunately Father has spent so much time making deals and looking for good financial investments while he's been here he's hardly noticed what I've been doing, so it hasn't taken too much enterprise on my part to creep out.'

The fire on her cheeks moved to her neck and the room suddenly seemed unbearably hot. 'Not that I ever do creep out, except to go to the theatre. And afterwards I come straight home, where Aunt Prudence is always waiting for me. And if I don't go to the theatre I always take a chaperon, either Aunt Prudence or my lady's maid. So I never really creep out.' Arabella knew she was still burbling, but it was essential that he knew she was not the sort of woman who flirted with men in public, or passed them secret notes, and she certainly had no intention of creeping out with him, tonight or any other night.

'Well, at least let me walk you to your room,' he offered.

'No, there's no need.' The last thing she wanted was Oliver anywhere near her hotel suite. It wasn't that she didn't trust him. It was that she wasn't entirely sure she could trust herself. Her own behaviour tonight had been so uncharacteristic and unpredictable, she was in danger of doing something reckless. She might even be tempted to encourage just one more kiss from him. She bit her bottom lip lightly to try to stop it from tingling at the memory of it.

She held out an unsteady hand to shake goodbye. 'That won't be necessary, I can find my own way to my room,' she said more emphatically than she intended.

Oliver took her hand in his, but instead of shaking it, he leant over and gave her a light kiss on the cheek.

Arabella froze.

His lips lingered.

Would he kiss her on the lips, too? Would he take her in his arms? Would he hold her body close to his? She knew she shouldn't want that. But she did. Like so many other women in the room, Arabella was falling for the charms of Oliver Huntsbury.

But she was not like every other woman in the room. She *refused* to be like every other woman in the room.

She took a step backwards, almost colliding with the wall. 'Well, goodnight,' she stammered. 'I suppose the next time we see each other will be at our engagement party.' She gave a fake laugh.

He released her hand and Arabella released her held breath.

'Until our engagement party.' His eyes once again sparked with wicked amusement.

Arabella turned and all but ran out of the restaurant, not bothering to say goodbye to her father who was still engrossed in his latest deal.

She hurried away, sure her almost-fiancé's eyes were still on her. Next weekend she would be engaged to him. Engaged to a man she didn't want to be engaged to. A man she didn't want to marry and, worst of all, a man who made her feel things she knew she shouldn't be feeling.

Oliver watched his fiancée leave, her silk dress rustling as she departed rapidly without a backwards glance, then slumped back down on to his chair.

On most nights the evening's entertainment would just be getting started at this late hour, but tonight he had no interest in visiting any of his usual haunts, no desire to see Lucy Baker or any of the other women who were currently providing him with delightful diversions.

Is this what happened when you became engaged? Oliver shuddered. Perish the thought. That was not him.

He pulled Lady Ambrose's note out of his pocket and read the contents. As expected, it was a reminder that she was hosting yet another party. A particularly salacious party, if the wording on the note was any indication, and it was being held at her town house later this evening. Normally Oliver would be pleased by such an invitation. Lady Ambrose's parties could even top his father's when it came to inventiveness. But tonight, it seemed he wasn't in the mood.

He looked towards the door through which Arabella had departed.

Nor, for some reason, did he feel compelled to follow up on any of the unspoken invitations he had received throughout the evening.

Instead he would return to his estate and tell his mother the news, that he was now engaged to be married.

At least his betrothal would bring pleasure to his dear mother. She, too, was an innocent and, despite being married to one of England's most notorious rakes, she refused to think anything bad about her husband and still saw marriage as a wonderful thing.

To maintain his mother's innocence, he had been forced to deceive her for many years. Oliver knew it would have destroyed her to know the man she loved and revered had been repeatedly unfaithful to her, with countless women throughout their marriage. So far his mother had continued to live in blissful ignorance, rarely coming to London and preferring to socialise with the genteel ladies in the Surrey countryside.

And now he was about to lie to his mother about himself. But it would only upset her if she knew the truth. That his engagement was not a love match, but merely a way to save one woman's reputation and allow another woman to defy her father and to continue to perform on the stage.

But even if he was forced to lie to his mother, he would not lie to Arabella. While his mother was never aware of what her husband was really like, at least Arabella knew exactly what sort of man she was now engaged to. She was entering this arrangement with her eyes wide open and had accepted him for who he was.

He had vowed he would not be like his father in the way he treated women as mere playthings, with no feelings of their own. He would do everything he could to avoid causing Arabella emotional pain and the best way to do that was for him to never see her again once the engagement party was over.

He looked again at the door through which she had departed. Keeping that vow would be so much easier if he was engaged to a woman who wasn't so damned attractive, a woman whose kiss did not hold so much promise of a passionate nature. But he had kissed her once, he would not do so again. He would not take her in his arms again. He would not feel that beautiful body pressed up against his, or taste those tempting lips again, not run his hands over her wonderful curvaceous figure.

He might not be able to forget their kiss, that would be asking too much, but it must never happen again. If it did, he was unsure whether he'd be able to stop at just a kiss and that would be a disaster. Arabella must retain her innocence until she met a man who was worthy of her, a man who could love her in the way she deserved to be loved.

He continued to stare in the direction she had departed and drained his champagne flute for the last time. No, a woman like Arabella was most definitely not for him.

He summoned the waiter and asked him to hail a hansom cab. Oliver would return to his town house, then catch the first train back to his Surrey estate and break the supposedly happy news to his mother. Then, next weekend, Arabella and he would go through the motions of an engagement party. After that, they would never have to see each other again.

Chapter Six

An engagement party should be a joyous time of celebration. Family and friends gathering together to mark the happy occasion. And the happy couple should be just that—happy.

But Arabella could see nothing to be happy about. As Nellie, her lady's maid, curled her hair, then lifted it into a bun high on her head and added the hair pieces that would give her already abundant hair an even more voluminous look, Arabella stared at the face reflected in the mirror. It was a face of a woman about to start a long prison sentence, not the look of a woman about to celebrate her engagement.

She just had to keep reminding herself it was not a real engagement. She was not going to be married. She had seven years in which to come up with a way to get out of this unwanted predicament. And it could be much worse, she could be tied to a man who repulsed her, instead of a handsome duke who made her heart beat faster every time he looked at her, whose kisses had caused her to forget who she was and what she was doing.

Arabella sighed. Was that better or was that worse?

Perhaps it would be better if he was some horrid old duke with bad breath and rotting teeth. Then there would be no problem, no confusion, she would know exactly how she felt and what she wanted.

Nellie teased out a few curls and allowed them to deliberately fall loose, so they had a carefree look about them, then stood back to admire her work. 'Perfect, if I do say so myself. It's just a shame that my perfect hair style is being worn by someone who looks as though she's about to have her head cut off.'

Arabella sent Nellie a sad smile. Originally from Ireland, Nellie had joined the van Haven household when she first arrived in America at the age of thirteen. Arabella was only fourteen herself at the time. They had grown up together and were more friends than servant and mistress.

'Sorry, Nellie. Yes, it looks lovely, as always.'

Nellie placed her hand gently on Arabella's arm. 'No, it's me that's sorry. I'm sorry you have to go through this, Arabella. Sorry your father is selling you off like this. Sorry that you can't just be left alone to live the life you want to live.'

Arabella patted Nellie's hand. 'I could say the same for you, Nellie. You could be so much more than just a lady's maid, if the world treated women better than it does.'

Nellie raised her eyebrows and sent her a mysterious smile. 'Oh, I have my plans and I'm not going to let the world tell me what I can and can't do.'

Before Arabella could question Nellie over what she meant, there was a knock on the door, and Nellie opened it to admit Rosie, Arabella's best friend. Recently married to the Duke of Knightsbrook, Rosie was glowing with health and happiness.

She hugged Nellie and gave Arabella a kiss on the cheek. 'Oh, Arabella, I was so sorry to hear about your engagement. I wish I'd been here to stop it.'

Arabella shrugged. 'Never mind, Rosie. It's only an engagement of convenience. Oliver is just as set against marriage as I am. He's like you, a great one for coming up with clever plans, so I'm sure we will never actually have to get married.'

Rosie screwed up her face. 'I hope he thinks things through a bit better than I did.'

Arabella smiled at her friend. She was referring to Rosie's plan to save Arabella from her father's last attempt to marry her off. Rosie had come up with what she thought was the perfect plan to put the duke off Arabella. While Arabella was pursuing work on the London stage, Rosie would meet him and pretend to be Arabella, then behave so badly that the Duke of Knightsbrook would have no interest in marrying her. Instead it had all gone terribly wrong, or gloriously right, depending on how you looked at it, and they had fallen in love.

'I'm sure Oliver knows what he's doing. And he has even more reasons for not wanting to get married than I do. So, no matter what, I'm sure he'll make sure this marriage never happens. In the meantime, while I'm engaged to be married, it stops Father from throwing me in front of every passing duke, earl or viscount.'

'Yes, I've heard the Duke of Somerfeld has quite a lot of reasons for not wanting to get married,' Nellie said and exchanged a knowing look with Rosie.

It seemed Oliver's reputation as a womaniser was known far and wide.

Nellie helped Arabella into a peach-coloured silk skirt and a matching embroidered jacket with a lacy neckline. Arabella had been tempted to wear black for mourning, but in the end had decided that might be taking things a bit too far.

While Nellie used a buttonhook to do up the buttons on Arabella's white boots, Rosie told them of all the plans she and her new husband had for modernising the Knightsbrook estate. She was so full of enthusiasm and Arabella had to admit that marriage suited her friend. She had never looked more lovely. But she had married the man she had fallen in love with. She hadn't been forced to become engaged to a man who was a notorious rake, whose sexual conquests were legendary.

Getting caught up in Rosie's excitement, Arabella found herself actually smiling and laughing. It might not be a day of celebration for her, but it was good to be with her two friends and with Rosie by her side she knew she'd get through this horrid engagement party.

Once Arabella was dressed, Nellie gave her a critical once over, then departed.

'Well, I suppose I had better get this over and done with,' Arabella said. The best friends left the room arm in arm, walked down the grand staircase, through the expansive hallway of Somerfeld Manor, and out through the heavy oak doors at the entranceway.

When Arabella and her father had first arrived at Oliver's estate, her father had wandered around, inspecting the house and the surrounding grounds with a satisfied smile. He had admired every piece of antique furniture and every ancestral portrait, and each time he saw the family crest, bearing two rampant stags and a shield, his smile had grown so wide he looked fit to burst. Arabella had quickly lost count of the number of times he had mentioned that the Huntsburys could trace their family back to the fifteenth century.

It was exactly what her father wanted. He could now boast that he was about to become related to a family with a country estate that had been in their family since before the time America was first settled.

Joining 'old money' was something he had desired for a long time. Despite being born in poverty, he now had more than enough money to gain entry to New York's highest social echelons. But Arabella was aware that, despite his money and his power, he was still looked down upon by those members of society who had been born to wealth and privilege. Now, through his daughter's marriage, he finally expected to gain the status that being part of such a long-established family would bring him.

And he didn't care that his daughter had to be sacrificed to achieve his dream.

While her father had walked round the estate with a self-satisfied air, Arabella had found herself somewhat overawed by the grandeur of the enormous four-storey house, with its maze of expansive rooms.

She had been raised in a luxurious mansion on Washington Square, which her father had spared no expense when it came to decorating, but Oliver's estate almost made their home seem humble. With its thousands of acres of land and countless rooms decorated with priceless objects and paintings acquired over many generations, it was impossible to ignore the fact that the Huntsbury family had been fabulously wealthy going back hundreds of years.

Under normal circumstances spending the weekend at such a grand stately home would have been a delight, particularly as the view from her room was so picturesque, with its outlook on to formal gardens, green rolling parklands, and woodland areas. But as the weekend had progressed her anxiety had only grown. Particularly as, despite the size of the house, it had been virtually impossible to avoid Oliver.

Every time she had been in his company, her nerves had taken another shredding, until she was now exhausted and just counting off the hours until the engagement party was over and she could put this all behind her.

She would have much preferred to have spent the weekend in London, doing what she loved. But instead she had been forced to get the understudy to take her part so she could take on a different acting role, that of a woman who was happy to be engaged to a man she knew little about, except that he was not the sort of man any woman in her right mind would want to be married to.

Standing at the top of the tiled steps that led down to the garden, she paused and looked out over the sweeping lawns in front of the house.

It was a pleasant summer's day, so the engagement party was being held outside. Linen-covered tables, laden with food and drink, had been set up on the grassed area beside the lake. An army of liveried servants were lined up, ready to serve the guests with as much food and drink as they required, and maids were at the waiting, to clean away dishes as soon as they emptied and keep the sumptuous banquet replenished.

It was a perfect day for an engagement party. The sun was shining brightly in a blue sky, dotted with fluffy white clouds. There was even a gentle breeze, so the guests would not get too hot. But this day was far from perfect.

Arabella's gaze moved to her fiancé, who was talking to his auburn-haired mother. Arabella had been introduced to Oliver's mother when she first arrived and had been surprised that the woman was so happy and carefree. Arabella had expected the wife of a man who had died in the arms of four women to be bitter and cynical. Instead his mother gave every appearance of being someone who had never been exposed to any of life's harsher lessons. And she was still an attractive woman, even though she was now in her early fifties. She must have been quite stunning as a young woman, but even that had not been enough to keep her husband from straying.

Oliver's affection for his mother was obvious. He treated her as if he was the parent and she the child, a delicate young child who needed to be protected and cherished.

Oliver turned and looked at Arabella and her breath caught in her throat. She wished that wouldn't happen every time they made eye contact. It was so hard to pretend she wasn't affected by how handsome he was when it was difficult to breathe and when her cheeks were glowing as if she'd caught too much sun.

Rosie gave her arm a small squeeze of reassurance as Oliver excused himself from his mother and walked towards them. Arabella tried to get her breathing under control and still her racing heartbeat, but she was fighting a losing battle. Every time she saw him, her heart responded in this inappropriate manner. And today was no exception. But then, he was looking particularly handsome, dressed in a cream three-piece suit with a waistcoat embroidered with silver thread. His perfectly cut jacket showed off the breadth of his shoulders, the tailored trousers draped around his lean hips, and she could see the faint outline of firm muscles under the fabric as he walked towards her.

Why did he always have to look so damn handsome?

As he crossed the lawn, those laughing brown eyes were fixed on her. Arabella couldn't ignore how mischievous he always looked, like a young boy who had just committed a prank that he knew his elders would thoroughly disapprove of.

When he reached the bottom of the steps those full, highly kissable lips smiled in welcome.

'Darling,' he said, amusement sparking in his eyes. 'You look beautiful.'

The term of endearment might be a joke, but the way his gaze swept up and down her body was nothing to laugh at. Nor was Arabella's reaction. Her body came alive under his gaze as if every inch of her skin was being caressed.

She coughed to clear her throat and to give herself time to get her traitorous reactions under control. 'May I present my friend, Rosie, the Duchess of Knightsbrook. Rosie, this is Oliver, the Duke of

Somerfeld. Rosie is my closest friend and she knows all about this sham.' She waved her hand in a circle to encompass the entire engagement party.

Oliver was standing two steps below Arabella and Rosie, but his six-foot-something height meant he was at eye level with the two women. He took Rosie's hand and bowed formally.

'It's a pleasure to meet you, Duchess.' Releasing her hand, he turned to Arabella. 'And I believe if we're to maintain our charade it might be more appropriate if you called me Oliver, or darling, sweetheart, my love, my cherished one, the love of my life, the light of my dreams, or some such,' he said with a laugh.

Arabella pulled a slight frown of disapproval. 'All right, Oliver it is, then.' A statement that caused Oliver to send her another of those heart-stopping mischievous smiles.

The Duke of Knightsbrook joined them, shook hands with Oliver and led his new wife away. Rosie was smiling at him coquettishly, her happiness making her glow.

Oliver's smile turned from mischievous to warm and tender. 'You *do* look beautiful today, Arabella. Only a fool would not want to marry a woman as beautiful as you.'

She gave a false laugh. 'Then I take it you consider yourself a fool.'

His responding laugh was genuine. 'I've never thought otherwise.' He held out his arm for her and Arabella fought the temptation to flee back inside the house. It was so hard to maintain a composed demeanour when she was being told she was beautiful by a man who made her pulses race, causing her to gasp for breath as if her corset was laced too tightly.

'Shall we greet our guests?'

She nodded and joined the receiving line with her father and Oliver's mother. The guests filed past and had already divided themselves into two groups, Oliver's friends in one and Arabella's friends from the theatre in the other. It appeared the two worlds were reluctant to merge, just like the engaged couple themselves.

She exchanged pleasantries with the elegantly dressed men and women, and tried to remember their names, but each one slipped immediately from her mind. All she could focus on was the way the women looked at Oliver. Some sent him looks that suggested they wanted to devour him, others gave him shy but equally inviting smiles, and many looked at Arabella in much the same way that Lord Bufford's thugs had looked at Oliver.

While these women were sending silent signals of invitation, the men on their arms seemed oblivious to what was happening. Oliver was seducing their wives right under their noses and the husbands were either completely unaware of it or didn't care.

Only Lord Bufford showed evidence that he did not trust Oliver with his wife, gripping Lady Bufford's arm tightly in a proprietary manner and smiling humourlessly, as if he had achieved a great victory over Oliver.

The introductions were no less irritating when they greeted the cast from the Limelight Theatre. Arabella had been pleased when her father had relented and agreed to hold the party on a Sunday which meant the cast were able to attend. But now she was having a small regret about making such a demand. It was obvious that some of the actresses had met Oliver before, but they were respectful enough to not make obvious overtures towards him. Well, not in front of Arabella, anyway.

But why should she be surprised? After all, weren't the women's reactions what she had already come to expect? Hadn't their first encounter been one where he was being pursued by the angry husband of one of his mistresses? And hadn't a woman blatantly slipped him a note while they were dining together at the Savoy? An invitation which she very much doubted had been one to take tea with a group of maiden aunts.

No, nothing about the women's reactions should come as a surprise to her. But that didn't mean it wasn't annoying.

But there was one person who was thoroughly enjoying the party. Throughout the introductions Oliver's mother had smiled with unabashed joy. She was obviously pleased that her son was to marry. With a stab of guilt Arabella was shamed that she, too, was now deceiving this kind, trusting woman.

Once the introductions were over Oliver took two glasses of champagne off the tray of a passing footman, handed one to Arabella and they walked slowly around the party.

'Your mother is lovely, Oliver. Not at all what I expected,' Arabella said.

'You probably expected someone who was worn down from years of misery living with my father, did you not?'

'Mmm.' That was the politest response Arabella

could give. That was exactly what she had expected. Exactly the effect being married to a rake would have on his wife. Exactly the reason why she would never consider a marriage to such a man.

'My mother managed to stay sweet, despite being married to my father. I believe it's because on their honeymoon she caught him in a compromising position with a young maid who worked in the Italian hotel in which they were staying. My mother was naturally distraught and my father managed to appease her by vowing she would never catch him with another woman again. And he stayed true to his vow.'

Arabella stopped walking and stared up at him. 'But I thought…'

'He stayed true to his vow that she would never catch him doing it again. And she didn't. He never vowed that he would remain faithful to her. And the trusting woman that my mother is, she thought her husband remained faithful to her from that day onwards.'

Arabella shook her head. 'But didn't she hear any of the rumours?'

'It helps that she rarely leaves the county, can't abide London and prefers the company of local people rather than society. My father was also a master at keeping rumours from her. Then as I grew into adulthood, I also did everything I could to protect her. Between us, we managed to stop any rumours from reaching her and to save my mother from a great deal of heartache.'

They resumed their slow stroll. Arabella was unsure whether that was a good or a bad thing. It meant he was kind to his mother, a good thing. But it also meant he was well experienced in keeping women in the dark. He was a master of deception. A very bad thing.

A friend of Oliver's joined them, and Arabella made her excuses so she could join Rosie and her new husband.

She walked across the lawn, wishing this party would finish so she could return to London, back to her life, away from all this emotional confusion. Her progress was halted when Lady Bufford suddenly accosted her. Arabella looked down at the fingers tightly clasping her upper arm, then back up at the woman, waiting for an explanation.

Lady Bufford sent her a false smile that was close to a sneer. 'So, you're the actress who managed to capture the Duke of Somerfeld.' The grip on Arabella's arm tightened. 'I wonder what you were able to do for him that no other woman before you has? It must have been quite something, but do you think it will be enough to keep him satisfied?'

The venom in her words sent a cold shudder running up Arabella's spine and she dragged in a deep, steadying breath. 'I don't know what you're talking about, Lady Bufford, but I insist you release my arm. Now.'

Lady Bufford shrugged and released her grip. 'You may think you've caught him, but you certainly won't be able to keep him.' She looked Arabella up and down. 'It won't be long before he tires of the novelty of being with an actress and wants a woman from his own class. Your father might have money, but I hear his father was some sort of miner. I mean, really?

A miner? What was Oliver thinking?' With a harsh laugh the loathsome woman walked away.

Shaken, Arabella took a moment to compose herself, then put on her sunniest fake smile and continued walking towards her friend.

Lady Bufford was wrong and she had wasted her anger on Arabella. She hadn't captured him. The only reason she was engaged to Oliver was because of her father's skulduggery.

No, she meant nothing to Oliver. She might not be like Oliver's mother, who was completely unaware that her husband was repeatedly cheating on her. Arabella knew that the man she was now engaged to was a complete philanderer, a fact he hadn't even tried to hide from her. But it was still humiliating to be engaged to a man who wanted just about every woman who came within range of his charming smile.

Her false smile faltered. And hadn't she been humiliated enough by men in the past?

Arnold Emerson's rejection had left her shaken and shamed. And now it seemed she was once again being humiliated in public.

She increased her pace. But it was almost over now. Her father had his engagement. Soon she would be able to leave Oliver to women like the poisonous, arm-grabbing Lady Bufford. A woman, who, unlike Arabella, was happy to share him with his multitude of mistresses.

Chapter Seven

It was wrong. So wrong. If Oliver needed further proof that Arabella van Haven was a woman he should not be involved with, the expression on her face during her encounter with Violet Bufford would provide it. Her lovely face had been contorted with an array of emotions, including shock, disdain and contempt.

Oliver had tried to intervene, but the encounter had happened so quickly he had been unable to cross the lawn in time. Now Arabella was in the company of her friends, where she was safe. Safe from him and safe from the likes of Violet Bufford.

Whatever the other woman had said had shaken Arabella. Violet had presumably taken delight in telling Arabella about their relationship and the details of their sexual activities.

But all it had ever been for either of them was a fun diversion. If it was jealousy Violet had been expressing, she had no more right to be jealous of him than he did of Lord Bufford or any of Violet's other lovers. And he doubted it would be genuine jealousy,

but whatever it was, it was completely unacceptable.
It was apparent he was going to have to have a discreet word with Violet so Arabella did not have to
suffer such an indignity again.

But one thing the encounter had absolutely confirmed to him was that Arabella was unlike any other
woman he knew. If Violet Bufford had confronted
anyone else he was involved with, she would have
merely ignored it, or laughed it off.

But Arabella had been visibly upset. Despite being
an actress, which usually equated with a certain degree of worldliness, she had an air of innocence about
her. And a man like he most definitely did not deserve the love of a woman who was so uncorrupted.

Not that Arabella would ever be silly enough to
fall in love with him. She was far too sensible and
intelligent for that.

But she did deserve to love and to be loved. She deserved a man who appreciated her, who would adore
her, who could commit to her and her alone. And
it simply was not in him to provide her with those
things. She needed to be protected from him, just
as his mother had needed to be protected from the
knowledge that she was married to a serial adulterer.

He looked over at his mother, deep in conversation with Mr van Haven. To his horror he watched
as his mother sent the wealthy American a shy smile
and coquettishly rose one shoulder. Was his mother
flirting with him? He prayed not. His mother could
not fall for that odious man, a man who was using his
daughter to further his own ambitions.

It wasn't inconceivable that his mother would
marry again. But to a man like Mr van Haven? After

marriage to an inveterate philanderer, surely she wouldn't now set her sights on a man who put money above people? It was an unfortunate side to his mother's innocence; she could not see the bad in anyone.

He strode across the lawn, determined to save her from the rapacious Mr van Haven.

'Mother, I think you're monopolising Mr van Haven. Perhaps you'd like to circulate,' he said, ruthlessly interrupting their conversation and taking his mother by the arm. He nodded to the older man as he led his mother away and received a glacial glare back from those cold blue eyes.

'You seem to be enjoying yourself, Mother. What were you discussing with Mr van Haven?' Not anything romantic, he hoped. Not marriage. Please, not marriage.

'Oh, he was very interested in the family's history. He's so happy that his daughter is marrying into a family with such a long and distinguished lineage. And so am I, Oliver,' she smiled at him, her eyes shining with tears of joy. 'You couldn't be marrying a more delightful girl. And fancy her being an actress.' His mother smiled playfully. 'I always knew you'd marry someone unconventional. You've always been such a rascal.' She looked around at the assembled guests, still smiling. 'Having these acting people here is causing such a stir.' She giggled quietly. 'We're becoming quite the bohemians, aren't we?' She turned back to Oliver. 'But she really is a beauty and I'm so pleased that you're marrying her. Your dear father would have been delighted by your choice, I'm sure. He was never a snob and he did admire actresses so much.'

Oliver cringed inside. There was no denying how much his father had admired actresses.

'You're right, Mother, she is a beauty,' he said, looking over at Arabella, still talking to her friends the Duke and Duchess of Knightsbrook. She turned and looked at him. When their eyes met, she blushed slightly and quickly turned back to her conversation.

Oliver exhaled loudly. Even this engagement party was more than Arabella should be subjected to. She should not have had to meet Violet Bufford, but her father had invited Lord Bufford so there was not much he could do.

A gong boomed out loudly above the sound of the chattering guests, causing every head to turn in the direction of Somerfeld Manor's entrance steps, where Mr van Haven was standing, his glass raised.

'Ladies and gentlemen, I'd like to propose a toast,' he shouted out. 'Arabella, Oliver, if you would please join me.'

Oliver looked over at Arabella and saw her take a deep breath, as if to brace herself for the ordeal ahead. Excusing himself from his mother, he walked across the lawn and offered his arm to Arabella. 'Don't worry. This will soon be over,' he whispered in her ear.

Like a couple heading up the steps to the gallows, they climbed the stairs and took their place beside Mr van Haven. Oliver sent Arabella a reassuring smile and took her trembling hand in his, trying to still her obvious nerves. She smiled back at him, but even her acting abilities couldn't stop the smile from quivering.

Her beaming father raised his glass higher. 'I'm pleased you have all been able to join us today here at Somerfeld Manor to celebrate the engagement of my daughter, Arabella, to Oliver Huntsbury, the Fifth Duke of Somerfeld. So please, raise your glasses to Arabella and Oliver, the Duke and future Duchess of Somerfeld.'

A sea of glasses raised in front of them. 'Arabella and Oliver,' the guests cried out joyously.

'But I'd also like to make an announcement to the cast and crew of the Limelight Theatre.'

Oliver felt Arabella tense beside him. He rubbed his thumb across the back of her hand to offer reassurance, but he could see the growing strain on her face from maintaining that false smile.

'I intend to make a sizeable contribution to the theatre.'

A murmur of surprise and excitement rippled through the guests.

'It can go to modernising your facilities, renovating the building, buying props, increasing the wages of all the cast and crew and it can provide all the necessary advertising to make your next production a success. Such improvements will increase patronage and make the theatre much more profitable. This is all part of my engagement present to my daughter.'

'Engagement present? Engagement ransom would be more accurate,' Arabella murmured so only Oliver would hear.

Enthusiastic clapping erupted from the cast and crew. They had no idea what a sacrifice Arabella was making so the theatre could survive. But Oliver did and it only increased his admiration for the young woman standing beside him.

'Three cheers for Mr van Haven,' one shouted,

followed by a resounding chorus of hip-hip-hurrahs, and the waving in the air of many hats.

Even Oliver's friends were getting caught up in the excitement, smiling and clapping approvingly.

Eventually Mr van Haven waved his hands, palms downwards, to bring an end to the rapturous applause. 'And after discussions with Oliver's mother, the Dowager Duchess, I have one more piece of good news to share with you.'

It was now Oliver's turn to become tense, for his false smile to become strained. He wasn't going to announce his engagement to Oliver's mother. Was he? Such a thing could not happen so quickly. Could it?

'The Dowager Duchess has recently shared some delightful information with me.' Mr van Haven turned to Oliver and smiled victoriously. Oliver narrowed his eyes and glared back at Mr van Haven, letting him know that an engagement to his mother would be a step too far. It was something he would never countenance. He would do everything in his power to protect his mother from that grasping, despicable social climber.

'I had been under the impression that the Duke would lose his title if he married before the age of thirty-five. It seems that my future son-in-law was mistaken.' Mr van Haven's victorious smile became a satisfied smirk. 'Personally, I would like to see the happy couple married off right here and now, but it seems I must abide by tradition. The banns will be read in the local church, and in four weeks' time my daughter and the Duke will be married. The Dowager Duchess has kindly consented to hosting the wedding at this magnificent estate, so I'd like to invite you all to return four Sundays from today to join the celebrations.'

The already excited crowd erupted into even louder cheers of enthusiasm. More hats were thrown in the air and a few couples were even dancing a jig. Everyone was excited by this wonderful announcement. Everyone, that is, except the future bride and groom.

Her father had won after all. How could Arabella have ever thought that he wouldn't? She should have known he'd have an ace up his sleeve. Didn't he always?

And now she was to be married. Married to a man who didn't want her. A man who no woman in her right mind would want to be married to.

But what choice did she have? Looking out at the jubilant crowd, she knew she could never disappoint her colleagues and tell them that there would be no wedding, that there would be no money for the theatre, that their jobs and their futures were not secure. She could not be so cruel as to take away from them something that had secured their futures, even if it meant destroying her own.

She looked at Oliver, his face as crestfallen as her own. Obviously, the thought of marriage to her was filling him with the same sense of foreboding.

But he was not trapped the way she was. He had choices. There was nothing to stop him from calling off this engagement, from refusing to get married. The cast and crew of the Limelight Theatre meant nothing to him. He was safe now from Lord Bufford's ruffians. He could walk away from this ridiculous proposal.

He smiled down at her and gave her hand a gentle squeeze. 'Don't worry, Arabella. Even if we do have to tie the knot, our marriage will be as false as our engagement. You have nothing to fear.'

She could not return his smile. It was easy for him to say there was nothing to fear. He was a man. He wouldn't be bound by the laws of the land that gave few rights to a married woman. When a woman married, she became essentially a man's property. While he had said he cared not a bit if she appeared on the stage, once they were married there would be nothing to stop him from changing his mind and insist she give up the life she loved. She did not want to give that power to any man and certainly not to this man she had only just met. No, there were many reasons for her to fear being married to Oliver Huntsbury.

The greatest fear being that, for her, she would actually want more from Oliver than he was prepared to give. She pulled her hand from his grasp. Having his hand touching hers was doing nothing to calm her agitation. No, she needed a clear head, so she could think about how she was going to cope with this intolerable situation.

Because it *was* intolerable, intolerable to be forced into a marriage with a man who didn't want her, intolerable to be engaged to a man who gave every appearance of wanting to bed just about every other woman in England.

'We're still not defeated, Arabella,' he whispered in her ear. 'Let's leave the guests to their celebrations and slip away so we can formulate a plan of action to get us out of this situation.'

Slipping away together was not a wise idea. Being

alone with him was never a good idea. But they did need to formulate a plan. She had no idea how they were going to stop this marriage, but perhaps Oliver did. After all, he had come up with the seven-year engagement idea. Perhaps he was capable of doing the impossible and thwarting her father's plans while still saving herself and the theatre. Arabella knew she was grasping at straws, but she nodded and followed him down the steps around to the side of the house, away from the sound of the celebrating crowd.

He took her to a small, white-painted pergola and once again he took her hands gently in his. And once again Arabella fought against her unwanted reactions. Her hands should not be burning. Her heart should not be racing at such a furious pace because he was touching her. And she most definitely should not be wishing he'd do more than just hold her hands.

'I am so sorry, Arabella. I should have told my mother not to say anything. Although, unlike my father, she is a terrible liar, so even if I had informed her of our plans she probably would have told the truth anyway.'

'You have nothing to apologise for.' She looked up into his brown eyes, eyes that were no longer sparkling with mischief, but were gazing down at her apologetically. Arabella was unsure which was harder to bear, that wicked glint in his eye, or this look of concern. Both ignited a strange response deep within her core, causing her to lean towards him as if drawn by an invisible but powerful force.

She told herself to stand up straight. 'None of this is your fault. It's all my father's fault. He has made it impossible for me to get out of this marriage without threatening the jobs of people I care about, but that shouldn't affect you. You don't have to go through with this.'

He stared at her for a moment, then slowly shook his head. 'I don't want to be the cause of your friends losing their livelihoods. They've done nothing wrong, so why should they suffer?'

She smiled at him. He cared about people he didn't know. He cared about his mother and had protected her from the pain of being married to a reprobate. Despite the way he lived his life, there was definitely a lot of good in Oliver Huntsbury.

He smiled back and she wished he hadn't. Not when it drew her gaze to his soft, sensual lips. Lips that had once kissed her. She bit the edge of her bottom lip and, with as much nonchalance as she could muster, she forced her eyes to move from his lips to his eyes. But that was no better. His warm dark eyes glittered, like sparkling black onyx, accentuating their devilish quality, causing her cheeks to erupt with heat and a tingling sensation to radiate out from her lips and race around her body.

She looked down at the ground. 'That's very thoughtful of you,' she said, her voice barely a whisper. She swallowed and slowly raised her gaze. 'It's very good of you to care about my colleagues,' she repeated in a more assertive voice. 'But it doesn't solve our problem. If we don't get married, my father will withdraw his money and the theatre and all the cast and crew will soon be ruined. But we don't want to get married, do we?'

He shook his head. Then that delicious smile grew wider. 'So, I'll make them a better offer.'

'You'll what?' she asked as he continued to smile that glorious smile.

'My money is just as good as your father's. There's nothing to stop me from offering the theatre whatever your father has offered them and more. Then your friends will be safe. You won't have to get married. We can tell your father we still plan to wed, but that we want a long, long engagement for propriety's sake. You'll be safe for a while yet from his matchmaking.'

Arabella's heart leapt. He had done it. He had done the impossible. He had found a way out of their dilemma. 'Oh, Oliver, that's a wonderful idea. You're so clever.' In her excitement she threw her arms round his neck.

His hands slid to her waist and he laughed. 'I never realised that one day a woman would become ecstatic because I promised I wouldn't marry her.'

'Oh, but that is the kindest thing you could do.'

He looked down at her, his laughter dying away. His dark brown eyes grew intense, staring into hers. As if mesmerised, she felt incapable of looking away. As she continued to gaze into the deep, fathomless depths a shiver rippled through her body. His hands were still on her waist, holding her firmly. His touch burned into her, through the fabric of her gown, into her skin, making it tingle with awareness. Her heart beating so hard she could feel it hammering against her chest, she knew she was incapable of breaking from him, did not want to break from his touch. Slowly, she moved her hands up his neck, her fingers curling through his thick blond hair. Parting her lips, she rose on her toes, moved her body closer to his, needing to feel the touch of his chest against hers, desperate to feel his arms close tightly around her. As if under the command of a puppet master, she pressed herself against him, rose even higher on her toes and tilted her head until her lips gently touched his.

And then he was kissing her.

Oh, this man definitely knew how to kiss! She had repeatedly dreamt of him kissing her again since the first night they'd met and now her dream was coming true. She parted her lips wider, her tongue lightly stroking his bottom lip, loving the masculine taste of him, the feel of his skilled mouth on hers.

He groaned slightly and pulled her in closer, his arms encasing her, holding her firmly. As if she was in one of her fervid dreams, she felt his tongue entering her mouth, tasting, probing, possessing her. She was hardly aware of what she was doing. All she knew was that she wanted this, wanted it with every inch of her aching body.

Like a starving man who had been invited to a feast, he deepened the kiss, pulling her in even closer. His powerful chest was now hard up against her breasts, breasts that were swollen with desire. Without thought she rubbed herself against him, desperately needing to be touched by him, to be desired by him, to be caressed by him.

As if following her unspoken command, he ran his hands down the back of her body, cupping her buttocks. His touch on so intimate a place released a tempest of need within her that was both exciting and frightening. Oh, yes, she wanted this man, wanted to experience every sensual pleasure he could give her. She arched her back, her buttocks moving sensually under his hands, letting him know how much she needed him, how much she had to have him, how desperate she was for him to relieve the fiery need burning within her.

'Marking the happy occasion, are we?' She heard a voice behind her, as if coming from a distant place.

He broke from her and she fell forward against him, her head tilted, her throbbing lips still desperate for his kisses.

'I'm pleased to see you two getting on so well. But you should leave all this until the wedding night, you know.'

Her father's voice invaded her foggy consciousness and she jumped back from Oliver as if from a raging inferno that was threatening to engulf her.

'Father? What are you...why are you...?'

'It looks like I'm saving you from giving yourself to this man before he's even sealed the deal and put a ring on your finger.'

He took hold of Arabella's arm and forcefully pulled her away. Oliver stepped towards her father, his eyes blazing with fury. But a fight between Oliver and her father would serve no purpose. Arabella had acted like a fool. Her kiss had revealed to Oliver exactly how much she desired his touch, something she had fought so hard to conceal. This whole incident had been embarrassing enough, without them fighting over her honour. An honour she had been more than happy to surrender to a man who was a master at the art of seduction.

She shook her head and placed her hand in the middle of Oliver's chest to halt his progress. 'It's all right,' she murmured, her voice cracking.

He continued to glare at her father but halted his progress and unclasped his clenched fists.

What had come over her? She was not going to marry Oliver Huntsbury. And she most definitely did not want to become one of his many mistresses, even if he *was* capable of kissing her into oblivion. This was all her fault. She should never have let her guard down and kissed him in the first place.

For once she had to admit her father's interference was all for the best. If he hadn't come along, who knew what might have happened. She might have given herself to him, just as countless other women had done before her and no doubt countless other women would do in the future.

Without another word to Oliver she turned her back on him and allowed her father to escort her back to the party, for once pretending to be the dutiful daughter she most certainly was not.

Oliver watched Arabella and her father walk away through narrowed eyes. 'Leave it for the wedding night,' her father had said. But there would be no wedding night. That meant he would never get to explore her tempting body, never get to fully taste what she had to offer. And if that kiss was anything to judge by it would be spectacular. She had kissed him with such passion, such urgency, such need. And the effect it had on him was devastating.

He had long ago lost count of the number of women he had kissed, the number of women he had bedded. He was all but blasé about kissing yet another woman. But Arabella, she was different. He didn't know what it was, but there was something special about her. It wasn't just her pretty face—he had kissed plenty of pretty women before—nor was it her gorgeous body, as tempting as it was. It couldn't be her innocence. He had always shied away from virtuous virgins, seeing them as nothing but trouble. And *he* most definitely would be trouble for *them*. While the idea of deflowering a virgin appealed to some men, it most definitely did not appeal to him.

Perhaps it was her passion. A passion that was also evident in her determination to succeed as an actress, to succeed against her father's wishes, despite the odds that were stacked against her. Perhaps it was that which made her so appealing to him. Or was it that she was utterly unimpressed by his title? For so many women his title was like a red rag to a bull. The thought of being the next Duchess of Somerfeld had seen many a young debutante throw herself in his path. But Arabella would rather have a minor acting role in a play at a rundown theatre than all the social prestige that came with being a duchess. Perhaps that's what he found so attractive. That and her pretty face, gorgeous body and very kissable lips, of course.

With that riddle still unsolved he headed back to the party. As the joyous crowd surrounded him, he could not get the conundrum of Arabella van Haven out of his mind. But the mystery would have to remain unsolved. They would not be marrying. He would make sure of that. He most certainly had no interest in marriage to anyone. She had no interest in marriage to him. So, he would make sure he found a way to halt this wedding.

Her father had said leave it till the wedding night and it was most definitely a shame that there would be no wedding night. But it could not be. He was not so much of a cad that he would subject such a lovely woman to the horror of being married to him just because he wanted to fully sample all that her passionate nature and beautiful body had to offer.

He looked over to where Arabella was talking to a group of excited actors, a fake smile once again on her lips, those plump red lips that had just moments ago been pressed up hard against his.

He sighed deeply. It was most certainly a shame that he would not get to experience the pleasure of their wedding night. And, of course, he would never take a woman like Arabella as his mistress. It was extremely tempting, but it was out of the question. He might not have much of a code when it came to women, but one rule he did abide by was that no one got hurt. And Arabella was a woman who could so easily get hurt.

He took a glass of champagne offered to him by a footman. As there would be no wedding, and hence no wedding night, the only thing left for him to do was to try to enjoy his own engagement party.

Chapter Eight

'What do you mean, you sold the business?'

'Exactly that. I've sold the lot. The entire building, which includes the theatre, the props and costumes, along with rights to the plays. Everything. I was made an offer I couldn't possibly refuse.'

Oliver glared down at the theatre owner seated behind his messy desk. The *former* owner of the Limelight Theatre. 'And dare I ask who bought it?' It was a question to which Oliver already knew the answer.

'Mr van Haven bought it.' The owner leaned back in his squeaking chair, put his hands behind his head and smiled. 'He offered me a ridiculous amount of money. He's closed the theatre for renovations, laid off the staff on full pay and pouring money into the place as if it's a bottomless pit. I must say I was a bit taken aback. I would have thought a man like Mr van Haven would have more financial sense than to spend such money on a third-rate theatre like this.' He waved his arms in the air as if to encompass the entire Limelight Theatre, the shabby office, the run-down auditorium and the severely neglected backstage area. 'But there you go. He can't be as clever or as good a businessman as people say he is. It looks as though when it comes to the theatre, he doesn't know what he's doing, but I made a tidy profit, which is all that really matters.'

Oliver shook his head in dismay. The theatre owner was wrong. Mr van Haven knew exactly what he was doing. He had spent that money to make sure his daughter was compliant with his plans to marry her off to a man with a title. To Mr van Haven it would be money well spent. Once again, the older man had outsmarted them and thwarted Oliver's plan.

'Well, at least his daughter will be happy that the theatre is doing well out of her father's money.' Oliver was desperate to see the bright side of this dismal situation. It had to be some consolation that the theatre would now be a success. He had to have some good news to take back to Arabella. Perhaps telling her that the theatre was to be greatly improved by her father might be the small silver lining to an otherwise very black cloud.

'His daughter? Why?' the former owner said, standing up and placing a wooden crate on his desk so he could pack up his belongings.

'Arabella van Haven. She's an actress here at the theatre.'

'She used to be.'

Oliver grabbed the man's arms and pulled him across the desk, halting his packing. 'What are you saying? What do you mean, used to be?'

The former owner stared back at him with wide eyes, a pile of old theatre programmes dropping from his hands. 'Just that—she used to be an actress here.

Apparently, her father told the director to find some-one to replace her. He said he didn't want to see Ara-bella van Haven's name on the bill ever again.'

Oliver froze, his face still inches from the other man's, then sunk down into a chair. With his head in his hands he released a growl of frustration. This was getting worse and worse. Not only would he have to tell Arabella that his plan to pay the theatre so he could stop their marriage had failed, but she was now also out of a job. She would be crushed. All her dreams would be shattered. This could not happen. He had to think of something to stop this ridiculous marriage and save Arabella's job. But what? That was a question to which Oliver had no answer.

He had agreed to meet Arabella at Hyde Park to tell her the good news. When he had set off to the theatre this morning, he had been full of confidence, certain that he would make everything right. All he had to do was offer the owner a better deal, give him more money than Mr van Haven. He had even con-sidered buying the theatre himself. Then it would be safe. All Arabella's colleagues would keep their jobs and Arabella would be saved from the terrible fate of having to marry him.

Instead, the only bit of good news he could give her was the theatre was indeed saved and everyone's job was safe. Everyone's, that is, except hers.

As he walked towards their agreed meeting place by the Serpentine, he felt like a man going to his ex-ecution. And not just because he was now committed to marrying in less than a month's time, but because he was going to have to disappoint Arabella on two counts. Her father could still hold the threat of destroying the theatre over her head and her dream of becoming an actress was now in tatters.

She was sitting on a bench staring out over the lake, looking as enchanting as she did on that first night when they met. Dressed in a blue-striped dress, with a jaunty straw hat sporting a blue ribbon on her ornately styled black hair and protecting herself from the warm sunshine with a cream-coloured lacy parasol, she was as pretty as a picture.

He paused to watch her and enjoy the sight before he had to destroy any sense of hope she might be feeling. She was staring straight ahead with unseeing eyes, not taking in the small boy in front of her, floating his ornate toy sailing ship on the placid water, or the little girl jumping around with an excited pug dog.

Oliver inhaled deeply to give himself courage and strode towards her in a manner more confident than he felt. The young lady's maid chaperoning her stood up as he approached and, as if by arrangement, she wandered off to give them some privacy.

Arabella looked up and sent him an expectant smile, then registered his stern look and her smile faded. 'It's bad news, isn't it? What has he done now?' Her shaking hands folded up the parasol and she gripped the wooden handle tightly.

He sat down beside her, his heart in his mouth. 'Your father has bought the theatre,' he stated bluntly, not knowing any way to soften the blow.

She released an annoyed sigh. 'I should have known he'd do something like that. He's got a reputation for anticipating what his business rivals will did not want to marry a title. Instead one was being thrust upon her.

'But I promise you, once we're married, we can part company,' he said, in his most reassuring voice. 'I'll make no further demands on you.'

Her smile was sad and suggested she didn't believe him. And why *should* she believe him? After all, all she really knew of him was that he was the sort of man who crashed into strange women's dressing rooms, grabbed them and kissed them. A man who had to run from irate husbands. A man with a scandalous reputation.

'And if nothing else, you will at least be safe from your father, Arabella.' He couldn't offer her much, but at least he could offer her that. 'After all, you'll be my wife. You'll be under my care, not your father's. He won't be able to stop you from doing anything, ever again. And I promise you your freedom.'

Arabella breathed in deeply, then exhaled slowly. 'It is so unfair,' she said, emphasising every word. 'I always have to be under someone's care, my father, my husband and, under normal circumstances, it would eventually be my son, just the way your mother is under your authority. It's simply not fair.'

Oliver shrugged. 'I can't agree more. And often women are under the authority of men less competent than themselves, but that, unfortunately, is the way of the world.'

'But it shouldn't be.'

'No, it shouldn't be.'

Once again Oliver felt as if that, too, was his fault. But he hadn't made the world the way it was. All he could do was ensure that one woman, Arabella,

do and I guess that's what we are now, his business rivals.'

They both looked out at the lake and Oliver steeled himself to impart the next bit of bad news. 'I'm afraid that's not all he's done.'

Her body tensed beside him and he heard a sharp intake of breath. 'What else could he do? He's got everything he wants now.'

'I'm afraid he's told the director that you can't work at the theatre any more.'

He had expected an immediate response: tears, foot stamping, angry words. But she continued to stare out at the lake, her body rigid as she silently seethed. 'Now he has gone too far,' she eventually said, through clenched teeth. 'He's already won, so why does he have to punish me even further?'

Pain gripped Oliver in the middle of his chest. Somehow, this all felt like his fault. Perhaps if he hadn't crashed into her room that night, if he hadn't taken her in his arms and kissed her, none of this might have happened. In some ways it was indeed his fault. And it was up to him to make it right. 'Please, Arabella, don't upset yourself. He might have stopped you acting at the Limelight, but he can't stop you acting altogether. You got the job there without him knowing, you can use your wits to find another job somewhere else. There are other theatres in London. He can't buy them all. It will be all right. I'll make sure it is.'

He didn't know how he would do that, but he would try. He couldn't bear to see her so unhappy, couldn't bear to see her dreams shattered.

'You're very kind, but this is not your problem.'

She turned to face him and he could see unshed tears in her eyes. 'I've said it before and I still mean it. You don't have to marry me. You don't have to get caught up in my father's scheming. He said he'd sue you for breach of promise, but he'd never do that, because the scandal might ruin his chances of marrying me off to someone else.'

Oliver shrugged. She was wrong. He didn't have a choice. If he didn't go through with this marriage, he would leave Arabella in a worse position than she already was. If they didn't marry, her father would withdraw all his funds from the theatre and it would be forced to close. And it was obvious that would not stop her father. He would eventually find some other titled man for her to marry and it might be one who did not respect and admire her the way Oliver was coming to, more and more.

'I've said I'd go through with it and, even though I've got too many faults to list, I'm always true to my word. Unless we can think of something your father hasn't already anticipated within the next four weeks, it looks as though we're about to become newlyweds.'

She gave a resigned shrug of her slim shoulders and sighed loudly. 'Thank you. It's very kind of you to go to all this trouble.'

Oliver swallowed a sudden ironic laugh. Many women had pursued him over the years, desperate to become the next Duchess of Somerfeld. They had all chosen to ignore the fact that they would be marrying a man incapable of committing to one woman. All they could see was a title, nothing else. He had dodged a bullet many times, saving himself and many a young woman from that terrible fate. Now he was

to marry someone who mistakenly thought he was a kind man, that he was kind because he was trying his best to save her from such a marriage. He could almost see the funny side of the situation. Almost.

'Hopefully it won't come to that,' he said. 'We've still got a month to think of a way out of this situation.'

She shrugged again and slowly shook her head. 'I've never known anyone to get the better of my father and he's been up against equally ruthless businessmen, ambitious politicians and bankers who are just as much in love with money as him, and he's thwarted them all. I don't think we stand much of a chance.'

They sighed simultaneously and looked out at the lake.

'I suppose being married to one another won't be that bad.' Oliver gave her an apologetic smile.

'No, I suppose there are worse things that happen to people. And I guess it could be much worse. He could be marrying me off to someone like Lord Bufford.'

He shuddered at the thought of Arabella married to a man like that and took heart from the fact that she considered him a better catch than a sixty-year-old man with a deeply florid complexion, bushy grey eyebrows, an overly waxed walrus moustache, a bulbous nose and a decidedly aggressive and irritating disposition.

Yet Violet Bufford had been more than happy to marry him. She, and her family had ignored Lord Bufford's flaws because it meant moving up the social hierarchy. But Arabella was not like that. Sh

his future wife, was free to live her life the way she wanted to, without the interference of any man, including her husband.

'And it's not fair to you either. You should be allowed to marry whomever you want, not be manipulated into marriage by my father.' She bit the edge of her lip. 'Is there anyone you really do want to marry?'

Oliver shook his head and smiled. 'No, there never has been and there never will be.'

She turned slightly on the bench and looked at him, her head tilted in question. 'But you're a duke. Don't all dukes have to marry, whether they want to or not, so they can produce the heir and the spare and keep the line going?'

Oliver laughed at her misplaced concern. 'I suppose the ones who care about such things do, but there's other members of my family who'll more than happily take up the title of Duke when I kick the bucket. And I think the world would be a better place if I didn't procreate.'

His smile died and he turned to face her. 'But what about you, Arabella? Don't you want children?' He held his breath while he waited for her answer. No matter what her response was, it was an added complication and one he hadn't considered.

Her gaze dropped and she stared at her hands, clenched tightly on her lap. 'I don't want to think about that now,' she said, her voice barely a whisper. 'We've only four weeks to think of a way out of this, that's what we should be concentrating on.'

Four weeks. That's all they had to think their way out of this impossible situation. Arabella looked back out over the calm water of the Serpentine and contemplated how they were going to achieve the impossible.

'So, do you have any more thoughts on what we can do to stop this marriage?'

He shook his head. 'I'm sorry, Arabella, I'm out of ideas at the present.'

Then it truly looked as though her father was going to win. Didn't he always?

The one time she had thought she had won a victory over her father was when she had insisted that he allow Rosie to live with them after Rosie's mother died. At the time Arabella had thrown a temper tantrum, had threatened to run away, until her father relented. She had thought she had won a victory. Now she suspected her father had merely decided that it would be to his advantage to make Rosie his ward. It gave Arabella a friend, someone to play with and entertain her when he was away from home pursuing his latest business venture. So, to some extent Rosie had become just another possession that he had given to his daughter. It had not been her victory. If her father hadn't seen all the advantages of having a ward, he would have made Rosie leave, despite the devastation it would have caused to an innocent young girl.

And Arabella was no different. She, too, was just a possession.

It was a terrible thing to think, but that was all she had ever been to her father. And now she was going to have to repay him for all the money he had spent on her over the years by giving him what he wanted, an entry to the British aristocracy. He didn't care who she married, whether the man loved her or not was of no concern, whether he was a scoundrel or a good man did not matter, as long as he had a title.

Was it even worth fighting a man who always won? 'Perhaps we should just go through with it,' she said, her voice resigned. 'After all, it won't be a real marriage. I wouldn't interfere with the way you live your life. My father will get his victory and we'll both be free to do as we please.'

It was most definitely not what Arabella wanted. She had no immediate plans for marriage, but when it happened, she had expected to be married to a man she loved, a kindred spirit who wanted to pursue the same dreams as herself. But then, wasn't that what she thought Arnold Emerson was? And hadn't she been wrong about him? Hadn't she completely misjudged the man she'd once thought she loved?

His love had been as phoney as her marriage would be. But with Oliver at least there would be no pretence. He didn't love her and he had no intention of pretending he did. And it could be much worse. She could be marrying someone who did not respect her work as an actress and would forbid her from continuing her life on the stage.

She would just have to resign herself to being married to a man who had countless lovers.

And she would just have to keep that thought foremost in her mind at all times if she was to avoid humiliating herself.

She had forgotten it when she had shamelessly thrown her arms around his neck at the engagement party and kissed him with an intensity that had surprised and shocked her.

And even this morning she had almost forgotten

who he was and what he was like. She had chosen her gown with such care and had even been tempted to apply a touch of rouge and lipstick, just to enhance her appearance. She applied make-up every time she appeared on stage, but never before today had she even considered doing something as risqué as wearing it in public.

It had all been so ridiculous. She should not be trying to make herself appear attractive to him. After all, she did not want to attract him. Did she?

No, of course she didn't. These affectations were going to have to be kept well under control if this marriage of convenience was to work. If her marriage was to be a success, she would need to ensure she had no feelings for her husband and that any physical attraction she felt towards him was squashed down so small that she was able to ignore it.

She glanced over at her husband-to-be. Except, squashing her feelings of attraction for him was going to be no small task. While she was pleased he wasn't an old duffer like Lord Bufford, being married to a man as handsome as Oliver Huntsbury was going to have its own complications. He was undeniably the most attractive man she had ever met and she had met some handsome men working in the theatre. But it wasn't just his stunning good looks that caused her to so easily forget her resolve. Nor was it just his easy, confident manner. There was something special about him. It was a quality that leading men strove hard to capture. It was a magnetism that caused every eye to turn in his direction and for women, even sensible ones like herself, to suddenly start preening themselves and acting in a ridiculously coquettish manner.

Yes, his masculine appeal was undeniable. But she was most certainly not the first woman to feel its attraction and she would not be the last. If she was to deny its pull, she had to keep reminding herself of Lady Bufford, Lucy Baker and all his other *very good friends*. She could not allow herself to be lured in, just because he was handsome. It did not matter what effect his kisses had on her. It did not matter that she could hardly remember who she was, where she was and why she was doing what she knew she shouldn't.

It was not going to be easy, but this unwanted marriage would only work if she kept her distance from Oliver, the reprobate Duke of Somerfeld.

Chapter Nine

A wedding day should be the happiest day of a woman's life. Isn't that what everybody said? But when you're being married against your will to a man who has been tricked into becoming your husband, happiness doesn't tend to be an emotion in great abundance.

A solemn Arabella stared at her reflection in the ornate mirror. It was like déjà vu. Just four weeks ago she was sitting in exactly the same place, staring at an equally sad reflection. The only difference was that time she was facing an engagement party. Today it was a wedding. And after today she would be a married woman.

'Cheer up, girls,' Arabella said with false enthusiasm, as an unusually gloomy Nellie dressed her hair, watched on by an equally despondent Rosie. 'It could be worse. I really could be going to my execution, instead of just becoming a bride.'

Her two friends sent her reassuring smiles.

'You're right,' Rosie agreed. 'It could be much worse. You could be marrying a man who wouldn't let you act on the stage.'

'And he could have bad breath and be desperate for an heir,' Nellie added. 'One thing about the Duke, he's definitely easy on the eye.'

Arabella smiled. There were some consolations, she supposed.

Her hair completed, Nellie tightened the laces of her corset, helped her into her silk petticoat and removed the wedding gown from the wardrobe. Using a pattern from a French fashion house and hand-embroidered ivory material, the London dressmaker had created an exquisite bridal gown. Despite her reluctance to marry, she experienced a slight thrill of excitement as Nellie helped her into the flowing folds of white satin. She did a small twirl in front of the mirror and watched the soft fabric of the long train swirl gently around her ankles. The gown was the epitome of elegance and romance even if today's wedding was nothing more than a business transaction.

Nellie fastened the line of small pearl-coloured buttons at the back of Arabella's gown, placed the gossamer-fine veil carefully on her head and secured it in place with a simple garland of orange blossoms. She removed a silver and diamond necklace from the jewellery box and placed it around Arabella's neck.

At the sight of the necklace Arabella bit her trembling lip. It had belonged to her mother, a gift from her father when they got married. Arabella couldn't help but wonder what her mother would have thought of this hastily arranged marriage. Would she have approved? Or would she have forbidden it and insisted that her daughter marry for love, not for social advancement?

Arabella would never know, but she could only

hope that her mother would have been a loving parent who wanted the best for her daughter.

As she buttoned up her lacy white gloves she looked at her sad reflection and sighed. The happiest day of her life? Not in the slightest.

'Well, I suppose we should get this over and done with,' she said to her friends. Rosie was dressed as her maid of honour and was wearing a flattering cream gown with a blue waistband. Unlike Arabella, marriage suited Rosie and every time she mentioned her husband her voice softened and her face lit up with pleasure. That's what a marriage should be like. It should be a love match. It shouldn't be about titles and improving one's social status.

The two girls made their way down the grand staircase of Somerfeld Manor, followed by Nellie, who was still fussing about the gown and straightening out the train.

Arabella took a few minutes to compose herself before walking out of the front entrance.

Her father was waiting for her, standing beside an open carriage decorated with garlands of flowers. The liveried footman moved forward. He offered his hand to help Arabella and Rosie into the carriage that would take them to the local church where the supposedly happy event would take place.

Her smiling father climbed in beside them. Dressed in a formal grey morning suit, a white orchid in his buttonhole, she had never seen him look more pleased with himself. This wedding might not be the happiest day of Arabella's life, but it was evidently the happiest day of her father's.

He had stopped her from marrying Arnold Emerson, the man she'd thought she loved, because he wasn't going to waste a potential asset on a man who would bring neither money nor prestige into the family.

Arnold had not loved her and had been easily bought off. Her father had inadvertently saved her from making a match that would have been a disaster. But that had not been his reason for offering Arnold money so he would withdraw his affections. If Arnold had possessed a fortune, or better still a title, they would now be wed.

And now her father had found someone with both money and a title. So, whether they were in love or not was of no matter to him, her father had what he wanted.

As they rode down the long, oak-lined driveway, the leaves rustled in a slight breeze and the carriage wheels crunched over the gravel. It was another perfectly sunny day. But that was the only thing perfect about this day, the weather.

The closer they got to the church the more Arabella's nerves jangled. She was about to be married. Her life was about to change for ever. She had no idea what it was going to be like to be married to the Duke of Somerfeld. He had promised her freedom, had said that nothing would change for her, but she had known him for such a short time. She knew virtually nothing about him. Nothing, that was, except the rumours she had heard and that did little to still her rampaging nerves.

The temptation to throw herself out of the carriage and make a run for it was becoming all but overwhelming. But where could she run to? Nowhere.

She was in the middle of the Surrey countryside and dressed in clothing that was hardly suitable for fast escapes. And if she knew her father well, and she did, he probably had burly men stationed along the path to drag her kicking and screaming back to the altar.

There was just one possibility left, that Oliver might have even colder feet than she did. Perhaps he had already decided to flee, back to the arms of one of his many mistresses. After all, there was nothing in this marriage for him. He said he didn't break his word, but how was she to know if that was true? He might have kept his word in the past, but he had presumably never been faced with the prospect of marriage before.

She shivered, as if the weather had suddenly turned cold, even though the sun remained shining in the cloudless blue sky.

Would it really be a good or a bad thing if Oliver didn't turn up? It would be good that she wouldn't have to get married, but bad as her father might withdraw his funding for the theatre. It would also be bad to once again endure the humiliation of being jilted, albeit this time by a man she didn't want to marry in the first place.

And all it would do was postpone the inevitable. Her father would find some other hapless member of the aristocracy to marry her off to and he would find some other method of tricking her into walking up the aisle. With a small dejected sigh Arabella knew she just had to accept the inevitable.

No matter how she looked at it, she was doomed. Doomed to become a wife.

The carriage pulled up outside a quaint stone

church, surrounded by happy villagers, all eager to get a view of the bride. No doubt many were wondering what sort of woman had actually captured the notorious rake, Oliver Huntsbury.

Arabella tried, with all her might, to look happy for their sake.

To the sound of an organ playing the wedding march, she entered the church on her father's arm, with Rosie walking behind. The sweet scent of roses from the flowers bedecking the church filled the air as they made their slow funereal walk up the aisle.

The congregation stood in the wooden pews and every head turned in her direction. Some were smiling, some were scowling and many had bemused expressions on their faces, as if they, too, could not believe this was actually happening.

Oliver turned to look at her and Arabella's slow progress momentarily faltered. Her husband-to-be looked magnificent. Dressed in a dove-grey morning suit, with a cream waistcoat and white cravat, he was more sublimely handsome than she remembered. Even from this distance she could see that seductive spark in his eyes. He was smiling with reassurance and Arabella tried to feel reassured. But how could she possibly feel calm when she could feel the blood pumping through her body and the hammering rhythm of her heart was so loud it was almost drowning out the sound of the wedding march?

And tonight would be their wedding night, their first together as man and wife. If Arabella's nerves weren't jittery enough already, reminding herself of that fact was enough to send them into agitated spasms.

She reached the altar and, like the possession she was, her father handed her over to Oliver. He smiled down at her and a frisson of awareness rippled through her. This man was to be her husband. This man with his laughing eyes and his devilish smile was to be her husband. This man, with a seductive charm that made him notorious among actresses and aristocrats alike, was to be her husband. Once again, she wondered whether it wouldn't be better to be forced into a marriage with a man who wasn't so attractive. Then she'd know exactly how to feel about this situation. She wouldn't be standing beside a man who caused her to feel disorientated every time he looked at her. A man whose kisses caused her to respond with a passion she had not thought she was capable of. A man who she knew she should never, ever fall for.

Arabella closed her eyes. She had to keep reminding herself of that fact if she was not to lose all sense of reason. No matter how much Oliver's charm and seductive manners disorientated her, she had to remember her resolve to keep her distance from him. She was not a real wife and she did not want to be one of the many women in his life. She did not want to be like his mother, in love with a man who was incapable of fidelity.

No matter what happened on their wedding night, and every other day and night that followed in their marriage, she would not let herself fall under his spell.

She opened her eyes and looked up at the vicar, dressed in his ornate vestments. Despite her determination to focus and not be distracted by the man standing beside her, she hardly heard a word the vicar said, apart from when he asked if anyone had just cause why this man and this woman could not be joined together in holy matrimony.

Arabella waited for someone, anyone, to say yes, because it was a joke, a farce, that it wasn't holy matrimony, it was a holy mess.

But the congregation remained silent.

She also heard Oliver promising to love and honour her, two things she doubted he would do. And as for *forsaking all others*—well, they had already agreed that would not be happening. But then again, she also promised to obey him in her own wedding vows. Something she had no intention of doing.

The vows completed, the best man held out the wedding ring for Oliver to place on Arabella's finger. Arabella removed her gloves, lifted her left hand and was horrified to see that it was shaking. Oliver gently took hold of it and covered it with both his hands, as if trying to calm her down and allow his strength to flow into her. But the touch of his skin on hers had the opposite effect. A rippling sensation rushed up her arm, causing her heartbeat to increase its furious tempo and her already agitated nerves to strain further until she was close to fainting.

She closed her eyes, took in a series of steadying breaths, then looked up at him and sent him what she hoped was a composed smile. But the tremor at the edges of her lips made a lie of any such pretence to composure.

'It's all right, Arabella,' he murmured quietly. 'Try to see this as a victory over your father. Once you're married you will be a free woman.'

Arabella nodded slightly and tried to smile with stiff lips.

The vicar coughed and sent Oliver a pointed look, reminding him to continue with the service.

Oliver picked up the ring, gazed down at Arabella and smiled. 'With this ring I thee wed, with my body I thee worship and with all my worldly goods I thee endow,' he said as he gently slid the ring up Arabella's finger.

With my body I thee worship.

A blush rushed to Arabella's cheeks. The last thing she wanted to think about right now was Oliver's body and she certainly didn't want to visualise him worshipping her. An image of being held by him, kissed by him, invaded her thoughts. Her cheeks grew hotter. Her heart pounded harder. She had to get her reactions under control. She just had to. She turned to face the vicar, who smiled at her benevolently and proclaimed them man and wife.

It was over. They were now married. Her fate was sealed.

'You may now kiss the bride,' the vicar said. No, it wasn't over. She had one more ordeal to endure.

She looked up at him and could feel her lips trembling. In fear? In anticipation? Arabella was unsure.

Oliver sent her one of those devilish smiles that always seemed to make her body react in the most inappropriate of manners. Although perhaps it was no longer inappropriate to react in such a way, now that he was her husband. Arabella pushed that thought away. He was her husband in name only, so, yes, it was still inappropriate.

He leant down and lightly kissed her on the lips. She closed her eyes. Despite herself she loved the

touch of his lips on hers, even if it was just a formality.

She parted her lips slightly, willing him to kiss her
more deeply. But unlike herself, he had the sense to
remember they were in a public place and his kiss remained light. Or was it because he was being watched
by a congregation that included at least one of his
mistresses and possibly several more?

The church bells rang out joyously and, as if in a
trance, Arabella was led back down the aisle on the
arm of her new husband.

A cascade of red rose petals descended on them as
they stood in the entrance of the church and the full
reality of the situation hit Arabella. She was now married to Oliver Huntsbury. Married until death parted
them. No matter what he said about nothing changing,
her life had just changed for ever in a fundamental
way. She was now a married woman. Nothing would
ever be the same again.

Oliver tried to smile as the rose petals danced
around them, caught in the light breeze. He was now
married, married to Arabella van Haven. A woman
he hardly knew. Just one short month ago, he had
no intention of marrying anyone, ever. And now he
was a married man. He had promised to honour this
woman in sickness and in health, for richer and for
poorer, and that, at least, he would do. But it was all
so much to take in. What sort of marriage would they
have? Would they really be able to work out an arrangement that suited them both?

Oliver hardly noticed the many people who shook
his hands, slapped him on the back and congratulated

him. All he could think was, *I'm now a married man. I've done what I vowed I would never do.*

And he had good reason for making that vow. He knew he was incapable of committing to one woman. He had discovered as a young man that he was exactly like his father. He loved women, but it was all women he loved—it would never be just one woman. And if he couldn't commit to one woman, then he wouldn't ever get married. It was a simple solution that had worked well for him in the past. But now he was married and to the type of woman he never, ever got involved with.

His gaze moved from his young bride to his smiling, happy mother.

He was not letting history completely repeat itself. Unlike his father's marriage to his mother, his bride was under no illusions about the sort of man she had married. He had not deceived his new bride, had never pretended to be someone he wasn't.

He looked back at Arabella, who was being hugged by her best friend. Remembering that she was not his would be so much easier if she didn't look so damn attractive. From the moment he saw her on the stage at the Limelight Theatre he had been entranced by her gentle beauty. Those crystal-blue eyes that sparked with intelligence, that heart-shaped face was undeniably attractive and she had immediately caught his eye. And how could he not be attracted to a woman who was so fiercely independent? She was determined to become a successful actress, to make her own way in the world. She had a father who was fabulously wealthy, who could buy and sell many members of the aristocracy. Yet she wanted nothing from him. She preferred to work in a shabby theatre in a rundown part of London rather than live a life of privilege and idleness. Her single-minded determination was something for which he had immense admiration.

His mother approached him, beaming with happiness. 'Oh, darling, that service was so touching.' She dabbed at her eyes. 'And Arabella makes such a beautiful bride.'

He kissed his mother's cheek and looked over at his bride. She did indeed look beautiful. The white gown suited her so much. It was a shame she was not a real bride, getting married to the man she loved. It was something she would never now experience and for that Oliver felt a deep sense of guilt. She should be marrying for love, to a man who loved her. She deserved that. She did not deserve this forced marriage. She did not deserve to have him in her life. If he hadn't burst into her dressing room chased by a group of thugs, her father might not have felt he could blackmail him into marriage. There was no doubt that her father would not have given up until his daughter was married to a titled man, but if she hadn't been forced to marry him, she might have met a titled man she could love, who could love her. He did indeed have a lot to feel guilty for, a lot to make up to Arabella. And the best way he could do that was to leave her alone, to let her live her life the way she wanted, without his interference.

Chapter Ten

Somerfeld Manor had been transformed for the wedding. Even to Oliver's undiscerning eye he could see that a great deal of effort had gone into making the house festive and inviting. Large bouquets of fragrant flowers decorated the great hall where the wedding breakfast was to be held. And musicians were tuning up in the adjoining ballroom in preparation for the dance that was to take place later that evening.

Tables had been set out for the large party of guests. Crystal sparkled, silver glistened and the tables were strewn with ivy leaves and scented lilac flowers. The house servants, along with an army of extras recruited for the day, were rushing about, attending to every need of the guests.

Oliver escorted Arabella to the head of the table, and, when she had seated herself, the wedding party sat down to the accompaniment of shuffling chairs and the sudden eruption of chatter.

Champagne began to flow immediately and the footmen made sure that glasses were topped up before they had a chance to be emptied. But Oliver took pains to ensure he moderated his drinking. It was essential that he keep himself under complete control. Something which he could tell was not going to be easy to achieve. Not when his new bride was sitting so close to him that he could smell her delightful jasmine perfume. But he knew from past experience that if he wanted to keep his amorous inclinations in check, then imbibing champagne would not help.

While the rest of the wedding party chatted, laughed, drank and ate, the couple at the head of the table exchanged only a few words as they picked at each successive course. Speeches were made, but Oliver hardly heard a word of what was said. He laughed when others laughed, looked solemn when others talked of the sacred importance of the institute of marriage. He even made a speech of his own, saying all the appropriate things about how beautiful his new bride was and how he would do everything he could to make her happy, all of which was true.

But it all happened as if he was watching someone else going through the motions of a wedding. One that had little or nothing to do with him. But then, that was exactly what he and his wife were doing, wasn't it? Going through the motions.

The wedding breakfast finished; he escorted his new wife through to the ballroom.

'It's almost over, Arabella,' he whispered in her ear as the band played and he led her out on to the dance floor for their first waltz together as man and wife.

As he slid his arm round her slim waist she gasped slightly and blushed, as if caught doing something that was forbidden. She placed her hand tentatively on his shoulder, standing well back from him as if she would get burnt if she came too close.

Oliver smiled. They must look a peculiar pair, a couple just married who were reluctant to even touch each other. He pulled her in closer. *Just for appearances' sake.*

They glided round the dance floor and her rigid posture relaxed as her soft curves moulded into his body. Unable to resist, his arm moved further round her small waist, pulling her still closer, until her soft breasts were touching his chest.

He registered the touch of her tight nipples against his chest and forced himself to suppress a growl of pleasure. Oh, what he wouldn't give to feel those lush breasts without that barrier of her clothing. To caress them, to rub his fingers along those hard nipples, to take them in his mouth and nuzzle them until she was screaming out for him.

It seemed his abstinence from champagne was not working and his amorous intentions were becoming painfully clear to him. He could only hope his new wife did not notice.

He loosened his grip on her waist and moved back, to minimise the contact he was having with her, so she would not be able to feel the effect she was having on him. He continued to lead her round the floor. How quickly he could forget his vow to himself when he had her in his arms. But it was a vow he had to abide by. He just had to remember she did not want to be in his arms. She had been caught up in things beyond her control. Under normal circumstances she would not even be dancing with a man like him and certainly not married to him.

She was in an intolerable situation and she needed his reassurance, not his lust.

Only a complete cad would allow himself to forget that. And he hoped he wasn't a *complete* cad.

He coughed lightly to drive out any lingering inappropriate thoughts, looked down into those soft blue eyes and sent her what he hoped was a comforting smile that was completely free of desire.

'Just remember, Arabella, that tomorrow everything will go back to how it was and we can try to pretend this wedding never happened.'

She sighed and tried to smile back. 'Except I'm no longer an actress. I'm just another young society wife. And I'm not even that, not really.'

He shook his head. 'You *are* an actress. And one day you'll be a great actress. You're just between jobs. Resting, isn't that what actors say when they're not working?'

She gave a small, resigned smile as he twirled them around one more time.

'And if it's any consolation, you're now completely free of your father's interference. You can do anything you want. As a married woman you won't need to be chaperoned. You can go anywhere, do anything, see anyone you want.'

A sudden thought hit him like a thunderbolt and he almost halted on the dance floor. What he had said was true. She would be just like all those married women he had taken as his mistresses. They, too, were women who could do anything, go anywhere and see anyone they wanted.

Arabella would indeed be free. Free of her father and also free of him. Just like him she could take a lover if she chose. Bile burned up his throat and his muscles suddenly clenched into tight knots at the thought of Arabella with another man.

Some other man would experience what it was like to make love to her. She would give herself to some other man, a man she actually loved.

But what right had he to object to such an arrangement? If she wanted to take a lover, who was he to stop her? Well, he was her husband, but he had said he wouldn't stop her from doing what she wanted and surely that had to extend to her taking a lover.

It seemed he was a complete cad after all. He could hardly bear the thought of his lovely wife having that amount of freedom. But bear it was exactly what he was going to have to do. He gritted his teeth more tightly. He had promised her freedom, even if that freedom meant she took another man to her bed.

Free. Is that what she was? All Arabella was feeling was confused. But it was good to be in Oliver's arms again, to have him hold her as he glided her gracefully round the ballroom. She could almost imagine that she really was his bride, that he loved her, wanted her. And her traitorous body was reacting as if that was true. It was as if this was where she belonged and it hadn't taken long for her to sink back into his arms, to surrender herself to him as he took the lead for their first dance as man and wife.

But even if her body was being deceived, her mind knew differently.

He didn't want her. He didn't want any woman. Or, rather, he wanted virtually every woman he met, but no woman in particular.

And he was free as well. Free to pursue any woman he wanted. And from what she had heard from the other actresses at the Limelight, his reputation for pursuing, and catching women was even more notorious than his father's.

She had let it slip that this was a marriage of convenience, that Oliver would be her husband in name only. Once the other actresses had heard that, then all attempts to keep the truth from her were extinguished. She had then been regaled with gleeful tales of Oliver's conquests and his athleticism in bed until her head had reeled with images that should not invade a young woman's mind. Images that were equally exciting and upsetting.

Several of the actresses had experienced that athleticism first-hand and Arabella had no doubts that Lady Bufford wasn't the only woman present at this wedding who had been his lover.

Yet tonight, would be her wedding night. He had kissed her twice before and she wondered if he would try to kiss her again tonight. Perhaps he would do more than just kiss her. He was her husband now, after all. In law that gave him certain rights. Would he try to exercise those rights tonight?

Would she finally discover what so many other women had done before her, what it was like to be seduced by Oliver Huntsbury?

She had little experience of men. Arnold Emerson had been as inexperienced as herself and had never done anything more than kiss her. And those kisses had been somewhat chaste affairs compared to what it had been like to be kissed by Oliver.

When Oliver had kissed her, it had been as if he

wanted to possess her. His fervour had been almost overwhelming, but it had also been exciting and had elicited feelings deep within her that she did not know existed.

Even now, in this crowded ballroom, she was feeling things she knew she shouldn't. She had loved the feeling of his body up against hers. Would she feel the touch of his body again tonight? Would he hold her again? Would he try to seduce her by kissing her, caressing her, relieving that demanding need for him that was almost painful.

She released a soft sigh, moved closer to him and looked up into his eyes. Eyes that weren't smiling. Eyes that were sparking with fire, burning into her with an intensity that was all consuming. And she wanted to be consumed, to be taken by him, to feel the heat of his passion.

Her breath coming in quick gasps, she was incapable of breaking free from his gaze. A small, sane part of her mind was telling her she should be wary. But she would not listen to her cautious brain. She loved having him look at her like that. Yes, perhaps he had looked at many other women like that, but tonight he was looking at her. And it felt wonderful.

Many other women.

Those three words that said it all hit Arabella like a lightning bolt coming out of a clear blue sky. Many other women.

Of course he knew how to make a woman feel special, to feel desired, as if she was the only woman in the room. He was an experienced seducer. That would be part of his usual technique.

And she had naively fallen for it.

Well, if he thought she would succumb to his charm he was going to be sadly disappointed. Tonight might be their wedding night, but this was a wedding in name only and he was going to find that out loud and clear. She would not be seduced by Oliver Huntsbury.

The music ended and the band struck up another piece. Arabella quickly released her hold on his shoulder and hand as if she were being scorched by his touch. She needed to get away from this man who made her forget herself so easily.

'Please excuse me, I think I should circulate with our guests.' Arabella all but ran off the dance floor. She wanted to talk to her friend Rosie. Rosie would be able to guide her out of this fog of confusion that Oliver seemed to wrap around her. But Rosie and her new husband were dancing, holding each other close and looking adoringly into each other's eyes. She didn't have the heart to break them up.

Instead she turned to the nearest person standing on the edge of the dance floor and used all her acting skills to force her lips into a welcoming smile. She had to talk to someone, to distract her mind and body away from treasonous thoughts of Oliver.

'How do you do? I don't believe we've been introduced.'

'I'm pleased to make your acquaintance, Your Grace. I'm Greta Jones,' the woman said, to Arabella's surprise. She had called her *Your Grace*. Then, to her even greater surprise, the woman bobbed a curtsy.

That's right, she was now a duchess, of all things, and people would start deferring to her in that manner.

'Please, there's no need to address me as Your

Grace. My name is Arabella van… Oh, no, it's not—it's Arabella, Duchess of Somerfeld now. Anyway, I'm still just Arabella.'

The woman smiled at her. 'Yes, Your Grace.'

Arabella smiled and ignored the woman's refusal to drop the formality. 'And how do you know the Huntsbury family?'

'Has the Duke not told you about me?' she said, her voice hushed as she gazed sideways at Oliver across the room talking to his mother. Arabella braced herself for yet another shock about her new husband. The woman looked too old to be his mistress. She was not much younger than his mother, but with a man like Oliver you never knew.

'Oh, you're Greta Jones. Yes, of course Oliver has told me all about you. I'm pleased you could make it to the wedding.'

She did not want the rest of the world thinking that Oliver kept her in the same state of ignorance as his father had kept his mother. This marriage was humiliating enough without having the world laughing at her for being Oliver's ignorant, gullible wife.

The woman beamed a delighted smile. 'I'm so pleased everything is so open between you and Oliver. That man really is a saint.'

A saint? Was this woman actually talking about her husband? She looked over at him. He had moved on from talking to his mother and was now chatting to a young woman, who was gazing at him wistfully. Arabella was sure it wasn't his saintliness that was causing her to give him coy, flirtatious looks.

'You're talking about Oliver, the Duke of Somerfeld?' Perhaps the woman was mistaken, perhaps there was some other man in the room who could more easily wear the title of saint.

'Oh, yes, such a wonderful man. When he found out that I'd had a child out of wedlock he did everything he could to help us. He bought me a really nice house. He provided me with a regular income and he's even paying for my Jenny's education. Oh, yes, the man's a saint.'

It wasn't her definition of a saint. Saints did not usually go around impregnating women. But instead of saying that, Arabella merely kept on smiling and nodding. 'So, does he see much of you and Jenny?'

'Oh, yes, he sees her all the time. After all, she is his half-sister.'

Half-sister?

Arabella tilted her head, unsure that she had heard correctly. 'She's what?'

'Half-sister. Didn't he tell you about Jenny? Oliver's father is also Jenny's father. They're half-siblings.' She gave Arabella a sideways glance, her brow furrowed.

'Oh, yes. That Jenny. Of course he did. I was forgetting.'

The woman gave a little laugh. 'Well, I suppose it is easy to forget. After all, his father did have a lot of children, so Oliver does have a lot of half-brothers and half-sisters. That's my Jenny over there, talking to the Duke.'

Arabella looked back at Oliver. She could now see that the young woman wasn't so much flirting with her husband as looking at him with affection and admiration. Perhaps she had merely seen what she had expected to see. Perhaps she *had* judged her husband a bit too harshly.

She looked back at Greta Jones, who was looking over at Oliver with the same smile of affection. 'And the Duke has made arrangements for all his father's children,' Greta said. 'The only condition he puts on his money is that we keep it secret from his mother. Oh, yes, he really is a saint. To us and to her.'

Arabella looked back at Oliver. Perhaps there was a small bit of saintliness hidden inside that sinner after all.

'And you've all managed to keep this a secret from Oliver's mother?' It was hard to believe when there were so many ex-mistresses, so many children.

Greta laughed lightly. 'Oh, yes, we're all so grateful that we're happy to abide by that one condition and an ability to keep secrets from women is something else Oliver inherited from his father.'

All Arabella's warm feelings towards Oliver instantly evaporated. Greta looked up at her and registered Arabella's expression and her smile faded. 'Oh, but now that he's married that will change, I'm sure he tells you the truth about everything. Now, if you'll excuse me.' Greta Jones quickly walked away, her face burning with embarrassment.

No, Arabella's initial assessment was right. There might be a saintly side to Oliver, but he was still more sinner than saint and that was something she would be wise to remember.

Chapter Eleven

The saint—or was it the sinner?—excused himself and walked across the room to join Arabella. She watched him stride towards her, unable to look away. There was no denying he was the most attractive man in the room. And Arabella's eyes weren't the only ones fixed on him as he cut a swathe through the crowded ballroom.

Yet, despite the numerous admiring gazes he was getting, his eyes never left hers and the effect on her nervous system was decidedly unsettling.

'Arabella, I'm sorry I've been neglecting you. But I see you've started talking to the guests.' He looked in Greta Jones's direction. 'What were you talking about?'

It was a casual question, but there was an underlying apprehension in his voice. Why he should be concerned that she was talking to her father's ex-mistress she didn't know? Was he worried that she had found out that he was financially supporting Greta and many more of his father's ex-mistresses and children? Surely what he was doing was a good thing. Or was he worried that she might start to see a side to him that didn't fit in with the way the rest of the world saw him, as an unmitigated rake? There was only one way to find out.

'She was telling me about the house you bought for her and how grateful she is that you're paying for Jenny's education.'

'Oh, that.' He rubbed his hand along the back of his neck and gave a strained smile.

Was the sinner embarrassed that his saintliness had been exposed?

'She also mentioned that you are supporting all of your father's ex-mistresses and children, and there's rather a lot of them.'

He gave a snort of derision. 'Well, someone has to. These women would be left on their own otherwise, struggling to survive in a world that is not easy for any woman and especially not a woman who has a child out of wedlock.'

'And did your father not make provisions for them?'

His jaw tightened. 'My father had no objection to me organising the allowances for them, but I'm afraid once he lost interest in a woman that was it. It didn't matter how much harm he had caused, it simply never occurred to him to even try to undo some of the damage. He would be too interested in moving on to his next conquest.'

There was anger in his voice. Like her, he'd had a father who pursued his own goals without caring about how much harm it might cause others.

'And you invited them all to the wedding?'

He looked down at her, his face serious. 'Only

Greta and her daughter. I've become quite close to them over the years and I didn't want them to feel excluded. I hope you don't mind.'

'Of course I don't mind. I think it's an admirable thing to do. I'm just surprised you've managed to keep all these secrets from your mother.'

Once again, he rubbed his hand slowly across the back of his neck. 'Well, unfortunately, thanks to my father, I've had a lot of experience in keeping things from my mother.'

Arabella couldn't stop a disapproving sigh from escaping. There might be a saintly side to this sinner, but he certainly had a lot of experience in keeping women in the dark. He was obviously a master at it.

She looked across the room at his mother. Was that to be her own fate, as well—to be kept in the dark and to have no idea what her husband was up to?

The Dowager Duchess looked in their direction, beamed a happy smile and walked over to join them.

'Oh, Oliver, Arabella,' she said. 'I don't think I've ever been happier, not since my own wedding day.'

'And you look beautiful, Mother,' Oliver said, leaning down and kissing his mother on the cheek.

His mother smiled coyly. 'But not as beautiful as this young lady. Arabella, you make a lovely bride. I'm sure you're going to be a wonderful Duchess of Somerfeld and wife for Oliver.'

Arabella forced herself to smile and hoped it looked genuine.

'And I truly hope the two of you are as happy as Oliver's late father and I were.'

Arabella looked sideways at Oliver, who looked somewhat uncomfortable.

'Mr van Haven was so excited that you and Oliver had married,' she continued. 'It was just a shame he had to leave so early. He said he had some urgent business to attend to.'

An exasperated sigh escaped Arabella's lips. Her father had been the first guest to leave. As soon as the wedding breakfast had finished, he had departed, not even staying for the ball. Now that he had achieved his goal, he obviously saw nothing to detain him. She had little doubt that he would now be taking the first steamer back to America, to his beloved bank.

'Yes, that was a shame,' Arabella replied truthfully. Everything about her father forcing this marriage upon her had been shameful.

'Well, I must circulate. There are so many lovely people here tonight.'

With that she departed and joined another group of women and Arabella wondered if they were yet more of her husband's ex-mistresses, causing Arabella to wince in sympathy for Oliver's poor, deluded mother.

'My mother is talking to her cousins,' Oliver said, seemingly reading her mind. 'And, as surprising as it is, even my father wouldn't try to seduce his wife's relatives.'

'No, he might have broken his vow and been found out.'

Oliver raised his eyebrows and gave a slight nod. 'Yes, unfortunately you're probably right. That most likely was his reasoning.'

The band leader announced the quadrille and couples took to the floor. Oliver sent her another of those mischievous smiles. 'So, Your Grace,' he said, performing a low bow. 'Would you do me the honour of this dance?'

Despite herself Arabella smiled back at him. Why did his smile always cause her to feel warm inside, even when she told herself not to succumb to his charms?

He held out his hand and she lightly placed her gloved hand on his. As he led her on to the dance floor, she caught sight of Lady Bufford, grabbing her husband and dragging the reluctant man in their direction. The assembled guests formed themselves into groups of four couples and it became apparent what Lady Bufford was up to. She bustled herself and her now red-faced husband into their set. She was obviously determined to get an opportunity to dance with Oliver.

Arabella forced her jaw to unclench and her body to relax. What did it matter if Lady Bufford wanted to dance with her husband? She had no right to be jealous. But still, this was her wedding night after all and she didn't want to share it with one of Oliver's mistresses.

The band struck up. Oliver took her hand and they danced the first set of steps. They parted and he joined Lady Bufford for the second set.

Arabella fought hard to keep that little green monster under control as she watched Lady Bufford simper and smile, and whisper something in Oliver's ear. Lord Bufford also appeared to be battling with his own demons and gave every appearance of a man fighting to restrain himself from leaping forward to pull his wife away from her lover.

Lord Bufford might be entitled to feel jealous at

this blatant display, but Arabella did not. Hadn't she promised Oliver freedom? Hadn't she said that she didn't care how many *good friends* he had? No, this was something she was going to have to learn to cope with. She was going to have to control her impulses to stamp her feet in rage, to pout, and to send her rivals looks that were designed to cut them to the quick.

But at the very least, she just wished Lady Bufford had the good manners to not be quite so obvious. Each time she danced with Oliver her face lit up like a modern electric lightbulb. She smiled up at him, giggled girlishly and continued to whisper in her ear. Surely she should have enough decency in her to restrain herself and keep her hands off the groom, even if it was just for this one night.

When the dance finally came to an end Arabella released her tightly held breath, pleased to be led off the dance floor, away from that despicable woman.

The temptation to ask Oliver what Lady Bufford had been whispering to him was almost overwhelming, but she would not do it. She clamped her teeth tightly together to stop the words from escaping.

They were joined by Greta Jones, who was all smiles. 'You two look perfect together,' she said, taking Oliver's hands.

Oliver bent down and kissed her cheek. 'I hope you're enjoying yourself, Greta.'

'Oh, I am, I am, Your Grace. I'm so happy to see you married. But it's time I went home. I just wanted to say goodbye to you and your bride. She really is delightful, Oliver. Just the sort of woman a good man like you deserves.'

Oliver and Arabella exchanged disbelieving looks.

Arabella knew she was neither the woman Oliver deserved nor wanted for his wife, but wondered what sort of woman he actually *did* deserve. Greta had called him a saint. Did he deserve a saintly woman? That most certainly was not Arabella. Surviving a marriage to a man like Oliver was going to demand the patience and forbearance of a saint, but her reaction to Lady Bufford's performance on the dance floor had shown her she definitely did not possess those qualities.

And as for the sinner, well, that man was obviously more than capable of getting as many women as he wanted, but whether he deserved them all was another question entirely.

They said their goodbyes to Greta and several other guests approached them to say farewell. The ball was starting to wind up and she would soon be alone with Oliver. Alone with her new husband.

While some guests would be staying overnight, they would be in a separate wing, far away from the rooms occupied by her and Oliver. Even his mother had announced that from the date of the wedding she would be moving into her own home on the estate and leaving Somerfeld Manor to the new Duchess.

So she would be alone with Oliver. What would happen then?

Several other guests approached them to say their goodbyes. Arabella made polite conversation, hardly aware of what she was saying. All she could think was that, with each departing guest, she was coming closer and closer to being alone with Oliver. Alone with a handsome rake with a notorious reputation. And she was his wife. Would it now be her turn to be the sole focus of his seductive charms? And how was she going to react if it was?

A tingling awareness raced round her body as heat erupted deep within her core. *She would be alone with him.*

As if sensing her body's reaction, he looked up from a departing couple and stared intently at her. Her nerves jumped in response and she stared back, transfixed. Fire flickered in those dark brown eyes as his gaze scanned slowly from her face down her body, then back up again. Every inch of her body burned under his gaze, as if his eyes had softly caressed her sensitive skin. He was looking at her as if she really was his. It was a look of possession, of desire, of passion. It was how he looked at her when he kissed her. Was it how he would look when he took her in his arms, when he laid her down on his bed? Was that how he would look at her when he made love to her?

A mixture of panic and excited awareness raged a war within her. She would soon be alone with this man. A man who could bring her body alive with just one look. A man who made her feel things she had never felt before, who made her body ache with need. A man she knew she had to resist.

A woman pulled at his sleeve and dragged his attention away, breaking the spell between them. Arabella blinked several times to bring herself back to reality.

What had just happened?

Had she just experienced a taste of his seduction routine? Was that how he looked at women when he was planning to bed them? She could see why he was so successful with women. It had certainly worked on her. One intense look from those dark brown eyes and she had lost all ability to reason. That one look had driven her imagination wild, sent thoughts of giving herself to him running through her mind, of letting him do anything he wanted with her, of *wanting* him to do anything he wanted with her.

She closed her eyes and took a series of deep breaths to force some control over her riotous nerves.

Well, if Oliver was planning on using his tried-and-true seduction techniques on her he would be wasting his time. He would not be seducing her, tonight or any other night. He was about to learn a valuable lesson: that not all women were his for the taking.

With each departing guest Arabella could feel that firm resolve fray more and more at the edges. She knew she was going to have to be strong. She just had to remember who he was, to keep in mind all those other women in his life. She might be his wife, but she did not want to be yet another one of his women, yet another *good friend* to add to the long list.

Finally, the last guests headed out of the room and departed in their carriages, leaving the couple alone in the suddenly quiet grand ballroom, with only a few servants remaining, who discreetly ignored the couple as they continued to clear the tables.

Now Oliver was about to learn his lesson. He was about to find out that she was not like other women. She would not be his latest conquest.

He turned towards her and Arabella's heart seemed to jump into her throat, her cheeks grew hot and her skin burned under his gaze. A reaction she knew she should not be having if she was to remain strong. She closed her eyes briefly and forced herself to take in a few calming breaths.

'It's been a long day, Arabella. Now we can finally retire,' he murmured. 'Shall we?' He held out his arm for her. Arabella nodded, unable to speak, and with trepidation she placed her arm through his.

This was it. They walked towards the stairs that led them up to their bedroom suite.

Arabella's mind blurred with confusion. All she was conscious of was his strong body close to hers as they ascended the staircase, so close she could feel his warmth, imagine the strong muscles under his shirt and jacket. Unable to stop herself she drew even nearer to him, their bodies almost touching, sending a thrilling ripple coursing through her body.

In silence they walked down the long corridor. Arabella could not imagine what was going through Oliver's mind as he led her towards their bedroom, but her own mind was a swirl of chaotic thoughts. Her body was even more confused and Arabella fought to slow the rapid drumbeat of her heart and get her breathing under control.

They reached the bedroom door and he stopped. Her breath caught in her suddenly dry throat as she looked up at him. He gazed down at her, those rich brown eyes staring deep into hers, as if penetrating through to her very soul. She waited, her treacherous body aching to feel his touch, a touch she knew she should not be wanting, but one her body desired with an insatiable need that could not be ignored.

He leant down towards her. Her lips parted in anticipation. She closed her eyes and moved towards him, her heart racing, her body throbbing. His lips caressed her warm cheek and she sighed. 'Goodnight, Arabella. I hope you sleep well.'

Her eyes flew open and she watched in disbelief as he turned and walked off down the corridor. Without a backward glance he opened the door to the adjoining room and entered.

As if frozen to the spot, Arabella continued to stare down the now empty hallway.

Was that it? Was that to be her wedding night? She'd had every intention of rejecting his advances, but he hadn't even tried to seduce her. The notorious rake, who desired almost every woman he met, did not desire one woman. His wife.

Well, so be it.

Abruptly Arabella turned and pulled open the door to her bedroom, slamming it shut behind her. Her hand flew to her mouth and she looked in the direction of Oliver's bedroom. She hoped he hadn't heard the bang of her door closing. It would be too humiliating if he thought she was in any way concerned that he had just rejected her.

She tiptoed across the room and reached for the bell pull to summon Nellie. Her hand paused in mid-air. If she called Nellie to help her undress, then her lady's maid would know that she was spending her wedding night alone. Nellie was her friend and she would not judge, but still Arabella felt ashamed that it would not be her husband who removed her wedding gown, her stockings, her undergarments.

Instead she would do it herself. With much wriggling and contortions, she managed to undo the small

pearl buttons up the back of her gown and release
herself from the tight corset. When she was finally
free, she threw the dress across the room. It landed
on a chair in an abandoned pile of white embroidered
satin and lace.

She released her hair and tossed the clips on to the
dressing table.

Dressed in her virginal white linen nightdress, she
climbed into the four-poster bed and scowled at the
closed adjoining door that separated her room from
Oliver's.

The door was only made of oak, but it might as
well be made of iron and be shut with a lock and
chain, it presented such a barrier between them.

Leaning over, Arabella blew out her lamp with a
decisive puff of air. The best thing she could do now
was to sleep and forget all about the man in the next
room. After all, it had been a long, tiring day. Instead
she lay on her side, staring at the carved wooden door
that connected their rooms.

Candlelight flickered along the gap under the door
and she could see a shadow moving around. He was
still up. Not yet in bed. Was he thinking of her? Was
he going to change his mind? Would the door open
and he would join her after all?

The shadow approached the door. It stopped moving. She sat up, pulled up the sheet to her chest and
gasped in a breath. The doorknob appeared to move
slightly. Or was that just a trick being played on her
eyes in the darkened room?

The shadow moved away. The light under the door
went out. He had retired for the evening. Arabella released her held breath. She lay back down. If he could

go to sleep as if today had been just another normal day, then so could she.

But instead she stared up at the ceiling for hour after hour, willing sleep to come.

Chapter Twelve

Oliver remained in bed until late in the morning, listening to the sound of carriage wheels crunching on the gravel driveway as the last of the wedding guests left the estate.

Perhaps he should have risen early to say good-bye. Although his absence would be excused—they would assume he was still in bed with his new bride.

But they would be so wrong. The first day of his life as a married man would not be spent in the arms of his wife. Nor would any other day or night during this arranged marriage.

Last night he had proven to himself that he *was* capable of achieving the seemingly impossible, he could walk away from his enchanting wife.

But it had taken every ounce of self-control he possessed to do so. When he'd looked down into her face, at her inviting lips, her blushing cream cheeks, her softly closed eyes, the temptation to kiss her had been so strong. As had the temptation to rip off that restricting wedding gown, to see her naked, to take her into his room and make her his own.

But he had done the unimaginable. He had resisted temptation.

Even though his mind had been clouded by desire, one rule had been able to cut through the obscuring clouds, a rule by which he had always lived.

He did not seduce virgins.

He had never done it before and he wasn't about to start now. Even if that virgin was his wife.

When it came to women, he might not have many restrictions, but even a man like him had to have some sort of code of conduct.

Arabella needed his protection, not his lustfulness.

But despite that rule nagging in his head, he had almost succumbed.

When she had tilted back her head, her pink lips parted, her blue eyes closed, the memory of kissing her had almost undermined his resolve. Virgin or not, there was no denying that when he had kissed her, he had felt a fire burning inside her. There was definitely untapped passion in his new wife and the pull to be the one to fan those flames until she burned up had been hellishly strong.

Yet he had resisted. He had walked away. Amazing.

Now he just had to ensure he continued to walk away from temptation.

He threw back the bedcovers. It was time to start his day. And this was to be a day like no other. After all, he was a married man now. That was going to take some adjustment.

He walked through to his dressing room, where his valet had discreetly laid out his clothes and shaving gear, presumably to avoid disturbing the newly married couple.

He washed and shaved, then pulled on his trousers, shirt and waistcoat, and stared at his reflection in the full-length mirror as he adjusted his cravat. Just how was he supposed to behave now he was a married man? he asked his reflection. They had promised each other complete freedom as if they were not married to each other, but she was still his wife. She was living in his house. She had taken his name. The world thought of them as a couple.

So how *were* they supposed to behave towards each other? As if they were friends? Acquaintances? Business partners?

He buttoned up his jacket. And if this was confusing for him, it must be even more so for her. In just a few short weeks her life had been turned upside down. She had gone from being a single woman pursuing a career on the stage to a married woman whose career had been destroyed.

While little had really changed for him, she must be devastated.

He must remember that at all times. He nodded to his reflection.

She wanted this marriage even less than he did, if that was possible.

He headed out the door and down the corridor to the breakfast room. As he walked through the house, he could see the servants had returned everything to how it had been. It was as if a wedding had not taken place the night before. And his new bride was nowhere in sight.

Perhaps she had already left and returned to London, or ridden off with her friends, the Duke and Duchess of Knightsbrook, to stay at their estate in Devon.

If that was what she had chosen to do, she had every right to do so. She did not have to explain herself to him, or even tell him of her intentions.

He served himself a generous breakfast and shook open the newspaper. No, the new Duchess of Somerfeld did not need to keep him informed of her plans. She was a free woman. She could go anywhere, do anything, see anyone she wanted. That was their agreement.

But she could have said goodbye to him, couldn't she?

He folded up the paper and pushed aside his plate, no longer feeling hungry as these questions continued to whirl through his mind.

Perhaps he could divert himself with a vigorous ride round the estate. Strenuous exercise would put an end to this unsettled state. It would drive out these constant thoughts of his marriage.

As he headed for the stables, he saw his bride, walking slowly in from the rose gardens, a posy of flowers in her hand. He stopped on the top of the steps and looked down at her, taking the opportunity to observe her before she was able to see him watching. Her black hair was tied back in a simple plait, making her appear even more innocent, and she looked so sad and wistful. The enormity of the grounds of the Somerfeld estate seemed to make her appear small and alone, and the expression on her face was so forlorn it broke his heart.

He rushed down the steps and crossed the formal garden.

'Arabella.' He hesitated, suddenly unsure what to say, uncharacteristically uncertain of himself.

She looked up at him and sent him a tentative smile. It seemed she, too, was unsure of how they were supposed to act with each other now that they were husband and wife.

With dark shadows under her big blue eyes, she looked tired. Had she spent the night worrying about what marriage would bring, what her duties would be? Well, she should have no worry on that account. He would expect nothing of her.

'Good morning, Oliver, I was just taking a walk round the gardens. They really are stunning.'

He nodded. 'Do you mind if I accompany you?'

She shrugged slightly. 'I can hardly stop you. After all it's your garden and I'm your wife, just another of your possessions.'

He dragged in a breath and winced. 'Please, Arabella. You know I don't think like that. You are not my possession. You are your own person. You are free to do as you want, to go where you want.'

She shrugged again and clasped her posy of flowers more tightly. 'I'm sorry, you're right. I should not have said that.'

They walked through the sculptured formal garden. Oliver was tempted to take her arm. Would that not be the polite thing to do? But his new wife appeared so tense, her body so rigid, he suspected she would be affronted by such a gesture.

He had to let her know that he meant what he said. 'Arabella, you have nothing to worry about. I will arrange with my man of business for you to have a regular allowance that is generous enough that you never have to worry about money,' he announced. 'That money will give you complete independence to live your life however you choose.'

She stopped walking and looked up at him. 'So, I'm to have an allowance, just like your father's ex-mistresses.'

There was bitterness in her voice. Why was she so annoyed with him? What had he done wrong? Couldn't she see that he would do everything in his power to ensure that marriage to him changed nothing for her, that it did not impede how she lived her life?

'An allowance will give you freedom,' he said softly, as if trying to calm a skittish colt.

'Freedom to do what? My father has destroyed my career and forced me into a marriage I didn't want. You say I have freedom, but what am I supposed to do with it now that I have it? I'm nothing if I'm not acting on the stage and that is all over now. All I am is a wife and I'm not even that.'

Oliver shook his head, unsure of what he could say or do to make things better. 'Well, my town house will be at your disposal any time you want. You can use that as a base to contact as many theatres as you like so you can secure another part.'

She exhaled a deep breath, shook her head and resumed walking. 'I'm so sorry, Oliver. None of this is your fault and I should not be getting angry with you. I'm feeling so confused by everything that has happened and I didn't sleep very well last night.' She blushed slightly and looked down at her posy of flowers. 'I just don't know what my role is now.'

He took her arm, determined to offer her reassurance. 'Nothing's changed for you. You can still act.'

She looked uncertain.

'You could even contact the Limelight Theatre again if you choose.' Oliver smiled as a thought occurred to him. 'After all, the manager was told he could not employ Arabella van Haven. He was not told he couldn't hire Arabella, the Duchess of Somerfeld.'

She paused, turned and looked up at him, her frown turning into a smile. A bright, delightful smile, as if the warm sun had just emerged from behind a grey cloud. 'You're right. My father *did* tell them they couldn't hire Arabella *van Haven* and she doesn't exist any more.'

The sadness had disappeared from her face and Oliver smiled back, pleased that something he had said had actually made her happy.

'That's exactly what I'm going to do.' Her walking pace increased; her body no longer rigid. 'I'm going to ask for my part back at the Limelight. It will be so good to pull the wool over my father's eyes after what he's done. He's such a stickler for contractual agreements. He's managed to fool many an opponent who didn't take the time to read the fine print. And now we'll return the favour. Oh, you're so clever, Oliver.'

Clever? That was not a trait usually attributed to him, but he rather liked the sound of it. Especially when being clever made her so happy.

'Right. Let's do that immediately,' he said. They turned around and walked briskly back to the house. 'And I'll send a telegram to the manager, so he knows that I, too, approve of you returning to the stage.'

Her smile faded, and she sighed audibly. 'Yes, I suppose now that you're my husband you do have to approve my actions, don't you? And I suppose that as a duchess the manager at the Limelight will feel obliged to hire me, whether they think I'm talented or not. It will be such a drawcard to have a member of the aristocracy on the bill. I'll be the freak that everyone wants to see.'

Her sadness had returned and Oliver knew he had to make things right for her. 'Then act under another name. Yes, some people will still know who you are, but the majority of people who go to the Limelight Theatre won't. You don't have to call yourself a duchess if you don't want to. You can be just plain old Arabella Huntsbury.' Although there could never be anything plain about the young woman standing beside him.

She stared up at him, her brow furrowed. 'Yes, that might work, I suppose.'

'Of course it will. And I assure you, I will never interfere in your life. You have my word. I can even draw up legal documents to ensure it, if you would like. With a substantial allowance and such legal agreements, you'll be more independent than you ever have been before. Marriage will not hold you back. I guarantee it.'

Her furrowed brow smoothed over and she sent him another of those heart-warming smiles. 'That's very kind of you.'

Clever and now kind—two descriptions largely unfamiliar to him. He was fearing she was starting to get the wrong idea about the sort of man he was.

They reached the foot of the steps and she paused.

'So, what about you? Will this marriage hold you back?'

It was his turn to furrow his brow. He was unsure how to answer that question.

'Don't worry,' she said before he could formulate an answer. 'I promise I won't restrict your freedom either. Like your father, your wife will never get in your way.'

At the mention of his father a pang of pain pierced Oliver's chest. He might be like his father in many respects, but he hoped he would never treat a woman the way his father had treated his mother.

'Arabella, I...' He was unsure how to continue. What could he say? *I won't be like my father?* He knew that would not be completely true.

'You don't have to say anything. I know the man I married.'

He cringed as they walked up the steps in silence. *She knew what sort of man he was.* Oliver also knew what sort of man he was and it had never bothered him before. So why was it bothering him now? That was a question he did not want to even try to answer. Instead he would focus on helping Arabella resume her career.

They walked into the drawing room. Oliver headed for the rolltop desk, sat down, removed a piece of paper and smiled up at her. 'Right, let's get your life back. You can tell me what to write. That way the letter to the manager will be from me, but you'll be completely in control.'

Arabella smiled back, regretting her earlier petulance. He was doing everything he could to make this easy for her and she was acting like a spoilt child, just because she was confused by her conflicting emotions. So what if she was the only woman in England this notorious rake had no interest in? That was what she wanted. She should be grateful that he did not try to seduce her last night. And she *was* grateful. So, it was time she acted that way instead of pouting and snapping at him.

She looked over his shoulder and laughed. 'If I'm to downplay the fact that I'm now a duchess, I don't think that stationery will be entirely appropriate.' She removed the piece of paper in his hand bearing the Somerfeld crest, returned it to the small shelf, took a plain piece of paper and placed it in front of him. All the while she tried to ignore the scent of him, all musk and masculinity, and the warmth of his body. She would not think of that now. She would focus on the task at hand, returning to the life she had before she met Oliver.

He dipped his pen in the ink pot and looked up at her expectantly. 'Right, what shall I write?'

She paced the room, thinking about the best way to convince the manager of the Limelight that they should rehire her. 'Well, I guess you can put the address of Somerfeld Manor at the top of the page. After all, they already know that I've married a duke so there's no point trying to hide that. I just don't think I should emphasise it by using stationery bearing your crest.'

Oliver nodded, and his pen scratched across the paper as he wrote out his address. 'Right, what next?'

'Well, *Dear Mr Hackett* might be a good start.'

Oliver dutifully wrote that down.

'I would like to announce that Arabella Huntsbury is now available for consideration in the part previously played by Arabella van Haven.'

She paused and looked over Oliver's shoulder as he took down her dictation. 'That way we're letting him know I go under another name without actually saying so.'

'Good idea.' Oliver finished writing and looked up at her, his pen poised above the paper.

'I am aware that my wife...' Arabella paused, finding it difficult to take in that she was referring to herself as Oliver's wife. *'My wife has been denied a part in your present production under orders from the new owner, Mr van Haven. Please be informed that Mr van Haven has since returned to America.'*

Arabella hoped the manager could understand that that meant her father was far away and would have no direct influence on the Limelight, so they were free to hire whoever they chose.

'While he has forbidden Miss van Haven from appearing at the Limelight, he did not forbid my wife from appearing, so I urge you to consider hiring her.'

Oliver wrote that down, but then his pen continued to scratch along the page. *'In doing so, you will be hiring a talented actress who I am sure you appreciate is destined for greatness.'*

'I didn't say that,' she pointed out.

'No, but it's what the writer thinks.'

Warmth flooded through her. He might just be saying that to encourage the manager to rehire her, but she loved hearing him say he thought her talented.

She resumed her pacing. 'Well, I suppose you'll also have to add that you give your permission.'

Oliver nodded, and continued writing. *'I have no objection to my wife, Arabella Huntsbury, appearing on the stage...'*

Arabella fought not to be annoyed. She should not have to get Oliver's permission. A woman should be free to choose her own path in life, whether she was married or not, but that was the way of the world. However, unlike many other women, she had a husband who would put no obstacles in her path.

'...and I feel I would be doing the world a disservice if I kept this superb actress from her public.'

He sent her a devilish smile that washed away her annoyance and she smiled back at him.

With a flourish, he signed his name at the bottom, blotted the ink, folded up the letter, addressed an envelope and rang the bell for a servant.

'Hopefully that will do the trick. And it seems I've acquired a new skill, being your secretary. How did I do?'

His teasing made her laugh. 'You were perfect.' And perfect he was, in so many ways.

'And as your new secretary, I will point out that we shouldn't put all our eggs in one basket. There are lots of theatres other than the Limelight. Why don't we contact a few more and see what response we get?'

When the footman arrived, Oliver handed him the letter and asked him to send it immediately so it would catch the next mail train to London. He also requested copies of the day's newspapers and for Cook to prepare some sandwiches for their lunch so they could eat while they worked.

'We'll scour the papers and get a list of the main

theatres and write to them all. I'm sure lots of them will have a part for a promising young actress.'

This was more than Arabella could have hoped for. Not only was he keeping his promise to not interfere in her career, but he was also helping her find work. Then a small voice inside her head questioned his motives. Was he trying to get rid of her? Was a wife going to be an encumbrance to his lifestyle? Would it suit him to have her busy on the stage so he could pursue his own interests? She forced that little voice to stay silent. It didn't matter what his reasons were, he was helping her and that was all that mattered.

When the newspapers arrived, they spread them out on the table and leant over next to each other so they could peruse the entertainment sections together. Arabella forced herself to focus and ignore the fact that she was now standing close to Oliver, so close that their arms resting on the table were nearly touching, as they scanned the list of theatrical establishments.

She moved her arm slightly away from his in an attempt to stop the tingling that being this near to him always elicited. 'The best ones to look for will be ones where the play is coming to an end.' Her voice came out unnaturally high. 'That means they'll be casting for the next play and starting rehearsals soon.'

Oliver picked up another piece of paper and dipped his pen in the ink pot. 'Right, I'll compose a list of likely candidates.'

He pointed to the advertisement for the Lumière Theatre. 'We should add that one as well. I know that their lead actress has recently left because she ran off with a viscount. I heard they're living together in Italy, so they'll be needing a replacement.'

He wrote that on the list and leaned back over again to survey the ads.

He showed her another advertisement. 'And the Neptune Theatre is probably a good bet, but they prefer actresses who can also sing and dance.' He leant on one arm and looked at her. 'Can you sing and dance?'

She quickly stood up. He was now far too close for comfort. 'You seem to know more about this business than I do,' she said more curtly than she'd intended.

He smiled up at her. 'Well, I have known a few actresses over the years and my father knew even more. I almost grew up in the theatre, you could say.'

Arabella's body tensed and she fought hard to stop her lips from compressing in a disapproving scowl. Of course he knew a lot of actresses. She already knew that. And it was not something she should care about. It *was* something she *didn't* care about.

'Yes, I can dance and sing,' she said as evenly as she could.

'Right. Well, let's put the Neptune Theatre on the list as well.'

He turned back to the newspaper and added a few more to the list. Arabella told herself to stop being so sharp. She knew that she was married to a rake. If she reacted like that every time she was reminded that he'd had countless lovers she was going to drive herself mad. So she breathed slowly and steadily, forced herself to smile and pointed to another advertisement. 'Add the Savoy Theatre to the list, it's worth a try, and I'd love to perform in a Gilbert and Sullivan production.'

When they reached the end of the advertisements, she realised Oliver had been right. There really were a lot of options available if the Limelight turned her down. And they'd only covered the theatres in London. If they got no response from them, then they could branch out and try the other cities, even the smaller towns. Her father might have forced her to marry, but in one respect he couldn't have chosen a better husband for her. Oliver really was determined to help her in her career.

He stood up, held up the list and smiled at her.

'Right, now we need to compile a list of your previous performances, so they know how versatile you are. Do you have any clippings of your reviews? We can include a few good quotes from them. And I'll arrange with a photographer to take your portrait and we can send copies to the theatres.'

Arabella laughed. He looked so serious and committed to what he was doing. 'You really do know the industry, don't you? Perhaps you should manage my career.'

He smiled back at her. 'That's not a bad idea. I'd prefer that to being your secretary.'

'I'm not joking, Oliver. Sarah Bernhardt and Lillie Langtry and all the other successful actors and actresses have theatrical agents. They deal with theatre managers, publicity and so on. It would put my career on a much more professional basis. What do you think?'

He tapped the end of the pen against his teeth as he considered her proposal.

Arabella instantly regretted her suggestion. If he was her agent, he would be in the company of a lot of actresses. Would she be able to bear it if he took one of her colleagues as a lover? She doubted she had such strength that she could bear such humiliation.

'On second thoughts. I don't think that would be a good idea. After all, we did agree to live separate lives.'

He lowered his pen and frowned. 'Yes, you're right. We did agree on that. But I do know a lot of people in the industry, so I'm sure I can be a help to you.'

It seemed he was disappointed that he wouldn't be spending his days in the company of young and available actresses. But he was right. He could help her career and she would be unwise to let her ridiculous jealousy get in the way.

'All right, you can be my agent,' she said tentatively.

'Excellent.' He smiled and held out his hand for them to shake on their new arrangement. As if putting her hand into a fire Arabella forced herself to extend her hand. At the touch of his skin a burning sensation ripped up her arm, causing heat to explode throughout her body. Her heart was beating so loudly he must be able to hear it, as Arabella could hear nothing else.

Why did his touch always do that to her?

She drew in a strained breath and looked up at him, fighting to keep her face impassive so she would not expose to him to her reaction.

But looking into those deep brown eyes was the worst thing she could do. Her heart thudding fast, she knew she should look away, but she couldn't. They imprisoned her. She held her breath as his gaze moved from her eyes to her lips, then back again. When his gaze returned to her eyes, she could see a change had come over him. He was no longer looking at her like a helpful friend, but like a hungry man staring at a feast. Her frantically beating heart increased its fierce tempo. She was the feast. He wanted her. He desired her.

She dragged in a slow breath and held it, waiting. Wanting him to do more than just look, to act on what he was feeling, to satisfy his hunger.

He inhaled long and deep, then looked away, released her hand and took a step backwards. Her burning hand now free from his grasp, she wanted to sink to the ground, her legs too weak to hold her. She had expected him to kiss her again. Had wanted him to kiss her again. To do more than kiss her. But he hadn't.

Humiliation and disappointment engulfed her. Why did she have to expose her need to him? He quite obviously did not want her. Hadn't he proven that last night? Hadn't he just shown her yet again?

Yes, he had fleetingly been interested in her, but just as quickly that interest had disappeared. And if he had satisfied his hunger, wouldn't he have then moved on to his next conquest?

Why did she keep forgetting that? Yes, his kisses had been earth-shattering. But they would be, wouldn't they? Of course he was a good kisser, a man who'd had an endless stream of lovers would be.

Arabella smoothed down her skirt and coughed delicately. 'As my theatrical agent you'll probably need to know all about my career to date.' Her voice was a little breathless, but there was nothing she could do about that.

He nodded his head rapidly, sat down and picked up his pen again. It was all business now. 'Yes, the first thing we need to do is make a list of all the plays you've appeared in and all the theatres you've performed at. You've worked in America so we'll also be able to say you've got international experience.'

She sat across the table from him. With a table between them she would hopefully not reveal to him just how much his touch, his look, affected her. 'Well, there was the Atrium Theatre in New York. It's just a small amateur theatre, but no one in England will know that. I played Lady Macbeth.'

He raised his eyebrows. 'I can't imagine you as someone capable of plotting murder, you seem too sweet for that.'

'I'm an actress, remember? I can be lots of different women,' she retorted.

'And do you have any reviews from that?'

'Yes. They were very good reviews. And not one of the reviewers said I was sweet.'

He sent her a long, appraising look, causing heat to rush to her face. Why was it so important to her to convince him that she wasn't a sweet little girl, but was as much a woman as every other he had known?

She looked away and in a garbled rush listed all her other performances until he had to ask her to slow down so his writing could keep up with her torrent of words.

At a slower pace she repeated the list of productions she had appeared in, and the parts she had played, while he wrote it all down.

When she had finished, he held up the page and smiled at her in satisfaction. 'That's quite a list. We should get it printed so it looks professional. We can send it out, along with your picture, then sit back and wait for the offers to come flooding in.'

Arabella smiled back at him. He really was being helpful and he would be a great asset as a theatrical agent. It was just a shame that she couldn't trust herself to keep her traitorous reactions to him under control.

A footman knocked on the door and entered. 'Your Grace,' he said with a bow, 'Cook would like to know when you would like dinner served.'

Oliver looked over at the engraved brass clock ticking on the oak mantelpiece and Arabella followed his gaze. To her surprise she realised they had spent the entire afternoon together and it was now late in the day.

'Tell Cook we'll be ready in an hour.' He looked in Arabella's direction and she nodded her agreement. 'And we'll dine on the terrace tonight. There's only the two of us and I believe it's warm enough.'

'Very good, sir.' The footman bowed and withdrew.

Oliver put his pen and ink away and picked up the lists they had compiled. 'I believe that is what you'd call a productive day. We'll have you back on the stage before you know it.'

He smiled at her. She smiled back. It was what she wanted with all her heart, to return to the stage. So why was that anticipation tinged with an edge of regret?

Chapter Thirteen

Oliver never felt nervous and certainly not because of a woman. Never. And yet, as he sat on the terrace and waited for Arabella, nerves were indeed getting the better of him. Ridiculous. Perhaps it was simply the unfamiliar situation of having dinner with a woman with the simple intention of eating, of making polite conversation and nothing more. Usually when he dined with a woman, both of them knew it was just a precursor to their time in bed together. And their conversation would be far from polite. It tended to consist of sexual innuendo, flirting and teasing.

But tonight, there would be no flirting, no teasing and definitely no sexual innuendos. And this dinner was most certainly not a precursor to bedding Arabella. It was to be food, drink and polite conversation, only. Nothing to be nervous about at all.

The footman opened the doors to the terrace and Arabella emerged. He rose slowly from his seat as if transfixed and took in the vision that had appeared before him. She looked stunning, wearing a light yellow, low-cut gown. There was more of her enticing soft flesh on display than he had seen before. He fought and lost the battle to stop his eyes from straying to that delightful décolletage, to those enticing cream-coloured mounds, rising and falling with each breath. How could he not look? After all he was just a man, a weak man, powerless in the face of such tempting beauty.

Exercising supreme willpower, he forced his gaze to move up to her face, her beautiful face. She had made quite the effort for tonight's meal. Not just with that wonderful gown, which exposed the tops of her breasts and the soft skin of her shoulders to his appreciative gaze, but also her midnight-black hair, which had been intricately styled. Although he had to admit, he preferred to see her with her hair in a long plait flowing down her back, as it had been today. Or, better still, he would like to see it loose, free from all restraint, so he could run his fingers through it, before...

He coughed to drive out that thought before it led him to places he knew he should not go. He pulled out her seat. As she sat down he inhaled her delightful scent—jasmine. He remembered it well from when he had taken her in his arms before. He paused, his hands still on the back of her chair, his body close to hers.

He felt her grow tense, reminding him that this was just a convivial meal between two people who had been forced together against their wills and his behaviour was becoming inappropriate.

He returned to his own chair and rang the small brass bell on the table. Two footmen immediately emerged from behind the doors, one to serve the soup, the other to fill their wine glasses.

Oliver raised his glass in a toast. 'To your brilliant acting career.' He smiled inwardly. That was the right approach. Keep it light. Keep it friendly.

She clinked her crystal glass against his. 'And to your new career as a secretary and theatrical agent.'

'Well, I don't know if it's going to be much of a career. There's only one actress I want to look after.'

He took a sip of the white burgundy, savoured the distinctive nutty taste, and tried to laugh off what he had just said. Yes, he was looking after one actress. But it was only Arabella's *career* he was going to look after. *Nothing more.*

He picked up his spoon and tasted the clear vegetable soup. 'I'm afraid there will only be three courses this evening. I hope you don't mind, but as there is only the two of us, I didn't want to put Cook to too much trouble.'

She smiled at him, that enchanting smile. 'Of course I don't mind. Compared to what actresses usually eat I'm sure it will be a feast.'

He took another sip of his wine and watched her as she ate her soup. She really was quite different from any woman he had known. 'The life of an actress is not one I'd have expected the daughter of a wealthy man to choose. After all, it's often long hours for low pay.'

She lowered her spoon and tilted her head in thought. 'I don't think I actually did *choose* to become an actress. I think the life chose me. The first time I appeared on stage I felt as though I had come home. It was like the other actors were the family I never had. And the audience—when they applauded it was like nothing else on earth. I felt so happy and being on stage continues to make me happy.'

They exchanged smiles. She lit up when she spoke of the stage, her blue eyes shone and her smile was nothing less than radiant. 'But what about your father? I suspect you being on the stage doesn't make *him* happy.'

She nodded and her forehead furrowed as her eyebrows drew together. 'Fortunately, for a long time my father took very little interest in what I did. I'd appeared in numerous performances before he even realised what I was doing. If it hadn't been for…'

She looked down and picked up her spoon again.

'If it hadn't been for what?'

She placed her spoon back in the soup bowl with a decisive clink and pushed the bowl away. 'I suppose you might as well know. After all, you are my husband, even if, you know, you aren't really.'

He waited. She had him intrigued. What on earth could she tell him that she thought he should know? He doubted there would be a scandal. And if there was, it was unlikely to be anything worse than many of the scandalous things he had done. Whatever it was, he would forgive her.

'My father found out about my acting because I wanted to become engaged to be married to an actor.'

Oliver sat up straighter in his chair. That was not what he'd expected. She now had his undivided attention. 'You were previously engaged? You wanted to get married? Who to? What happened?'

She inhaled deeply and exhaled slowly through pursed lips. 'It was an unofficial engagement. His name was Arnold Emerson and we appeared together in that amateur production of *Macbeth* in New York. I thought he was in love with me. He said he was in love with me and I believed him. When he approached my father to ask for my hand my father was horrified. He said he was a charlatan and was only after my money. I was sure my father was wrong and was only saying that because Arnold had no money and no status. Not exactly the sort of man my father wanted me to marry.' She picked up her spoon and clenched it tightly. 'But it turned out that my father was right. To prove his point, he offered Arnold a large amount of money to leave New York and never see me again. And that's exactly what he did.'

'That's appalling. The man's a complete bast— dastard.'

She looked up at him. 'Who, my father?'

'Well, yes, him, too, but, no, this Emerson fellow. He's a dastard and a fool, and you're better off without him.'

'Yes, that's what my father said.'

'For once I'm in agreement with him.' Oliver steeled himself to ask the question to which he both wanted and did not want to hear the answer. 'Did you love him very much?'

She shrugged. 'I thought I did. But I didn't really know him, did I?' She gazed at him, those big blue eyes staring into his. 'I was angry at the time, but I think I was more angry that Father had been proven correct than because I wouldn't be getting married to Arnold. So I suppose that means I wasn't really in love with him after all.'

Relief flooded through him and his tense shoulders relaxed. 'I'm so sorry, Arabella.'

She shrugged again. 'Well, it's all in the past now.' She bit lightly on her lip and looked over at him. 'So what about you? Have you ever been in love?'

Oliver couldn't help but laugh at the absurdity of the question. Him? In love? Never. 'No, most certainly not. In fact, I doubt if such a thing actually exists. Countless women thought they were in love with my father, including my mother, but like you with Arnold Emerson, they never really knew him. If they did, I doubt that there would be much love in their hearts for that scoundrel.'

'So your father taught you that love doesn't exist and my father taught me that when it comes to love and to men, I can't trust my own judgement. What a great married couple we make.'

Oliver lifted his wine glass. 'In that case, shall we toast our fathers, the old scoundrels.'

'Our fathers.' She laughed and clinked her glass against his.

The footman arrived, removed their soup bowls, replaced them with the fish course and began serving out the vegetables.

'Just leave them, thank you,' Oliver said. 'We can serve ourselves.'

With a bow the footman departed.

'But your mother loved your father?' Arabella asked as she served vegetables on to their plates.

'Yes, she did. And in her case love was very, very blind.'

She looked up at him, a spoonful of carrots suspended in mid-air. 'So how many mistresses do you think your father had?'

Oliver frowned. That was a question he couldn't possibly answer. 'I don't know. I doubt if I could even take a tally of how many he had each year.'

She nodded; her face thoughtful. 'So, they were all short-lived affairs?'

'I suppose some lasted longer than others, but none for very long. They only lasted until the next pretty face caught his attention.'

She bit the edge of her lip. 'And how many children did he have, apart from you? How many half-siblings do you have?'

'At the last count there were eighteen.'

'Eighteen.' The serving spoon clattered back into the silver terrine and she stared at him with wide eyes.

'Yes, but I suspect there are more. I have people investigating to see whether there are any that I have missed, so that I can make sure they are supported by the estate and not left to try to cope in poverty.'

'And what about you, Oliver? Do you have any children?' she asked quietly, picking up the serving spoon and clenching it tightly.

'No,' he stated emphatically.

She tilted her head, as if waiting for him to prove why he was so certain. Oliver coughed, unsure how he should explain, without going into details that might embarrass her, the precautions he and his mistresses took to avoid pregnancy. 'I know I have no children because there are things a man can do to prevent such things happening. And the women I am involved with have their own methods of...' He waved his hand in the air. Was it her embarrassment that he was trying to prevent or his own?

'I see,' she said, colour tingeing her cheeks. 'So why did such techniques never work for your father?'

Oliver laughed, a humourless laugh. 'Because he didn't use them. He didn't care. It was as simple as that.'

'Oh, I see.'

Oliver hoped that was the end of her questioning. With most of the women he associated with the conversation could quickly get downright bawdy and he would be far from embarrassed, but discussing how to prevent pregnancy with Arabella was a decidedly disconcerting experience.

They ate their meal, with only the sound of silver cutlery on porcelain breaking the silence. Once the fish course was over the footmen served the dessert. Oliver waved it away, but Arabella's face lit up at the sight of the strawberry tart and cream. She ate the sweet treat with obvious enjoyment, occasionally closing her eyes and licking her lips, causing Oliver to smile.

When she had finished, she looked at him and winked. 'Delicious.'

As if by sixth sense the footman reappeared and removed her plate. Oliver refilled both their glasses and sat back to look out over the estate. He took in the long shadows cast by the plants and topiary in the formal garden and watched as a group of swallows dived and swooped in the soft early evening light, as if putting on a show for their benefit.

He smiled again at Arabella and she smiled back.

He couldn't remember the last time he had done this, just sat outside and watched the last of the sunlight disappear. It was such a pleasant evening he was pleased he could enjoy it with Arabella. But such pleasure was just an interlude before their real lives recommenced.

'Hopefully you will hear from the Limelight Theatre soon,' he said. 'Then you can get back to doing what makes you happy.'

'Hmm, and what about you, Oliver, what makes you truly happy?'

She waited for his answer, then colour exploded on her cheeks and she looked away. She had obviously answered the question herself.

Oliver smiled. 'I take it from your blushes you think you know exactly what makes me happy.'

She picked up her glass and took a nervous sip. 'Well, I wouldn't know about that.'

He stifled a laugh. 'But there are *other* things that make me happy, too.'

'Really? I wouldn't have thought you'd have the time or energy for anything else.'

He laughed lightly. 'I suspect my reputation far exceeds reality.'

'Well, I should hope so.' She placed her glass firmly on the table, the wine nearly spilling over the rim. 'Just so I don't experience any surprises, how many *good friends* do you actually have at the moment?'

'At this precise moment?'

She nodded.

'None. I know you have a poor opinion of me, but I'm not quite the rascal you think I am. And I do have some rules that I live by, you know. I'm not a complete cad.'

She shook her head, her lips pursed. 'Rules? What sort of rules?'

He took another drink, not sure if he liked the direction the conversation was going, but she deserved to know about the man she was now tied to. 'I've already told you I only get involved with women who want to have fun with no commitment and that is almost invariably married women who are unhappy with their husbands for various reasons. But I also have a rule that I never seduce anyone, ever.'

'You *never* seduce anyone?' She gave a small, fake laugh and a deeper blush tinged her cheeks. Her discomfort at this conversation was obvious, but despite that she continued. 'You can't be much of a rake if you don't seduce women—isn't that the very definition of a rake?'

'I never said I *was* a rake. And, no, I don't seduce women. I would never take a woman to my bed unless she was more than willing.'

Her lips pinched into a narrower, more disapproving line. 'So, is that your only rule? You never seduce anyone?'

He shrugged. 'No. I have another rule, I never bed virgins.'

The colour on her cheeks burned a deep crimson red. She picked up her wine glass, put it back down on the table, then picked it up again, her hand clenching the stem. 'That rules me out then, doesn't it?'

she said with another false laugh. 'I might be a married woman, but I'm a virgin and I guess I'm going to stay that way.'

It was Oliver's turn to feel embarrassed. He looked over at her, both shocked and surprised by her frank statement. 'I'm sorry, Arabella. This situation should not have been forced on you. You should have been allowed to marry whomever you wanted. To marry a man who loved you.'

'I thought you didn't believe in love, said it didn't exist.' She looked up at him, a challenge in her eyes.

Oliver squirmed in his seat. 'I don't, but I suspect you do. All I'm saying is, don't give your virginity to just any man. Wait until you think you are in love.'

'Well, that's hardly your business, is it?' She stared at him defiantly. 'If I don't object to whom you take as a lover, you can hardly object to any man who becomes mine.'

Acid burned up his throat at the thought of Arabella with another man. His hands clenched into tight fists, as if he wanted to commit an act of violence on this unknown lover. 'You're right, I'm hardly in a position to object,' he said through gritted teeth.

'Well, I'm pleased you have accepted that,' she said, her voice sounding anything but pleased. 'So, perhaps you can find a suitable lover for me, one who doesn't live by your rules.' Her false laugh now had a jeering quality. 'A man who doesn't mind seducing married virgins.'

Her words were like bullets fired straight at his heart. Rage boiled within him and blood pulsated in his ears. He stared at her in shocked disbelief, hardly able to believe what she had just said. He knew she had a low opinion of him, but this…? This was sinking to lower depths than even he was capable of plummeting.

He glared at her; his jaw so tense it ached. 'I…will…do…no…such…thing.'

Chapter Fourteen

Arabella stared out at the garden, seeing nothing. She had gone too far. But his so-called rules had made her angry. How could he have rules when it came to women? This one he could take to his bed, but not that one. It was outrageous. And it didn't help that all this talk of bedding and seduction had caused a decidedly unsettling reaction deep within her. All those women he had bedded, they knew what it was like to be held by him, to be caressed by him, to be desired by him. Something she would never experience.

There was no denying she *did* desire this man, her husband. The way her heart beat faster every time he looked at her told her that, loud and clear. But it was a desire she should not be feeling. And it was a desire he did not feel for her in return. She was a virgin. She might be his wife, but she was against the rules.

But her anger at his ridiculous rules did not excuse what she had just said. She had wanted to shock him, and the anger flashing in his eyes showed that she had succeeded.

Perhaps she was acting so out of character because last night she had hardly slept a wink. Instead, she had tossed and turned in her bed all night, unable to get comfortable, unable to stop her mind from going over and over everything that had happened during their time together. When she wasn't tossing and turning, she was lying on her side, staring at the closed door that separated them, thinking about the man behind it.

No wonder she was tired. No wonder her nerves were strung as tight as a long bow. No wonder she was so quick to become offended. But still, that didn't excuse what she had said.

She took a tentative sideways glance in his direction. His strong jaw was clenched so tightly she could see the bulge of muscles at the side of his face. He, too, was staring out at the garden, but she doubted he was taking in the scenery and his hand was gripping the wine glass so tightly he was in danger of breaking the stem.

Only the sound of the birds tweeting in the trees interrupted the uncomfortable silence stretching out between them.

She had to put this right. She had to apologise for saying something so offensive to him.

'I'm sorry, Arabella,' he said, still staring straight ahead. 'I should not have reacted so strongly to what you asked.'

He was sorry? *He* had nothing to be sorry about.

'No, Oliver. I'm the one who should apologise. What I said about…' She waved her hand in the air, not wanting to repeat the words. 'I didn't mean it. And I should not have said it.'

He turned slowly to face her. Despite his apology,

rage still burned in those dark brown eyes. 'So, I take it you don't want me to find you a lover?'

She swallowed and shook her head.

He held her gaze and heat burned brighter on her already flaming cheeks. She swallowed again, aware that there was only one man she wanted as her lover and he was staring at her right now.

The realisation hit her, hard. She struggled to breathe, her eyes grew wider and her heart thumped so wildly she could feel its pulsating rhythm through-out her body.

It shouldn't be true, but it was. She wanted Oliver, not just to be her husband, but to be her lover. How had she let this happen? She hadn't wanted it to hap-pen, had been determined that it wouldn't happen, but it had and she couldn't deceive herself any longer.

She lowered her eyes and dragged in a breath to try to slow the turbulent beating of her heart.

This was an impossible situation. He was a rake, for goodness sake, a man who moved from one woman to another without a backward glance. And she wanted him. Desired him. Had her experience with Arnold Emerson taught her nothing? It would seem not. She was once again falling for the wrong man.

'No, I don't want you to find me a lover,' she stated with all honesty. The only one she wanted was sitting beside her, glaring at her with his hard, brown eyes.

He looked back out at the garden and took a sip of his wine. 'Good.'

'Obviously that would be an inappropriate role for a husband.'

He laughed without humour. 'Obviously.'

'When I take a lover, it will be a man of my own choosing.' But how was any other man going to match the man she was married to? Arabella shook her head and looked up at Oliver.

His grip on the wine glass intensified and those clenched muscles at the side of his jaw reappeared. He breathed out slowly and deeply, then drained his glass in one long draught.

He was still angry. But why should he care who she took as a lover? Was it simply because she was his wife, his possession and, even if he didn't want her himself, he didn't want any other man to have her? Would he be so petty? Nothing about him had suggested he was a petty man.

But there was no denying that he was enraged. Was there a possibility that the thought of her with another man was making him jealous? His reaction to her taunt that she wanted him to find her a lover could have been due to his pride, but his obvious anger at her statement that she could find her own lover, that was different.

Or was it merely wishful thinking on her part? If he was jealous, did that mean he desired her, wanted her?

A footman appeared with a lamp and placed it on the table. Arabella had hardly noticed that the last of the twilight had faded and they were now surrounded by darkness. The lamp cast an arc of yellow light around the table, enclosing them in an intimate circle.

Slowly Oliver turned towards her. 'Arabella, you are a free woman,' he stated in a clipped monotone. 'I have said it before, but it is worth restating. I will do nothing to interfere in the way you live your life. But I know men. You should be careful whom you get involved with.'

She stared him straight in the eye, determined not to be cowered by the turbulent emotions that were waging a war within her.

'So, do you think I should also compile a list of rules for choosing a lover the way you have?'

She watched his reaction carefully. His jaw clenched tighter as he gripped the now empty wine glass. 'Perhaps,' he said in that same monotone.

'Well, obviously they will have to be different from your rules,' she said ruefully.

'And whatever those rules are, Arabella, they are ones you are going to have to compile yourself. I have no interest in helping you.'

He stared down at her, his unflinching eyes making it clear that this conversation was over. Arabella was now seeing a completely different man from the brazen one who had rushed into her dressing room and taken her in his arms, or the man with the mischievous smile and devilish sense of fun.

This man was serious. He saw nothing funny in her taunting.

And nor did Arabella. She did not want any rules. She did not want a lover. She only wanted him.

'I shall leave you to think about your list. Now, if you'll excuse me, it is getting late. It is time to retire for the night.' He stood up and bowed formally. 'I believe you can find your own way to your room.' With that he departed, leaving Arabella sitting alone, staring out at the dark estate.

* * *

Oliver never retired early, at least not alone. But he could not remain in Arabella's company a minute longer. Not if she insisted on discussing her plans for finding a lover. That was more than any man should be expected to endure. It was a form of torture that could rival the medieval rack.

He reached the foot of the stairs and stopped. After undergoing such torture the likelihood of him being able to sleep was extremely remote. He turned and headed along the corridor, down the back stairs, through the kitchen.

As he passed through the servants' area, he waved his hands, palm down, to signal that they should remain seated and ignore his presence.

Once outside he breathed in deeply to relieve the constriction in his chest and began walking, briskly. This was another first. When had he ever been forced to take exercise to rid himself of his reaction to a woman? Never. But his pent-up energy had to be expended somehow and, for once, it would not be in a bed with a willing lover.

He walked along the dark avenue of trees, shimmering in the light evening breeze. This situation really was impossible. It would be funny if it wasn't so damn tragic. He wanted to bed his wife. Under normal circumstances that was a perfectly acceptable thing to want to do—more than acceptable, it was expected, it was part of the marriage contract. But these were not normal circumstances. He had known his bride for a few short weeks. They had married against their will. And she deserved so much more than to lose her virginity to a man like him, a man who was incapable of commitment. She did not deserve to live the life that his mother had been forced to live, sharing a man with a multitude of other women. He would not subject any woman to such a life, particularly Arabella.

Not to mention that bedding her would break two of his cardinal rules.

He increased his walking pace, heading into the woodland area. But that was something he did not want to think about. The sooner Arabella left Somerfeld Manor and returned to her life in London the better. Then he wouldn't be tormented by that bewitching face, that gorgeous body, or that silky skin, and the memory of those creamy breasts rising and falling above the bodice of her beautiful yellow gown.

Crashing through the thick undergrowth, Oliver knew that he most definitely had to get all thoughts of Arabella out of his mind.

He spotted the dark form of a tenant, hiding behind a tree, a shotgun under his arm. The man was presumably out poaching. Well, good luck to him. He presumably had a family to feed and was using some initiative. Oliver tipped his hand to his head in a gesture of greeting as he quickly passed. He smiled at the thought of the man's surprise. He must make a ludicrous sight, the lord of the manor, dressed in formal evening wear, all but running around his estate in the middle of the night.

He slowed down and headed back towards the house, physical exhaustion starting to overcome him. Hopefully this would not be a regular occurrence. Hopefully he wouldn't have to spend every night running around his estate like a mad man. As soon as

Arabella found employment as an actress she would be out of his house, out of his life. That would make her happy and her absence, while perhaps not making him happy, precisely, would most certainly be the best for both of them.

He entered the house and headed up the stairs to his bedroom. After such exercise he could only hope that he would now be able to sleep, that he would not lie in bed, awake, thinking of the woman lying in bed in the room next to his, with only an adjoining door between them.

Instead of calling for his valet, he undressed alone, drew on his robe and paced the room, his body still agitated. It seemed sleep wasn't going to come. He walked over to the window and stared out at the estate, lying in quiet darkness. The sooner she left Somerfeld Manor the better. Until then he was going to have to learn to endure this torture.

What was it that someone said, in one of Oscar Wilde's plays? That they could resist anything except temptation. Much to Oliver's annoyance, that applied equally to him. Resisting temptation was something he had such little practice at.

A creaking noise behind him interrupted his thoughts. He turned and saw his wife standing in the doorway. Wearing a white nightgown, her long black hair flowing freely, she was temptation itself. One Oliver knew it would take a man much stronger than him to resist.

Chapter Fifteen

It had taken every ounce of self-confidence Arabella possessed to turn the door handle to the adjoining room. And now here she was, standing in his bedroom, staring up at him, and it was taking even more strength to stay and not flee back to her own room.

When she had seen the light from his lamp appear under the door, she knew she did not want to spend another night staring at that light and wondering. She did not want to lie in bed thinking about him, wishing and wanting. So, she had got out of bed and opened his door. But she hadn't thought about what she would do once she was in his room.

He continued to stare at her, not moving from the window. He was dressed in a loosely tied maroon robe and her gaze was drawn to his muscular chest, visible at the robe's opening. He was naked underneath. She gulped, her startled gaze moving back up to his face.

Surely he would take some action. Do something. Not just stand there. Surely he knew why she was here. Was that all he was going to do? Just stay exactly where he was, staring at her? It seemed it was.

Her heart thumping loudly against her chest, she gasped in a series of breaths to give herself courage. If he wasn't going to do anything, then she would have to. She placed her hands at her neckline, closed her eyes and pulled at the laces holding the front of her nightgown together.

'What are you doing, Arabella?' he asked, his voice thick and constricted.

Instead of answering she continued to fumble at her laces with clumsy fingers.

He crossed the room, took hold of her hands and stilled the action. 'Arabella, I've told you. I don't seduce virgins.'

She pulled in another deep breath and spoke as clearly as she possibly could. 'In case you haven't noticed, you're not seducing me. I'm seducing you.' Well, that was what she was trying to do, but it was a bit difficult when she couldn't even unlace her nightgown.

She looked up at him, praying she would not see him laughing at her. Instead there was an unmistakable look of passion burning in his eyes. Passion for her. She had not been wrong. The way he had spoken to her over dinner, the things he had said to her, the way he had behaved had all led her to think he wanted her. And the look in his eyes confirmed that. It was the same as she had seen before he kissed her, the same as when he'd stared at her with such hunger earlier today.

'Arabella, are you sure?'

She nodded. Of course she was sure. She had never been more sure of anything in her life. 'Yes,' she said, her voice little more than a whisper.

He lifted her fingers to his lips. 'You know what sort of man I am. I can't offer you commitment, I can't offer you fidelity.'

She shook her head. 'I'm not asking you for either of those things.'

He lowered her hands and held them close against his chest, so close she could feel his heart pounding, could sense the tension in his body. His eyes never left hers and the intent of that look was undeniable. He most certainly wasn't laughing at her. He was looking at her as if he wanted to devour her. And that was exactly what Arabella wanted him to do.

That look in his eye making her bold, she smiled up at him, teasingly. 'I'm just a married woman who wants some fun.'

His lips slowly curled into that mischievous smile she loved so much. 'Well, in that case, my dear, let's have some fun.'

His hands slid around her waist, pulling her towards him. His kiss was gentle, but that was not what she wanted. She wanted him to kiss her the way he had when he'd burst into her dressing room. That kiss had possessed her, taken her over, caused her to lose herself, to forget everything and everyone around her until she'd kissed him back in front of everyone. And she wanted him to more than just kiss her now. Did he still require permission? Then she would give it to him. She wrapped her hands around his neck, running her hands through his thick blond hair and holding him tightly against her.

Parting her lips, she kissed him back, her body hard up against him, the touch of his naked skin against her breasts, her legs against his, letting him know she wanted him to deepen the kiss.

His grip on her waist tightened and he pulled her possessively towards him, his fierce kiss crashing over her, hard, demanding, potent.

Yes, this was what she wanted. She released a quiet moan of pleasure as his tongue entered her mouth, plundering, probing. Her body melted into his. Oh, yes, this was most definitely what she wanted. This was why she had risked everything and entered his room.

His hand slid down from her waist, cupping her buttocks. Every inch of her body pulsated for him, ached for him. Her mind going blank, she clasped him tighter, her swelling breasts rubbing against his muscular chest, wanting to feel his skin against hers, his body surrounding her, his hands caressing her.

He stepped back from her and desperation gripped her. No. He could not be stopping now. She would not let him. She looked up at him, her confused mind trying to formulate the words that would make him kiss her again.

'Raise your arms above your head,' he said, his voice a low growl.

Arabella followed his command and in one swift movement he lifted up her nightgown, pulled it off her body and tossed it to the side of the room. She was now standing naked in front of him.

Any fleeting embarrassment was swept away when his lips found hers again, kissing her, devouring her.

Still kissing her, he lifted her up in one smooth movement and carried her over to his bed. Placing her carefully in the middle, he stood back, looked down at her and smiled.

'You really are beautiful, Arabella. The most beautiful woman I've ever seen. And this is how I imagined seeing you from the very first time I laid eyes on you.'

Lying naked in front of him, Arabella knew she should be feeling embarrassed. But she didn't. *He had wanted her in his bed from the moment he had first seen her.* That admission sent a heady wave tingling through her body and any residual shyness evaporated. He desired her, had always desired her. And right now, with him looking at her with such fierce passion, that was exactly how she felt—desirable.

His robe dropped to the ground and it was now her turn to admire his body. And it was a body worthy of admiration. Her gaze took in the firm, strong muscles of his chest and his flat hard stomach, with a scattering of dark hairs drawing her gaze down his body. And if she had any remaining doubt of his desire for her, she no longer did. His desire was standing, firm and hard in front of her.

Her eyes returned to his and she saw that devilish smile on his lips. He had seen where her gaze had travelled.

Arabella bit the edge of her lip and smiled back at him. 'So, are you going to show me some of that fun you promised?'

He laughed lightly and joined her on the bed. 'Happy to oblige.'

Arabella arched towards him and wrapped her arms around his neck, longing to feel his touch. He smiled down at her and watched her reaction as his hands moved slowly over her sensitive skin. His fingers lightly ran over her stomach and up her ribcage. A low groan escaped her lips and she closed her eyes, surrendering herself to the sensation of his touch.

His hand reached her breasts. He cupped each one in turn and his thumb moved over the now achingly tight buds. She writhed on the bed as his hands tormented her nipples. A pounding deep within her core possessed her body and her moans came louder, faster, her mind and body consumed by his caresses. When he leant down and took one nipple in his mouth it felt as if she was about to die from pleasure. His tongue rasped over the stiff nub, licking, sucking. Her moans became cries of ecstasy. Louder and louder, in time to the rhythm of his tongue.

His hand slid down her body and moved between her legs. She felt his fingers gently stroke along her folds and enter her most intimate of places. His palm pressed between her legs, intensifying the throbbing that was engulfing her, while his lips continued to tease and torment her nipples. Surrendering herself to the experience, she rubbed herself against him, her back instinctively arched, matching his rhythm, increasing the pleasure, a pleasure that kept mounting, growing, intensifying until a forceful, ecstatic wave crashed over her. She released a loud, shuddering cry and collapsed back on the bed.

When she opened her eyes, he was smiling down at her. She blinked away a few tears that had sprung to her eyes and smiled back at him. 'That was…that was…' She couldn't think of the words.

'So, do you want some more of that?' he asked gently.

'Oh, yes,' she replied. 'Yes, yes, yes.'

He kissed her again and she melted into his kiss. His tongue entered her mouth and she once again savoured the masculine taste of him, inhaling that wonderful musky scent she loved so much. Her hands wrapped around his shoulders, moving down his strong back, loving the feel of his hard muscles under her fingers, then down to those firm tight buttocks.

But she wanted more than his kisses, more than his caresses.

She withdrew from his lips and lifted herself up towards him. 'Make love to me, Oliver,' she urged.

He hugged her closer, his chest hard against hers. 'I don't want to cause you any pain, Bella.'

'You won't. I want this, Oliver.' She rubbed the inside of her thigh against his leg and smiled at his quick intake of breath. Unable to stop herself, even if she wanted to, Arabella parted her legs and arched her body towards him.

'Make love to me, now, Oliver.'

He did not need to be asked again. He wrapped her in his arms, his strong thighs moving between hers. As if under their own command, her legs wrapped themselves around his waist. She felt the tip of him at the edge of her feminine folds, but still he hesitated.

'Stop me at any time, Bella,' he murmured.

But Arabella knew she would not stop him, could not stop him. He pushed himself slowly into her. She gasped out loudly, but in pleasure, not pain. Slowly he withdrew and even more slowly he entered her again, watching her carefully as he did so. She cried out in pleasure and clasped his buttocks tightly, pushing him towards her, letting him know this was what she wanted.

She looked up into his eyes. Concern was now gone, replaced by a look of primal hunger, a hunger that only intensified her need for him. He entered her more deeply and she cried out his name, urging him on. He responded immediately, pushing into her again and again, deeper, harder.

With each stroke her cries became louder, her body moving against his, in time to his thrusting rhythm.

Her eyes closed, she lost herself to the sensations swelling up inside her, taking her higher and higher, until they reached a pitch of intensity that was almost more than she could bear and a convulsive shudder whipped through her, causing her to dig her fingers into his buttocks and cry out, before collapsing back on to the bed. Just as her body went limp, she felt his heart suddenly pound harder against her sweat-slickened breasts. He muttered her name on a soft moan and pulled out from her just before he released himself.

Wrapped in each other's arms, they held each other tightly while their panting breaths slowed down and Arabella could hardly believe that such a feeling of fulfilment was possible.

When his breath returned to normal, Oliver lifted himself up on to one arm, smiled down at her and brushed a stray lock of hair from her face. 'Well, I don't know about you, Duchess, but personally I feel thoroughly seduced.'

Arabella laughed, wrapping her arms tightly around him as he kissed her once again.

Chapter Sixteen

Oliver gazed down at his sleeping wife, at her long black eyelashes resting on her soft, porcelain-cream skin, at her full red lips, swollen from his repeated kisses. She looked so angelic in repose, but last night there had been nothing angelic about her behaviour. He smiled at the memory of her standing in the door-way, dressed only in her nightgown. The light from behind her had made the gown almost translucent and he had been able to see the outline of her beautiful body, those luscious curves and long, shapely legs.

It had taken a level of iron willpower he didn't know he possessed to not move, to not cross the room and rip off that nightgown so he could feast on her beauty. Like a mantra he had kept reciting to himself, again and again, *You do not seduce virgins, you do not seduce virgins* in order to keep himself fixed to the spot.

But even iron can bend if exposed to a high enough temperature. And his iron willpower had been unable to withstand the fury of the heat generated when she had whispered those words in his ear, 'You're not seducing me, I'm seducing you'.

He ran his finger gently down the side of her face and curled a strand of her long black hair around his finger. She had made it clear to him that he was not taking advantage of her innocence. She had given him permission to stop fighting his attraction to her and to give vent to the surging passion that had been building up inside him like a volcano.

And he had discovered his initial assessment of her had been correct. When he had kissed her on the night they had first met he had suspected there was a well of untapped passion simmering within her, just waiting to be ignited.

And last night he had definitely stoked those fires. They had made love repeatedly. Each time she had become more adventurous, continually surprising him, and her appetite had been as ravenous as his own.

Last night had been unlike anything he had experienced with a woman. The intensity, the passion, the intimacy, it had been utterly intoxicating. And like a drug that had entered his bloodstream and taken him over, he had craved more, much more.

Why he should have experienced such a strength of feeling he had no idea. He couldn't be that cliché, a man who became puffed up with masculine pride because he was a woman's first lover. Could he?

Oliver knew it wasn't that. Was it because Arabella was so different from any other woman he had known?

He continued to gaze at her lovely face. She had a delicate beauty, but that disguised a strength of character that was admirable.

Her determination to succeed on the stage, to carve out a life of her own, despite being the daughter of an extremely wealthy man, made her unique in his world. He knew no other woman, or man for that matter, who was prepared to forgo all that wealth could give them, to risk it all so they could achieve their dream.

And last night, by coming into his room, she had shown that strength in a different way. She had been so nervous, her hands shaking as she'd tried to free herself from her nightgown, yet she had forced herself to continue. He smiled with warm pleasure. She had been willing to take a risk and expose her vulnerability to him.

He really was a lucky man to have a woman like Arabella in his bed, not just because making love to her had been so magical, but because she was so special, unique.

His smile turned to a loud, exasperated sigh. But he would have to enjoy it while it lasted. They would soon be returning to their own lives. Their time together was just an interlude, a very enjoyable, very satisfying interlude, but an interlude all the same.

He rolled over on to his back, put his hands behind his head and stared up at the ceiling. Last night he had told her he couldn't offer her commitment and fidelity and she had accepted that. He only hoped she meant it and they weren't idle words. It was true, he had never committed to a woman. Experience had taught him he was incapable of doing so.

But he could not subject Arabella to the life his mother had led with his father, waiting dutifully at home while her husband moved from woman to woman without a backward glance. That was not the life that she should be leading. But it was also a life he knew a woman like Arabella would never accept. His jaw tensing, he knew that one day she would find someone who could offer her what he couldn't— commitment, fidelity, love. When that happened, he would have to accept it.

He rolled back to his side and gazed down at her. But that was all in the future. Right now, they were here together and he should be just enjoying the moment, not worrying about what would one day happen. Right now, she was with him, here, in his bed. And right now, he had no interest in any other woman. He was exactly where he wanted to be and with the woman he wanted to be with.

But how long would that last?

A leopard never changed his spots. He was not a one-woman man.

Eventually he would revert to type. He just had to ensure that he had set Arabella free before that happened.

He pushed away that thought. He did not need to think of it now. He ran his fingers down the soft, creamy skin of her shoulder and arm. She moved sensually in the bed. Her eyes opened and she smiled at him. Soon they would be parting and life would return to normal, but one more taste would do no harm. He leant down and kissed his wife's waiting lips, then took her in his arms to make love to her one more time.

Making love to Oliver…it had to be the perfect way to start the day. Arabella smiled and stretched lazily in the four-poster bed, her body tired and sated. She was so happy. Last night and this morning had been more thrilling than she could possibly have imagined. Now all she had to do was ignore the little voice in the back of her head that was asking, *What happens now?*

She did not know how this was going to work. Last night, she had promised Oliver that she would not interfere in the way he lived his life and she would abide by that promise. There would be other women in his life and that was something she was going to have to accept. She would just have to learn to control the pain that clenched her heart whenever she thought of him with someone else.

That was the deal. He had promised he would do nothing to interfere with her career on the stage and he had abided by that. More than abided by it, he was actually helping her achieve her goals. And Arabella would do the same for him.

Well, she wouldn't actually help him pursue other women. She wasn't a complete martyr and he hardly needed any help in that area anyway.

But she would at least do nothing to stop him. No matter how much heartache it caused her.

In the meantime, she would enjoy this moment while it lasted. Feasting her eyes on her husband's gorgeous body, she moved them slowly over every inch of him, as if committing each sculpted muscle to memory. Her fingers then followed the same path as her eyes, moving up those strong arms, across his wide shoulders, down the rock-hard chest to that flat, firm stomach. She smiled wickedly, her hand slowly moving lower.

It was amazing how last night had changed her. Those initial nerves had soon disappeared. She had felt so safe in Oliver's arms, safe enough to release a delicious wantonness she had not known she possessed, a wantonness she had thoroughly enjoyed exploring.

He grinned when her teasing fingers reached their destination. 'Again? Already? You will be the death of me.'

She laughed as his arms surrounded her.

'But this would definitely be something worth dying for,' he said, his lips finding hers and stifling her laughter.

They spent the day in bed together, never moving except to eat. When each discreet knock came at the door, Oliver would retrieve the tray left by the servants and they would picnic among the bedclothes, feeding each other an array of delicious treats prepared by the cook. Then they would make love again. Each time, when she fell back on to the bed, wondrously replete, Arabella was sure her hunger for him had finally been satisfied. They would remain in bed, talking and laughing, but before long that ache would start again, an ache that only he could soothe.

And so they passed another day and night together.

On the third day, the ever-thoughtful Nellie left a note to say she had prepared a bath in Arabella's dressing room. Leaving the tangled knot of sheets and blankets, Arabella led a naked Oliver by the hand through to her rooms, stepped into the bath and lay back as the warm water wrapped around her.

'Allow me,' Oliver said, picking up a sponge and slowly lathering her body.

Bliss, was all Arabella could think as she closed her eyes and surrendered herself to the touch of the sponge, the warmth of the water and the scent of lily of the valley from the soap.

But there was something that would make this experience even more blissful. She opened her eyes and smiled invitingly at Oliver. 'Join me.'

He frowned slightly. 'There's hardly room.'

'Then we'll make room.' She sat up straighter and curled in her legs.

His frown turned into a mischievous smile and he climbed into the bath. The water level rose, lapping at the rim. His large frame filled the other end of the bath and he wrapped his long legs around her.

'Right, now it's my turn.' She picked up the sponge, pulled herself into a kneeling position and rubbed the sponge along his shoulders, chest and slowly down his stomach.

Her attempts were thwarted when he grabbed her round the waist and kissed her, sending a tidal wave of water sloshing over the side on to the carpeted floor.

They both peered over the side at the mess they had made, then back at each other. 'This is not going to work, is it?' he said.

Laughing, she shook her head.

'In that case...' He scooped her up, dripping from the bath, and lowered her to her feet, her wet skin gliding against his glistening body. Taking one of the fluffy white towels left on a nearby wooden chair, he wrapped her in it and dried her slowly, then quickly ran the towel over himself.

'Right, now that we're clean, there appears to be a bed we haven't christened yet,' he murmured, scooping her up again and carrying her into her bedroom.

'So how many bedrooms does Somerfeld Manor have?' she asked as he lowered her on to her bed.

'I've never counted them, but I believe there's around forty.'

Arabella smiled, her toes curling in excitement. 'It looks as though we've got a lot of christening ahead of us.'

Oliver laughed, joining her on the bed. 'Then I'd better get busy, hadn't I, and get this one ticked off our list.'

Another rapturous day and night had passed. It was as if the outside world hardly existed. There was only this room, this bed and this man. And that was just how Arabella wanted it to remain.

Another discreet knock at the door alerted them to the arrival of more food. Arabella was famished. She had never felt more in need of sustenance, but then she had been indulging in some rather strenuous exercise recently.

Oliver disentangled himself from the sheets and strode across the room. She hummed with satisfaction as she surveyed his naked form from behind, all taut, powerful muscles. Was there anything more attractive than his firm round buttocks? Arabella doubted that very much.

He opened the door and retrieved the tray. She sat up, anxious to see what tasty food had been prepared for them. She had lost count of the time, did not know which meal it would be, but was sure that Cook would have once again prepared something delicious. It was funny how food tasted so much better when it was eaten in bed with your lover.

Removing the lid from the serving dish, she saw it was a selection of cold meats, cheeses, pâtés and bread. It must be lunch time, perfect.

Then she spotted a letter, standing upright between the silver salt and pepper shakers. She picked it up and turned it over. It was from the Limelight Theatre and addressed to Oliver.

Suddenly struggling to breathe, she handed it to him. 'This is for you,' she whispered.

He put down his plate and took the letter from her outstretched hand, read the address and handed it back to her. 'It might be addressed to me, but it will be about your future. You should be the one to read it.'

With trembling fingers, she picked up the ivory letter opener that had been placed on the tray and slit open the envelope. She quickly scanned the contents, then re-read them again, more slowly, her stomach clenching as she absorbed each word. She handed the letter to Oliver and watched him carefully as he read it.

When he had finished, he looked up at her. They held each other's gazes, his solemn expression reflecting exactly how she was feeling.

Chapter Seventeen

It was good news. Of course it was good news and Oliver would be selfish to think otherwise. But he *was* selfish. He wished they could continue to stay in bed together, let the world pass them by and forget everything and everyone else.

But for once in his life he would not be selfish. Arabella deserved more than that.

'That's excellent. Exactly what you wanted,' he said, jumping out of bed and grabbing his robe. 'You must return to London immediately.' He pulled the bell cord to call for a servant and forced himself to smile at her with as much excitement as he could summon.

Arabella remained in bed, still clutching the letter in her hand. She didn't look particularly pleased, Oliver mused. Perhaps it was because it was unexpected. Or maybe she was nervous about the part she had been offered in the new play, which, while not one of the leads, was more substantial than her previous role.

She smiled tentatively at him, slowly climbed out

of bed and looked around for her discarded nightgown. After four days of being continuously naked,
she suddenly appeared uncomfortable and self-
consciously crossed her arms, covering her breasts.
He picked up her nightgown and handed it to her.
She took it from his outstretched hand and quickly
pulled it over her head. Her body disappeared from
his gaze. Oliver hoped and prayed he had not seen it
for the last time.

She once again looked around the room, as if uncertain what to do next.

'You *are* happy, aren't you, Bella? This is what
you want, isn't it? You're not worried about anything,
are you?'

She nodded. 'Oh, no, I'm not worried, and yes,
yes, of course I'm happy. I'm just a bit taken aback
that the reply came so quickly. That's all. But, yes,
of course I'm happy.'

It wasn't how happy usually looked. Happy didn't
normally appear so confused or pensive.

A quiet knock at the door stopped him from questioning her reaction. He opened the door and told his
valet to arrange for her trunks to be packed and for
the carriage to be prepared so they could return to
London on the next train.

Arabella tilted her head. 'Will you be returning
to London as well?'

Oliver nodded. 'Yes, I have business to attend to
there, so I might as well join you. Plus, it will give you
a chance to get settled in at my town house.'

Business? What business?

Oliver was unsure. All he knew was that he did
not want to leave Arabella. Not yet.

She remained standing in the middle of his room, staring up at him.

'Perhaps you should summon your lady's maid so you can prepare for the journey,' he suggested.

Her gaze moved to their unmade bed, at the tray of now-abandoned lunch. 'Oh, yes, of course.'

She exited through to the adjoining room and closed the door behind her. Another quiet knock came at his door and he opened it to admit his valet, carrying his shaving equipment and a bowl of hot water.

Oliver always preferred to shave himself, so while he lathered his face his valet prepared his clothing for the journey.

He would be returning to London. Back to his old life.

He paused and stared at his reflection in the shaving mirror, his razor poised at the edge of his soaped cheek.

Wasn't that what he wanted? To go back to the constant round of parties, the gambling dens and the other delights London had to offer?

Of course it was. Why wouldn't it be? That's who he was, after all. He ran the razor along his cheek, then washed the soap off the razor in the hot water. It was a good outcome for both of them, *wasn't it*? The last few days had certainly been enjoyable, but it was time for things to get back to normal. And Arabella being offered a part in a new play was certainly all for the best. While he returned to his old life, she would be busy forging a career on the stage.

It had all worked out perfectly. So why wasn't he more pleased? He tilted back his head and ran the razor up his neck, scraping off several days' stubble.

The answer to that question was obvious. Because he was selfish. He wanted to spend more time in bed with Arabella. He had not yet completely satisfied his need for her.

He rinsed the razor again and stared down at the bowl. When had that ever happened before? Never. He had never had to move on from a woman before he was ready. But it looked as though this time he was going to have to. And if he was to avoid acting like a petulant child who'd had his favourite toy taken away from him, he would have to keep his feelings to himself.

He finished off his shaving and rubbed a warm towel over his face.

This was a brilliant opportunity for Arabella and she did not need a husband who was thinking only of his own carnal needs holding her back.

He pulled on his shirt and his valet buttoned on the stiff white collar, then helped him into his waist-coat and jacket. All was not yet lost, Oliver reminded his reflection in the full-length mirror while his valet brushed down his jacket. They would be together at his London town house and maybe there, with any luck, he would have ample opportunity to satisfy his need for his wife and finally get her out of his system.

Arabella was meant to be happy. After all, how could she not be? This was wonderful news. So why did she feel as if she had suffered a defeat, not a victory? Until a few days ago the only thing that really gave her pleasure was the thought of being back on stage. Now she had experienced another source of exquisite pleasure, in the arms of her husband. And it was a pleasure she wasn't ready to give up, not yet.

She sat in silence in front of her dressing table mirror as Nellie styled her hair. Like it or not, she was going to have to give up that pleasure. She was returning to London, back to where she had first met Oliver, back to his world, a world inhabited by an array of beautiful women like Lady Bufford and Lucy Baker. Here, at Somerfeld Manor, she'd had him all to herself, but now she would have to share him.

Getting a part at the Limelight was a victory, but losing Oliver to his real life was most definitely a defeat.

But she had told him she would accept him the way he was and put up no objections to the way he lived. It was now time to keep that promise.

She stood up so Nellie could help her into her travelling dress. There was no reason why she should feel sorry for herself. Didn't she have everything she wanted? She was to resume work as an actress and had just experienced a few days of pleasure, the level of which she previously didn't know existed. No, she had nothing to feel sorry about. So she wouldn't. She would celebrate the victory and ignore the defeat.

Because when it came down to it, she had no other option. It was a defeat of her own making. Hadn't she promised she'd make no demands on him? Hadn't that been the only reason he had made love to her, gone against his rules of not seducing virgins?

She nodded decisively at her reflection. No, she had absolutely no right to feel sorry for herself. And there was no question about whether she would abide by her promise. Of course she would.

She forced herself to smile as Nellie brushed down her dress. She *would* be happy. She would return to London, her old life, her real life, the life that she loved.

She joined Oliver, waiting for her outside the house beside the carriage already loaded with their trunks. With as much enthusiasm as she could summon, she smiled at him as he helped her into the carriage which would take them to the train station.

Forcing herself to maintain a façade of gaiety, she made polite conversation throughout the trip. As the Surrey countryside passed them by, outside the train window, she worked hard to ignore that annoying voice reminding her that this was indeed the end of their journey together.

Arriving in London, they took a cab from the station to his Mayfair town house. The quiet of the neighbourhood was a stark contrast to the bustle of the railway station and the busy, chaotic streets they had travelled through, with horses, carts, carriages, omnibuses and pedestrians all jostling for position on the teeming roads. It was hard to believe that they were in the centre of a busy city. It was so tranquil, the only sound being the twittering of birds, singing in the large trees that lined the pavement, and the subdued chatter of two passing nannies, pushing their large, black perambulators.

'Rather pleasant, isn't it?' Nellie whispered to her, her hand on her hat as she looked up at the three-storey brick façade. 'I'm going to enjoy living here.'

'Don't get too comfortable, Nellie. We're not staying here. We'll be moving into the boarding house along with the rest of the cast.'

Nellie rolled her eyes, but followed Arabella through the columned entranceway and into the house. Servants were rushing up and down the staircases, still making the house ready for their sudden arrival. Arabella looked up at the ornate carved ceiling, soaring above them three storeys high, each storey with a carved wooden balcony overlooking the entrance.

Yes, Arabella had to admit it was quite an improvement on the boarding house where the actors stayed. But she was committed to returning to her old life. Now that her father had left the country, she did not have to stay at the Savoy. While the cast and crew always treated her as if she was no different, Arabella was always aware that she came from a privileged background and, unlike them, was not dependent on the paltry wage that acting brought in.

So to prove to them that she would not be adopting any airs, now that she was a duchess, she would organise to join them at their humble boarding house. And it would prove to Oliver that she was really committed to returning to her real life.

'Let me show you to your rooms,' Oliver said, leading her up the stairs. She caught Nellie's eye, who gave her an encouraging smile and nod. But Nellie would have to accept disappointment. They would not be staying at this house, and she would soon be explaining this situation to Oliver.

He opened the door to her room and smiled at her. 'I hope this is satisfactory.' If she was actually staying, it would be more than satisfactory. The spacious room, with floor-to-ceiling windows overlooking the garden courtyard, had a light and airy feel. It was a delightfully feminine room, with delicate red and cream wallpaper with a Japanese blossom motif, Persian rugs on the wooden floor and a large four-poster bed. Nellie was right, this would be a very comfortable place to stay. And, once again, her rooms would be adjoining Oliver's with only an interconnecting door between them.

That was another very good reason for her to not stay at his town house. How many other women was Oliver going to entertain in the room next door to hers? She had promised him freedom, but it did not mean she wanted to be present to witness him exercise it. She shuddered, despite the warmth of the summer's day. No, that would be asking too much of her. She would have to get used to the thought of him with another woman, but she wanted it all to happen out of sight, then hopefully, it might just be out of her mind as well.

'Well, I think I'll go straight to the theatre.'

Oliver moved to one side as she barged past him. 'But surely you want to get settled in first,' he said to her retreating back.

She headed towards the stairs. 'No, the letter said they're starting rehearsals immediately, so I don't want to miss a single day.'

'Then I'll accompany you.'

'There's no need.' Arabella quickly rushed down the stairs. She did not want Oliver at the theatre. She most definitely did not want to risk some other actress capturing his eye. 'Honestly, there really isn't,' she called back to him.

He caught up with her at the bottom of the stairs. 'I'd like to accompany you. I love watching you perform and I've never seen a play in rehearsal before.'

Arabella paused at the entrance, trying to think of an excuse as he asked a footman to arrange for his carriage to be brought to the front of the house. She could hardly tell him the real reason she did not want him to accompany her. She had already told the other actresses that their marriage was to be one in name only and she knew there were several who more than adequately fitted Oliver's requirements of wanting to have fun with no commitments. If he was going to have other women in his life, she would rather it not be any she knew.

It looked as though her resolve was about to be sorely tested. With the greatest reluctance she nodded and tried to ignore his obvious smile of delight.

Chapter Eighteen

Arabella's father had been true to his word. He had promised to inject much-needed funds into the Limelight Theatre and, looking up at the once crumbling façade Oliver could see the transformation. The flaking plaster had been removed, the exterior freshly painted and the broken brown and cream tiles in the entranceway replaced. It now looked like a professional theatre ready to welcome its eager patrons.

The interior was as much a revelation. The previously shabby chairs in the auditorium had been re-upholstered in plush red velvet, a gold-ruched curtain was suspended above the stage and a new, thick purple and gold carpet had been laid to replace the old, threadbare floor coverings.

He looked around the walls and could see modern electric lighting had also been installed. Arabella's father must have had men working round the clock to complete the renovations before he left for America. It was an impressive sight. The Limelight now rivalled any theatre in the city in terms of opulence.

The cast were assembled on stage and Arabella

rushed forward to join them, as if she couldn't get away from him fast enough. He took a seat in the auditorium to watch his wife embrace her new life, one that didn't include him.

As soon as she appeared on stage, she was surrounded by excited actresses, all eager to see the rings on her finger and from Arabella's awkward stance they were also presumably asking her about married life. Her taciturn answers told Oliver just how reluctant she was to share any information and how uncomfortable she was with their questioning. The director hushed the chatter and Oliver saw a look of relief pass over his wife's face.

But what else should he expect? Neither of them had wanted to be married. It was hardly a love match or a whirlwind romance. It had all been arranged against her will. She was unlikely to be acting like a love-struck newlywed, all girlish blushes and coquettish simpering.

Their marriage was simply a convenient way for Mr van Haven to get the title he wanted and for Arabella to continue to live the independent life she wanted, unrestricted by the demands of either her father or a husband. Oliver had been true to his word by marrying her. Now it was time for him to step out of her life.

He settled down more comfortably into the plush chair. It would hardly matter if he watched just one rehearsal first.

The cast began a read through of their lines. After a few tentative glances out into the auditorium Arabella seemed to forget about him and he watched as his wife transformed herself before his eyes. She became completely lost in her part, taking on the appearance and the mannerisms of her character, that of a poverty-stricken young woman trying to protect her family from an evil landlord.

Oliver felt himself swell with pride as he watched her performance. There was no denying his wife was extremely talented. He was also pleased he had played a small part in ensuring that she was able to continue doing what she loved and that the world would be able to share her talent, too.

But he wasn't *completely* invisible to her. Each time the director interrupted with instructions, she looked out into the auditorium. He sent her what he hoped was an encouraging smile, although he doubted she could see him in the darkened theatre.

When the rehearsal came to an end the cast all gathered around, talking and laughing, excited by the progress they had already made.

Oliver joined them on stage and everyone except his wife appeared pleased to see him. She was standing alone, staring down at the script clasped in her hands. He would have assumed she was still engrossed in learning her lines, if it wasn't for the quick, furtive glances she kept sending in his direction.

Slowly the hubbub died down and people started taking their leave, with much kissing of cheeks and theatrical waving of hands.

'Right, your carriage awaits, m'lady,' Oliver said with a low bow, getting caught up in the theatrics surrounding him. 'Shall we return home?' He extended his arm for her to take.

'Um…actually, I've decided I'll stay at the boarding house with the other actors.'

Oliver's extended arm dropped to his side. 'You'll *what*?'

'It's just that I don't want the others to treat me any differently,' she said, her words coming out in an embarrassed rush.

She had nothing to be embarrassed about, just as he had no right to feel disappointed. It was her choice how she decided to live her life. But that didn't make it any easier. They would not be spending any more time together. She would not be sharing his bed each night.

'As you wish,' he said, trying hard to disguise his disappointment. 'But allow me to escort you to your new accommodation.'

She shook her head. 'No. If I'm to try to act like one of the crew, arriving in a carriage with your crest on the door would hardly be appropriate.'

Oliver laughed. 'I very much doubt if it will be the first time a carriage bearing a duke's crest has delivered an actress home.'

Her mouth drew into a tight line and she scowled. He had said the wrong thing.

'If it will make you feel any better, I can offer other members of the cast a ride as well.' He looked around and gestured towards the group of actresses watching them with interest from the wings.

'That won't be necessary,' she said hurriedly, frowning in their direction. She inhaled deeply. 'I'm sorry. Yes, thank you, Oliver, I would like you to give me a ride to my lodgings and if you could please arrange for my trunk to be delivered as well, I would be grateful.'

The boarding house was even shabbier than Oliver had expected. He accompanied her into her room and tried to hide his shock. With bare wooden floorboards, it was much smaller than her bedchamber at his town house, but contained four single beds. It seemed she would be sharing with three others. The one window, which let in minimal light, looked out on to the brick wall of the neighbouring building, and from the musty smell he suspected the dark paint on the bedroom walls was disguising damp and possibly mould.

And she chose to live here, rather than with him at his town house. Unbelievable.

'Are you sure about this, Bella?' He patted a mattress, feeling how thin it was and causing the rusty springs to creak.

'Yes, of course I am.'

There was a hesitation in her voice. It was clearly his opportunity to convince her of her mistake.

'You don't have to stay here. You can always come home to my town house. No one will think any less of you. I'm sure if any of the other actresses had the opportunity to exchange this...' he gestured around the room '...for their own suite of rooms in Mayfair they'd jump at the chance.'

She pulled back her shoulders and glared at him. 'I don't care what any other actress would or would not jump at. This is where I want to be.'

He shook his head in disbelief and stared at her.

She held his gaze for a moment, then turned and looked out of the window at the non-existent view. He was tempted to argue with her, to insist she come home with him, but he knew it would fall on deaf ears. And who was he to tell her what she could and couldn't do? She was an independent woman who could make her own choices.

She turned from the window. 'Now, if you don't mind, I'd like to get settled in. Will you please arrange for my trunk to be delivered?'

He stood helplessly in the middle of the room, unwilling to leave, even though she was making it clear that his presence was no longer required or wanted.

But leave he must. 'As you wish.' He remained standing, unable to move. Once again she looked out of the window at the brick wall.

He gave a slight bow, even though with her back turned she couldn't see it, and headed down the narrow wooden stairs to his waiting carriage.

It was ridiculous. She was being ridiculous. He climbed into the carriage and looked up at the shabby exterior. She really was determined to do things the hard way. If she didn't want to stay at his town house, the allowance he had allocated to her meant she had enough money to stay in any of the best hotels in London if she wanted to. Was she also reluctant to take his money? It would seem so. It was obvious she wanted nothing more from him.

Oliver returned to his town house alone. He was now, once again, a free man. He could do anything he wanted.

He looked around the drawing room. It appeared different somehow, as if something was missing, but it was exactly how he had left it just a few weeks ago. He quickly poured himself a glass of brandy, the crystal decanter clinking against the glass. He knew exactly what was missing. Arabella was missing. He had expected them to spend some more time together, had wanted to spend more time with her. He had not tired of making love to her, far from it. He had expected to have her in his bed tonight and for many nights to come. He had hoped to continue what they had started at his Surrey estate. Instead he would have to find other ways to entertain himself. He poured another glass of brandy, tossed it back and wondered how he would spend his evening.

Perhaps he should ask his wife to dine with him.

She didn't want to live in his house, but that didn't mean she didn't want to spend time with him. And once they had finished dining, maybe she would like to come back to the town house for a nightcap, and then, perhaps, he could encourage her to stay the night. After all, what harm would one more night together do?

He dismissed that idea. It was ludicrous.

That was not what she wanted. She had made it clear they were now to live as if their marriage had never happened.

And if that was what she wanted, then there was one thing he was certain about. He could not remain at home alone. He had never been a man to ruminate or agonise over what might or might not have been and he wasn't about to start now.

He grabbed his hat and gloves and asked the footman to hail a cab. He would start at his club and then let the night unfold the way countless other nights had in the past. He might be a married man, but Arabella was getting on with her own life, so it was time he did the same.

Nellie stood at the entrance of the bedroom, looking just as disapproving as Oliver had earlier that evening.

She placed her suitcase on one of the beds, turned to face Arabella and tilted her head, waiting for an explanation.

'I know, I know, Nellie, it's a bit grim, but I had to let Oliver know that I expect nothing from him. And that meant I wouldn't be living at his town house, nor would I be taking his allowance. I want to do this on my own, to prove to everyone I'm capable of making my way in the world as an actress.'

Nellie sat on the bed, grimaced as it emitted a pained creak, and stood up again.

'An actress with her own lady's maid? That's a bit unusual, though, don't you think?' Nellie ran her finger along the dusty mantelpiece and frowned.

'Yes, about that. I hope you don't mind, Nellie, but I've arranged for you to work at the theatre doing hair, make-up and helping with the costumes.'

Nellie brushed her hands together to rid herself of the dust and smiled. 'No, of course I don't mind. It will be fun. And I suppose this won't be too bad once we've got used to it.'

She looked around the room and Arabella could see Nellie was trying to put on a brave face.

'And after all it's only temporary,' Nellie continued. 'You'll soon be a famous actress living it up in your own luxurious home and then I'll have my own hairdressing salon and beauty parlour and be making all those frumpy old toffs look more gorgeous than they thought possible.'

Arabella smiled at her. Nellie was always so supportive and optimistic.

'Thank you, Nellie,' she said and began helping her lady's maid unpack their bags.

Laughter suddenly filled the room as Flora and Harriet, the two other actresses they would be sharing with, burst through the door.

When they saw Arabella, their laughter died and they stared at her as if she was a green-skinned monster.

'You're *staying* here?' Flora said. They looked at each other, then back at Arabella, their mouths open.

Arabella had expected their reaction. It was the same reaction she had got when she had told the theatre manager that she wanted to stay at the boarding house, but it didn't make it any easier to bear.

'Why aren't you staying with the Duke?' Flora asked. 'What's gone wrong? He hasn't chucked you over already, has he?'

Arabella bristled, but forced herself to continue hanging dresses in the small wardrobe. 'No, he *hasn't* chucked me over.' She forced herself to continue in a calm manner. 'In case you haven't heard, the Duke and I merely married because my father was determined that I would marry a man with a title. Neither of us wanted the marriage and we have both agreed that we will be man and wife in name only.'

The two wide-eyed actresses looked at each other, then back at Arabella. 'Well, I had heard something like that, but I didn't really believe it. If I was you, I wouldn't care if it was in name only,' Flora said. 'I'd be taking advantage of being his wife. I'd be living at his town house and doing my best to keep that one on a short leash.'

Flora looked over at Harriet, who nodded enthusiastically.

Arabella shrugged, moved the coat hangers along the rack, then back again, and wished they would change the subject.

Flora approached her and placed her hand gently on Arabella's arm. 'You do know what sort of man the Duke of Somerfeld is, don't you, Arabella? He's a bit of a one for the ladies.'

Yes, Arabella knew that already. Knew it very well indeed. 'What he does is his own business.'

Flora dropped her hand from Arabella's arm and narrowed her eyes. 'So, what are you saying? The Duke can carry on living in exactly the same way as he did before he was married? Seeing who he wants, doing whatever he wants, and you won't care?'

Arabella's jaw clenched tightly and her hands gripped the fabric of the nearest dress. She breathed deeply and exhaled slowly to try to free her constricted chest. 'That's exactly what I'm saying.'

She could not ignore the gaze that passed between the two pretty actresses. It was obvious what they were thinking. The Duke of Somerfeld was available for the taking, that any woman after some fun with a fabulously wealthy man just had to bat her eyelashes in his direction and she could have everything the Duke had to offer, even if it was just for a short time.

Arabella swallowed to relieve the burning in her throat. That was a reaction from women she was going to have to learn to deal with. She might have shared a few wonderful days with the Duke of Somerfeld, as had many other women before her, but he was not hers. Never had been. Never would be. And she needed to put aside any unwanted feelings of jealousy, to concentrate on her career, to move on and leave the Duke of Somerfeld in the past.

Chapter Nineteen

Oliver rose uncharacteristically early the next morning and arrived at the Limelight Theatre just as rehearsals were commencing. He crept into the auditorium and took a seat upstairs near the back, where he would not be noticed. Then he settled down to watch his wife perform. It wasn't long before he became absorbed in watching Arabella act, just as she became absorbed in her own performance.

It was so obvious she was doing what she loved and her determination to be just one of the cast was obviously working. No one was deferring to her. No one was treating her like a duchess or an heiress.

This was definitely her home, where she wanted to be, where she belonged.

It might not fit in with what he wanted, but he would do nothing to stop her achieving her dream, even if it meant stepping back from her life.

As he watched, hour after hour, he could see the play coming together, the performances becoming more polished. Even though the actors had gone over their lines again and again, the more they repeated them the more spontaneous they appeared. It was a pleasure to watch.

And his greatest pleasure came from watching Arabella. He was biased, of course he was, but he could tell that Arabella's performance was particularly stunning. His eyes were constantly drawn to her when she was on stage, whether she was speaking or not.

She definitely had something special and he was sure he wasn't just thinking that because she was his wife, or even because they had spent four incredible days and nights in bed together exploring each other's bodies.

The longer he watched, the less he noticed the other actors and actresses, until he barely registered when they were speaking. He could only see Arabella. Watch her performance grow, her confidence increase.

She was a superb actress and acting was what she was born to do.

Her father might have dominated her off the stage, structured her whole life, even forced her into an unwanted marriage, but on stage she was a different woman. She commanded the stage and became the part she was playing. The director would give her instructions and like a chameleon she would instantly assume the form he required. It was brilliant and impressive to watch.

When the rehearsal drew to a close, he quietly slipped out of the theatre before anyone noticed. It was already early evening. The entire day had passed without his noticing. He summoned a cab to take him home so he could make ready for the evening's entertainment. He had no idea how he would spend it, but he knew exactly where he would be the next day, and the days after that. Seated right at the back of the Limelight Theatre, watching his beautiful, talented wife.

Arabella was being foolish. She knew she was. But at every rehearsal it was as if she was performing only for Oliver. She wanted him to be proud of her, to think highly of her acting abilities, so she gave it her all and imagined him saying how impressed he was.

Yes, it was ridiculous, but thinking that Oliver was watching her as she worked was certainly doing wonders for her performance. She was receiving so much praise from the director and the other cast members that it was almost going to her head. But it was one man's praise she really wanted and that was something she would not be getting. She had cut him from her life, had let him know she wanted her independence more than she wanted him. And he had given her exactly what she wanted. What she'd *thought* she wanted.

And when she was in rehearsals, she could almost convince herself that she did indeed have exactly what she wanted. But as soon as rehearsals were over that empty void was waiting, threatening to swallow her up, and she had to work hard to keep it at bay. She had to force herself to keep smiling, to pretend that everything in her life was exactly as she wanted it to be.

Now, after a week of intense rehearsals, opening night was looming large.

The final dress rehearsal had gone well and tomorrow night they would be performing before the live audience. The entire cast was tired from working hard all day, but they were still bubbling with enthusiasm as they returned to the boarding house, confident they would have a stunning opening night.

Arabella had tried hard to join in with their enthusiasm. And she *was* enthusiastic, but part of her still felt as though something was missing. As much as she tried to ignore it, she knew that she was missing Oliver. She was missing him so much that some days she could hardly bear it. But bear it she must.

She had exactly what she wanted, didn't she? She might be married, but to a man who had given her complete freedom. Her father was back in America and leaving her alone to live her life the way she wanted to. She had a major part in a play. She was surrounded by the cast and crew of a tight-knit theatre group. Everything she had ever dreamed of had come true. She had no right to feel miserable. And she wouldn't be feeling miserable. If she had never met Oliver Huntsbury, she would be unaware of any other life, would not know what true happiness felt like.

As usual the actresses were getting ready for a night out. They went out most evenings, either to parties or to dine with their various admirers, and tonight, with opening night just one night away, everyone was in a party mood. No one would be staying home at the boarding house. No one, that is, except Arabella.

Nellie, too, had gone out for the evening with her latest conquest. She had offered to stay home and keep her company, but Arabella had insisted that she was perfectly happy on her own and that she would prefer it if Nellie went out.

But she wasn't happy. Far from it.

Oliver had said she was a free woman. She was free to do anything she wanted. If she wanted to go to parties, she could. If a man showed interest in her, there was nothing to stop her from taking him as her lover. But that was the last thing she felt like doing. There was only one man she wanted as her lover and he was out of bounds. Instead, while the other actresses were out enjoying themselves, she had stayed at the boarding house, until she was starting to go mad with boredom.

And once again she was facing a night alone. As the other actresses preened in front of the mirror and chatted about the night to come, Arabella could feel that empty void starting to surround her and drag her under.

This had to change. She had to take action.

'Going anywhere special tonight?' she asked Flora with as much nonchalance as she could summon.

'To a party in Mayfair. Nicholas de Valle has been showing rather a lot of interest of late and has invited all of us. You can come, too, if you like. It should be fun. He's a duke, you know, and is rather partial to actresses,' Flora laughed. 'Aren't they all, these posh gents? You should come. It'll get you out of yourself.'

Arabella kept smiling as she cringed inside. Yes, weren't they all like that. And one duke in particular. No, she did not feel like going to a party where *posh gents* would be chasing after actresses. But nor did she want to be alone. Alone with her thoughts. Alone with the dark void.

She very much doubted that Oliver would be alone tonight. She couldn't picture him moping around in his town house. So, what was sauce for the goose should be sauce for the gander, or in this case the other way around.

'All right. I will.'

She reached into her wardrobe and removed her most stylish gown, then put it back and selected something a bit less fashionable. She did not want to stand out from the other actresses.

With Nellie off pursuing her own dreams, Arabella did her best to fix her own hair, until Flora took pity on her and helped.

They ordered a carriage, which Flora assured her the party's host would be paying for, and six of the actresses set off, laughing and talking loudly, all looking forward to the night's fun.

Arabella forced herself to join in, to laugh and jest along with them. She *would* enjoy herself tonight. She would push aside all her sadness and have fun. She would replace the dark void with lightness, happiness and laughter.

The carriage pulled up in front of a brightly lit town house and the sound of laughter, loud talking and music spilled out on to the pavement.

The actresses pushed their way through the crowds milling at the entranceway and joined the noisy, jostling throng. Arabella could see that the guests came from all walks of life. Well, the women did. There were wealthy women, dressed in the latest fashions, women like her actress friends who did not have money for expensive gowns and jewellery, and other women dressed in a manner that suggested they worked in somewhat more disreputable professions.

But there was one thing that all these women had in common: they were all young and good looking. The men, however, were of all ages and all bore the signs of privilege and wealth. Another thing the men had in common was the way they were looking at the women. As Arabella and her friends made their way through the crowd, they were being stared at as if they were fresh delicacies being served up for the men's appreciation.

Arabella paused at the entrance to the drawing room, which was packed wall-to-wall with a boisterous crowd. Did she really want to be part of this world?

But what was her option? Return alone to the boarding house? Alone with those unhappy thoughts that kept churning through her head.

She forced herself to enter the room and took the glass of champagne that was thrust into her hand. It was obvious from the loudness of the crowd, the array of florid complexions and the raucous laughter that a lot of champagne had already been consumed.

Arabella looked around for a familiar face. Flora had already disappeared, presumably with the host, and the other actresses had instantly been swallowed up by the party. Unlike Arabella, they had no problem entering into the spirit of the occasion, flirting and laughing with circles of adoring men.

Arabella tried hard to smile, but it just wouldn't happen. Her lips just wouldn't move.

This was a mistake.

She did not want to be here. She might not want to be back at the boarding house, alone with her thoughts. But she was no less alone in this crowd. If anything, this boisterous party was making her feel even more lonely.

She placed her untouched glass of champagne on a table and looked around for a footman who could summon her a cab.

Then she saw him.

Oliver entered the room, laughing, surrounded by a group of attractive women. They were all smiling up at him as if he was the most amusing man they had ever met. And they were all sending him undeniably provocative looks.

He looked as though he didn't have a care in the world. Let alone a wife.

Now she most definitely wanted to leave. She turned quickly. A servant stepped into her path. She bumped into him, sending his tray of champagne flutes crashing to the floor.

A wild cheer of enthusiasm went up from the partygoers, as if she had done something amusing and entertaining, rather than a clumsy act brought on by her panic.

She looked around the room, her face contorted into a rictus of a smile. Everyone was laughing and applauding.

Everyone except Oliver.

He was staring straight at her, his cold eyes boring into her, his lips a thin line of disapproval.

Her strained smile froze as their gazes locked across the room. The cheering crowd merged into a swirling mass. The raucous sound of their laughter disappeared. All she could focus on was the scowling man across the room, glaring at her.

Chapter Twenty

He had no right to look at her like that. He had absolutely no right to condemn her for attending this party. She had as much right to be here as he did. Weren't they both free to do as they pleased? And Oliver certainly was doing something that pleased him very much, if the coterie of admiring young women surrounding him was anything to go by.

As if she were emerging from a trance, the noise of the crowd exploded into Arabella's consciousness, even louder than before.

No, she would not be cowed by his disapproval. Using all her skills as an actress, she sent the room her most radiant smile, made a theatrical curtsy, took a glass of champagne from another servant's tray and raised it in a toast to the cheering crowd. Much to the partygoers' enthusiastic response.

Only one man was not cheering. The man she was married to.

Arabella forced her smile not to quiver as she saw him excuse himself from his group of adoring women, push his way through the jostling partygoers and cross the room towards her.

She would not show any sign of nerves. Would not let him know how much seeing him had unsettled her.

'Hello, Your Grace, fancy meeting you here.' With false joviality she made another deep curtsy.

'And I'm equally surprised to see you here, Arabella,' he responded, no hint of a smile on his face. 'This is not the sort of party I would expect you to attend.'

She shrugged. 'But it is obviously the sort of party *you* attend, judging by how well known you are here.'

She nodded in the direction of the group of attractive young women, who were still watching them from across the room with undisguised interest. 'I assume they are a few more of your good friends. So how many good friends of yours are actually here tonight?'

She looked around the room, as if taking an inventory, her false smile still frozen on her face.

Her sweeping gaze returned to him. He glared down at her. That mischievous smile was nowhere in sight. There was no laughter in his cold, dark eyes.

She cringed. Had she let a hint of jealousy enter her voice? She did not want to sound jealous. After all, she had no right to be. And she most certainly did not want him to think she was.

Yes, they had made love, but that had been under her instigation. He owed her nothing. Yet here she was, feeling jealous because he was doing exactly what she told him he could do.

'This is no place for you. You need to leave. Immediately.'

She gave an incredulous laugh. That was exactly what she had intended to do until he had seen her. Now she was determined to stand her ground. 'Surely you're not telling me what to do? Wasn't freedom to do as we pleased part of our agreement?'

He inhaled deeply through clenched teeth. 'Listen to me. You do not want to stay here. If you think this party is loud and raucous now, it is nothing compared to how it will soon become. It's time you left.'

Still smiling, Arabella looked around the room and noticed several couples involved in decidedly amorous encounters, encounters that should only be conducted in private. She was unable to suppress a gasp when a man ran his hand up the inside of a woman's leg, under her gown. Surely the woman would object. Surely someone would stop them. But no one noticed. The drinking and carousing continued around them.

He was right.

This was most definitely not the sort of party she wanted to attend. But the same could *not* be said for Oliver. This was his world. A world where she did not belong. A world in which she did not want to belong. A world full of women who wanted to have fun with no commitments. His sort of women.

Her scan of the room moved to a woman staring at her from across the room. Lady Bufford. With eyes narrowed, like an assassin assessing her target, she sauntered over to join them.

'Ollie, darling, I see you've brought your wife to tonight's entertainment,' she said, her voice dripping with derision. 'Delightful. If you're not otherwise occupied, perhaps the two of you would like to join me upstairs. Your wife can show me what techniques she used to get a man like you to the altar. She must be able to do something for you that I can't do and lord knows I've tried every trick in the book.'

Arabella gasped and her face exploded in a fiery blush while Lady Bufford laughed at her obvious discomfort.

'Hold your tongue, Violet. You go too far,' Oliver said, taking hold of Arabella's arm. 'We were just leaving.'

'Oh, I am sorry. Do I take it from her blushes that it wasn't her experience that attracted you? Oh, you men, you're all the same. You can't resist a virgin.'

He turned his back on Lady Bufford, ignoring her, his grip tightening on Arabella's arm. 'I don't care what we agreed. You are leaving this place and you are leaving it now.'

Shaken by Lady Bufford's words Arabella lost the will to protest. Deflated and embarrassed, she allowed Oliver to bustle her out through the crowd. He flagged down a passing cab and all but lifted her inside, then gave the driver the address of his town house before climbing in beside her.

After the noise of the party, the silence inside the cab almost had a physical presence, with the clip-clopping of the horse's hooves the only sound as they drove through Mayfair's quiet streets.

'I'm so sorry, Arabella. Violet Bufford has a cruel tongue,' Oliver said quietly, breaking the heavy silence. 'You should not have been subjected to that.'

'It's of no matter.' She blinked away the tears that had embarrassingly sprung to her eyes and shivered. The summer's evening must have been chillier than Arabella had expected as she suddenly felt very cold.

'And you didn't have to leave on my account. You can return me to the boarding house and go back to your party.'

Oliver took off his jacket and draped it round her shoulders. 'You've had a shock, Arabella. You should not be alone. I'll take you back to our town house until you recover and then return you to your lodgings.'

Arabella wanted to protest, but she did not want to be alone. He was right. She'd had a shock. The party, all the women flirting with Oliver, and then Lady Bufford's acid comments had left her shaken. And Oliver's coat around her shoulders, still containing the warmth of his body, went some way towards assuaging that shock. She closed her eyes, breathed in deeply and inhaled the masculine scent of him.

That scent was both comforting and arousing. It reminded her of how it had felt to be held in his arms, to be made love to by this strong, attractive man. But those thoughts battled with images of the women at the party. They, including Lady Bufford, also knew what it was like to be made love to by Oliver. And if she hadn't unexpectedly arrived at the party, he would have been making love to one or more of them tonight.

She shrugged off his jacket from her shoulders and handed it back to him. 'Thank you, but I'm perfectly fine. You can ask your driver to return me to my lodgings now.'

He shook his head, but took his jacket from her outstretched hand. 'I will do no such thing.'

They slipped back into silence and Arabella couldn't stop herself from replaying everything that had happened during the short time she was at the party. The riotous noise, the inappropriately amorous behaviour between the guests, the women giving Oliver looks that could only be described as lustful. Despite the shivers still running through her body, her cheeks once again exploded with burning heat. That was Oliver's world and it could never include her.

The carriage drew up outside his town house.

'I said I want to go home. This is not my home. I want to return to where I really live, where I belong.'

He opened the carriage door as if she hadn't spoken and held out his hand to help her descend.

'I said I want to go home.'

He exhaled loudly. 'Arabella, please, just come inside for a while. I can see how upset you are and, despite what you think of me, I will not let any woman, even my wife, go home by herself in such a distressed state. Once you have settled down, I'll order my driver to take you back to your boarding house, but for now I insist that you come inside.'

She stared straight ahead. He remained standing at the door, his hand outstretched. She knew she was being petulant, but she felt petulant. She was angry. Angry with him and angry with herself. But he was right, she did not want to be on her own.

Reluctantly she accepted his hand and allowed him to lead her up the stairs and through the entrance to his house. He asked the footman to prepare coffee and they entered the drawing room.

Arabella sat on the *chaise longue*, feeling like a chastised child. But she had done nothing wrong. All she had done was go to a party that he was also attending. But she *did* feel she had done something wrong. He was right, that party was not the sort of place she would usually frequent. She should have known that Flora would take her somewhere wild. But even if she *had* made a mistake, he still had no right to judge her.

Leaning on the marble mantelpiece, he looked down at her. 'So, are you going to explain what you were doing at that party?'

Arabella pulled herself up, squared her shoulders and lifted her chin, determined to give him a defiant answer. She would not let him know how out of her depth she had been. Nor would she let him know that she had already intended to escape before he had seen her. 'My roommate, Flora, had been invited so I decided to join her. I thought it might be a bit of fun.'

'And was it?'

She shrugged. 'But why should it matter to you? You have no more right to question why I was at that party than I have to question you. That wasn't in our agreement.'

He stared at her, then frowned. 'Yes, I suppose you are right. But we didn't agree that we wouldn't offer each other advice. I know that world, Arabella. It's not for you. If you want to have fun, find it somewhere else, not at parties hosted by men like Nicholas de Valle. The man's a notorious rake and his parties are legendary.'

Arabella shrugged again. 'And he's a friend of yours?'

Oliver gave a quick nod.

'So, it's all right for you to go to such parties, but not me?'

'I'm a man, Arabella. So, yes, it is all right for me, but not for you.'

Arabella felt her eyes grow wide and her mouth almost fell open. *Had he really said that?* Had he really told her what she could or couldn't do? Had he really said it was all right for him, but not her? Was he worried what people might think if his wife went to such parties? Or was it that he did not want to be seen consorting with other women in front of his wife? Or did he think it might put off some of his conquests if his wife was present? Although it certainly wouldn't put off women like Lady Bufford.

Well, he was soon going to discover that if he wanted an obedient wife, he had married the wrong woman. Standing up, she put her hands on her hips and stared him straight in the eye. 'How dare you? How dare you say I can't go to such parties because I'm a woman? Next you'll be saying that as my husband you forbid it.'

'Sit down, Arabella,' he said firmly. 'You know you're being ridiculous. Why don't you just admit it? You made a mistake and went somewhere you didn't belong.'

'Oh, so I didn't belong there, did I? But you did. And Lady Bufford did. And all those other simpering women hanging on your every word as if you were some sort of god, did, but not me. Not your wife.'

She had intended to shame him, but he remained standing at the mantelpiece, unmoved by her outburst. 'Yes, it was a party for women like Lady Bufford and those so-called simpering women, but not for you.'

'And what makes me so special? Is it because I'm your wife that you don't want me seen at such places? Or are you worried that I might just find myself another lover and people might think that the famous rake Oliver Huntsbury can't satisfy his own wife?'

Her words had hit their intended target. Oliver's skin darkened, his jaw clenched and he stared back at her, his brown eyes unflinching.

'Is that what you want? To find another lover?' he asked, his voice dangerously quiet.

'Perhaps.' She glared back at him with more defiance than she felt. 'Isn't that what you were there for? To find another one of your sort of women? Well, perhaps I'm starting to become just that sort of woman as well.'

He gripped the edge of the marble mantelpiece, his back rigid, his eyes granite hard. 'You are not that sort of woman. You never have been and you never will be.'

Arabella bristled at his curt dismissal. 'And how could you possibly know what sort of woman I might be, or the sort of woman I might become? Things have changed for me, haven't they? A few weeks ago, I was a single woman and I was a…a…' She paused.

'A virgin.'

Heat exploded on her cheeks. 'Yes, a virgin. I'm neither of those things now. So perhaps I'm changing.'

'You can't change who you are, Arabella. And why would you want to?'

So I can become the sort of woman you would be attracted to.

'Why not? Why shouldn't I change? Why shouldn't I find a lover as well? Why shouldn't I have some fun?'

'If it's a lover you want, you don't have to go to parties to find one.' He quickly crossed the room.

Before Arabella had time to fully register what was happening, she was in his arms. His lips were on hers. Hot, hungry lips, devouring her. She kissed him back, unable to halt the reckless desire that the touch of his body had ignited deep within her. Her body aflame, she moulded herself into his strong arms and chest, her lips and tongue tasting him. Her fingers moved through his hair, wanting to hold him close, wanting to never let him go.

'Is this what you want, Arabella? Do you want a man to make love to you?' he ground out harshly, before kissing a line down her neck.

She tilted back her head and gasped in a breath. 'Yes,' she whispered, her heart pounding so hard she could feel blood pumping through every inch of her body.

Yes. This was exactly what she wanted. This was what she needed to fill that aching void caused by being apart from him, what she needed to quench the fire that raged within her. She needed him. She wanted him.

Breaking from her, he took her by the hand and led her up the stairs to his bedroom.

Chapter Twenty-One

It was not how Oliver had expected the evening to end, but he couldn't have wished for a better conclusion. To have his wife back in his bed—it was what he had hoped for, but had never thought would happen.

She rolled over and gazed up at him, her long black hair falling over her creamy shoulder and curling round her full breasts. His gaze followed the line of that tress, then continued along her body, across her small waist, to her rounded hips, down her long, slim legs, then back up to her blue eyes.

'Good morning, Husband.' She smiled at him. 'So it seems we both got what we went to the party for. I found a lover and you took a married woman who wants to have fun to your bed.'

Her smile grew wider to let him know it was a joke, but Oliver still cringed. Was that what she thought of him, like a tomcat always on the prowl? It might have been true once, but was it any longer?

He ran his hand gently along her cheek. 'Going to the party was as much a mistake for me as it was for you, Bella. I had hoped it would provide me with a diversion, but it failed. Just as it has failed every night since you left.'

She propped herself up on her elbow and stared at him, her brow furrowed. 'What do you mean?'

He sighed and fell back on to the pillows. 'I forced myself to go, just as I have every night since we returned to London, but when I got there I wondered why. Nothing about the party interested me. In fact, it all seemed a bit desperate. I felt surrounded by people who were trying to drown their unhappiness in noise, drink and other people's bodies.'

'So, you didn't want to be there? You weren't interested in any of those other women?'

An urgency had entered her voice and he smiled up at her. 'There's only one woman I'm interested in. I was actually about to leave when you arrived. You thought you saw me surrounded by a group of simpering women, but what you actually saw was me saying my goodbyes.'

She bit the edge of her bottom lip. 'So, you weren't interested in any them? Truly?'

He smiled. It seemed she needed even more reassurance. 'No, Bella, the only woman I'm interested in is the one I've been watching in rehearsals every day.'

Her blue eyes grew wide. 'You've been attending my rehearsals every day?'

'Yes, I've been watching you from up in the gallery, where you wouldn't see me.'

Her smile grew tentative. 'So, what do you think of the play?'

He laughed, wrapped his arms round her waist, and rolled her beneath him. 'The play is wonderful.

You're wonderful. I have no doubts that the play is going to be a big hit and you're going to be famous.'

She wrapped her arms around his neck and joined in his laughter.

'So, before you become famous and throw me over for some backstage Johnny, I'd like to make love to my wife one more time.'

'Just the once?' She laughed, wrapping her legs around his waist. 'Surely you've got more stamina than that, Your Grace.'

Stifling her laughter, he kissed her, determined to prove his stamina was more than up to the challenge.

Arabella lay on her side, Oliver's arms wrapped around her, his breath warm on her neck. She could stay like this for ever. Could spend the rest of her life making love to this wonderful, virile man. Her husband.

But she couldn't. Tonight was opening night. She had to go to the theatre.

Opening night.

Tonight was opening night.

She should be at the Limelight getting ready for tonight's performance. She sat up quickly and looked frantically around the room. 'What's the time?'

Oliver stretched out a lazy arm and grabbed his waistcoat, abandoned beside the bed. He pulled out his fob watch and, still lying on his back, opened the clasp. 'It's five o'clock.'

Arabella threw back the covers, jumped out of bed and grabbed her gown. 'I need to get home. I need to get changed. I have to get to the theatre.'

How could she have forgotten? In the past it would

have been the only thing she'd have been able to think about from the moment she woke up. But she had been completely distracted.

And it was no surprise. Being in Oliver's arms—how could that not be a distraction of the most wonderful kind? But she had to get dressed and get to the theatre. Now. It was almost unbelievable that she had forgotten, even for a moment, that tonight was opening night.

'Oliver. I have to leave,' she reiterated to the man still stretched out on the bed like a contented cat. 'Tonight's opening night.'

She scanned the room for her clothes, strewn chaotically around the room from when Oliver had all but ripped them from her body last night. She picked up her corset and one shoe, and searched the room for its companion.

Oliver rose from the bed and she paused in her anxious search to take a quick scan of his taut, muscular body, then went back to gathering up her clothes.

'Well, I'd hate to interfere with your panicking,' he said as he picked up her silk stockings and handed them to her. 'But if you slow down, I can arrange for some clothes to be collected from your boarding house while you're at your toilette. Then we can take my carriage to the theatre and we'll get there in plenty of time.'

She took the stockings from his outstretched hands. His calmness helped her tense body relax and her churning stomach to settle down. He was going to take care of everything. He was going to arrange everything for her, so she didn't have to panic. She smiled at him. It was so nice to be looked after.

* * *

In a much calmer frame of mind, she had got ready and was soon travelling with Oliver to the theatre. As they rode through the busy streets, he took her hands in his and murmured gentle words of encouragement and support in her ear, helping to keep those nerves at bay. Oh, yes, it was very nice to be looked after like this by a strong, supportive man.

When they arrived at the Limelight Theatre, she left him to join the cast in the dressing rooms. Backstage, without Oliver by her side, her pre-performance nerves started to bubble up within her. And she wasn't the only one. Everyone was tense, going through their own calming routine to get themselves ready for tonight's performance and working hard to not let their own anxiety affect anyone else.

Some had their little superstitious rituals they performed, others were doing breathing exercises and some were staring at their reflections and giving themselves silent pep talks. In among this Nellie was running around, making sure everyone's make-up, hair and costumes were perfect.

A stagehand called through the door that there was five minutes to show time and the cast whispered break a leg to each other, as a final good luck wish, and made their way to the wings.

As Arabella would be appearing in the first scene, she entered the stage along with the leading actors and waited anxiously for the curtain to be raised. Tonight she would not only be performing for an audience, but she would be performing for Oliver as well. He would be sitting in the auditorium, watching her, just as he had done every day during rehearsals. She prayed she would make him proud and not get struck by the dreaded curse of stage fright.

The curtain started to rise. The cast all breathed in, deeply and audibly, then the leading actor confidently projected his first line out to the darkened auditorium, capturing the audience's attention.

From that moment Arabella's nervousness dissolved. She forgot about everything except the play in which she was acting. Her absorption into her part became complete as each actor gave it their all, the energy on stage becoming almost palpable.

When the entire cast assembled on stage at the end of the performance, took each other's hands and made their final bow, Arabella could tell it had been a resounding success. The audience stood as one, clapping and stamping their feet. Arabella lost count of how many curtain calls they had made as they returned again and again to ever-rapturous applause. She also couldn't fail to notice how loud the applause grew each time she took a solo bow.

The performance had exceeded the cast's most optimistic expectations and they were united in their sense of euphoria, as they finally gathered in an excited huddle at the edge of the stage, laughing, talking loudly and slapping each other on the back.

Arabella's happiness was complete when Oliver joined them, wrapped his arms around her waist, lifted her off her feet and kissed her. 'What can I say? That was magnificent. You were magnificent. I have never felt more proud of you.'

She smiled down at him, certain she was about to burst with happiness.

Rosie and her husband joined them. They had come up to London especially for the opening night and Arabella was so happy to see her best friend again. 'Oh, Bella, you were at your very best,' Rosie said. 'That truly was a virtuoso performance.'

Even the smiling director joined their group and kissed her on both cheeks. 'Arabella, you were marvellous, simply marvellous. You shone tonight. Whatever you did last night it certainly put that extra spark in you, so please keep doing it. You were superb.'

Oliver winked at her as the director wandered off to congratulate another actor. 'You heard what the man said,' he whispered in her ear, his arm around her waist. 'You're under strict instructions to keep doing what you did last night.'

Arabella giggled, reached up and kissed him. 'Oh, well, if I'm going to keep that spark, I'll have to do that every night of the play's run. And then there will be more plays after that. I'm going to need that spark for a long time to come.'

Oliver laughed, picked her up and whirled her around. 'Happy to oblige.' Lowering her to her feet, he turned to the assembled crowd. 'The champagne is on me,' he called out to a roar of approval. 'The Savoy is booked and the champagne is already on ice.'

The jubilant crowd tumbled into waiting cabs and, with much banter being shouted between the racing cabs, they made their way to the hotel.

The champagne immediately started to flow freely and the exuberant cast and crew took advantage of the food and drink on offer. The entire patronage of the Savoy seemed to get caught up in their excitement and soon everyone in the restaurant was joining in with the celebration.

Arabella was so pleased she could share this occasion with Oliver, who looked as triumphant as she felt.

The celebrations continued well into the small hours of the morning. It wasn't until the stagehands arrived with the early editions of the morning papers that a hush descended.

A suddenly anxious cast and crew crowded round the director as he opened the first newspaper on the top of the pile. The reviews could make or break a play. They could determine whether they played to a season of full houses or to rows of empty seats. Arabella held her breath as the director began reading.

The first newspaper had a rave review, then the second, the third. With each review the volume of the happy voices grew until the director was having to shout to be heard above the high-spirited noise.

The champagne started to flow again, even more freely. The hugging and cheek kissing resumed, and people began dancing and singing, unable to contain their excitement.

'It seems I'm married to a woman who shines, a woman who captures the audiences' hearts and is destined for greatness,' Oliver said, repeating some of the flattering comments made by the reviewers about her.

Arabella smiled at him. 'Oh, Oliver. I couldn't have asked for more. The play will be a success now. The theatre is saved. I doubt if it will ever need money from my father again.'

'And I like to think I played a small part in your

success.' Oliver laughed. 'So, if you've had enough of the celebrations, let's get you home so I can put some more of that spark in you.' Oliver sent her that mischievous smile she loved so much. 'After all, you have been given strict instructions from your director to keep doing what you did last night and there's another performance tomorrow.'

Arabella nodded her head enthusiastically. She could think of no more perfect way to end this perfect evening than in Oliver's bed, making love to that magnificent man. 'While you order a cab, I'll just freshen up in the powder room.'

He nodded and turned to leave. She grabbed hold of his arm to halt his progress. 'And make sure you order a cab with fresh horses. I want to get home as quickly as possible. I can already feel that spark starting to fade. You need to renew it urgently.'

With a playful salute Oliver headed towards the door and Arabella retired to the powder room, determined to make herself as attractive as she could for the rest of the night's entertainment.

Arabella smiled at her reflection as the attendant helped her to fix her hair. Happiness had definitely improved her appearance, her eyes sparkled and her skin was glowing.

She did a little twirl in front of the mirror and thanked the attendant for her help. She headed towards the door, but her exit was halted when Lady Bufford entered.

Arabella's smile faltered before returning as large as before. She would not let that toxic woman ruin her evening.

'Good evening, Lady Bufford,' she said in her sweetest voice.

'Good evening, Your Grace. And congratulations on tonight's performance. I didn't manage to catch the play, but I hear you performed rather well.'

'Thank you.' Arabella nodded and turned to leave.

'A better performance than the one I hear you gave on your wedding night.'

Arabella froze, her body suddenly turning cold, as her legs weakened beneath her.

'I suppose that was why Oliver didn't stay in your bed but came to mine instead.'

Arabella turned slowly. She saw her reflection in the mirror, standing behind a preening Lady Bufford, her pink cheeks now white, her eyes dull and lifeless, her shoulders slumped.

'I thought it a bit strange for a man to be with another woman on his wedding night,' Lady Bufford continued in a sing-song voice. 'But I suppose after he'd deflowered you, he wanted a bit of real satisfaction so he decided to join me in my bed.'

'You are a cruel, nasty woman,' Arabella said, her voice strained and shaking.

Lady Bufford shrugged, smiled at Arabella and left the room.

Arabella groped her way to the nearest chair and collapsed on to it, her shaking legs no longer able to hold her up. The attendant passed her a hand towel to wipe away the tears Arabella had been unaware were coursing down her cheeks.

While she had been lying awake on her wedding night, wishing that Oliver would join her, he was in

another woman's bed. How could he have done that?
On her wedding night? Yes, they had agreed to give
each other freedom. But her wedding night? Could he
not have slept alone for one night? Did he not know
how much that would shame her? Did he not realise
how humiliating that was? Did he not care? He might
say he cared about her now, and she did not doubt that
was true, but they were lovers now. On the night of
their wedding they were not. On that night he didn't
care how much he hurt her, how much he humiliated
her. How could he be so selfish?

The door opened again, and Arabella attempted to
rise. She would not let Lady Bufford see her in this
condition, would not let her know how much her cruel
words had pierced her heart.

But it wasn't Lady Bufford, it was Rosie, who instantly rushed to her side, knelt down beside her chair
and took her hands in hers.

'Bella, what is it? What's wrong? Why are you
crying?'

Arabella shook her head. 'Rosie, can I stay with
you this evening? Can you take me away from here
without Oliver seeing? I'll explain everything when
we get back to your town house. But I want to leave,
now.'

'Of course I will. I'll tell my husband to get us a
cab and I'll be back soon.' Rosie rushed out and Arabella put her head in her hands and dissolved into
tears of pain and humiliation.

Once again, she had misjudged a man, had seen
only what she wanted to see. She had thought Arnold
Emerson loved her, that he wanted to marry her and

cared nothing for her money. It was only her father's cruel action of offering him money so he wouldn't marry her that had proven what that man was really like. And the cruel words of Lady Bufford had proven once again that when it came to men, she was completely naive.

Oliver pushed his way through the partying crowd, looking for Arabella. She was nowhere in sight. He had expected her to be ready and waiting by the door, wanting to get back to their town house and to their bed as anxiously as he did. Could she still be in the powder room? If she was still fixing her hair and making herself attractive for him, she was wasting her time. He would soon be dishevelling her carefully styled hair and she could not possibly make herself any more beautiful to his eyes than she already was.

He spotted Arabella's lady's maid, dancing with one of the actors, and cut in between them.

'Nellie. Can you please go into the rest room and tell Arabella her carriage awaits?'

Nellie nodded and Oliver diverted himself by watching the cheerful crowd while he waited for his wife. They were still in high spirits and he doubted they would be retiring soon. While the party was certainly fun, he was looking forward to having much more fun when he got home.

Nellie returned; her face surprisingly sombre. 'She's not in there and the attendant said she left with the Duke and Duchess of Knightsbrook.'

He shook his head. 'No, there's some mistake, Nellie. Arabella asked me to order a cab to take us back to our town house. Perhaps she's waiting somewhere else.' He looked around the room.

'No, you're the one who's made the mistake. The attendant told me all about it. You ought to be ashamed of yourself.'

He looked down at the scowling Nellie. 'What? Who told you what? What are you talking about?'

The lady's maid's nostrils flared in disgust and she looked him up and down. 'She's gone. That's all you need to know.' With that, she turned her back on him and joined the partygoers.

He looked at Nellie, then around the gathering, as if somewhere in this crowded room he would find the answer to his confusion. What on earth was going on? He scanned the room again, hoping to see Arabella smiling at the trick she had played on him. But she was still nowhere to be seen. And neither were the Duke and Duchess of Knightsbrook. Perhaps Arabella *had* left with them. But why would she do that without telling him? And what was all that nonsense about the powder-room attendant? This was all very peculiar. But there was only one way to find out what had gone wrong. He would have to ask his wife.

He pushed his way back through the crowd, jumped into the waiting hansom cab and gave the driver the address of the Duke of Knightsbrook's town house.

The sooner he put this ridiculous confusion to rights the better.

When he arrived, the house was in darkness, except for one upstairs light. Despite the unsociable hour Oliver pounded on the door, which was almost immediately opened by the footman, followed by the Duke still in his evening clothes.

'I believe Arabella is here. I need to speak to her. Now.'

The Duke's stern expression suggested he had no interest in seeing Oliver and even less inclination to let him into his house. 'My wife is upstairs comforting your wife. Neither of them wishes to see you so I suggest you leave, immediately.'

Oliver shook his head. This was getting more and more confusing. 'What's going on? Why would Arabella need to be comforted? And why did she leave the party so suddenly?'

'Don't push your luck,' the Duke said through clenched teeth. 'If it was left to me, I'd give you a good thrashing for causing that lovely young woman such distress, but out of respect for my wife's wishes all I'll do is bar your entrance.' With that the Duke shut the door in Oliver's face. He stared at the closed door, inches from his nose, momentarily stunned.

This really was ridiculous. And getting more ridiculous with every passing minute. Something had obviously happened while he had been ordering a cab, but whatever it was he couldn't do anything about it until his wife spoke to him and explained her actions.

But what was he supposed to do? She didn't want to see him and unless he broke down the door there was no way he was going to get access to this town house.

He looked up and down the outside of the three-storey house. There was no easy way of scaling the outside and getting up to the only room which still had a light. The room where Arabella was presumably being comforted by her friend over the distress caused by some crime he had no knowledge of committing. And even if he could find a way up to the second storey, hanging tentatively outside a closed window would hardly be the easiest way to have a serious conversation with his wife about what had upset her.

This was something that was going to have to be left until the morning. With reluctance, he turned from the door, climbed back into the cab and made his way home through the quiet early-morning streets.

Oliver rose early after a sleepless night and took pen to paper. If he couldn't see Arabella in person, then he would write to her. They could solve whatever the problem was through correspondence. He scribbled a quick letter asking her why she had left and if it was due to anything he had done, or not done, said, or not said. Then he asked her to give him an opportunity to explain himself. Surely that was only fair.

Instead of getting his footman to deliver the letter he carried it round in person. When the footman opened the door he took the letter, but was obviously under strict instructions not to let Oliver in as he immediately closed the door in his face.

With no other choice Oliver returned home and waited for a reply to arrive. Several hours passed. No letter arrived. He took another piece of paper from his writing desk and dipped his pen into the ink well.

This time he took his time composing the letter. He apologised for whatever transgression he was being accused of and begged Arabella to return. It was hard to believe. He had never apologised for his behaviour before and had certainly never begged a woman for anything. But he had no reservations about doing it now. Whatever had upset Arabella he wanted to put it right. If he had said or done something to upset her, then he *was* profoundly sorry and he had no hesitation in apologising.

There was no point delivering the letter himself. He could all but guarantee he would not be allowed entrance, so he sent it with his footman. Then he waited. And waited. The first post arrived. There was no letter. It was the same with the second post. But finally, with the third post, there it was. The letter he was waiting for.

He grabbed it off the footman's silver tray, immediately ripped it open and scanned the contents.

It wasn't from Arabella. It was from his mother, informing him that a woman had arrived at Somerfeld Manor, claiming that her child had been fathered by the previous Duke.

This was a disaster. Another disaster.

The two women who meant the most to him in the world demanded his attention at the same time. He could not allow his mother to deal with this situation on her own, but he had to set things straight with Arabella and he had to stay in London if he was to do that.

He read the letter again. A shock like this would have a devastating effect on his mother. He could not leave her to cope alone. He had to return to his Surrey estate.

In haste, he penned another letter to Arabella, told her how reluctant he was to leave London until they had sorted out their problems, but that his mother needed his immediate help. Then he asked his valet to pack his bags. He would have to get the next train back to Surrey.

But the last thing he did before he left was to remind all the servants that if any mail arrived for him, it had to be forwarded on to his estate—immediately.

The stack of unopened letters was mounting up. Arabella just couldn't bring herself to read them. She didn't want to hear any of his excuses, any of his explanations. She had married a man with an insatiable sexual appetite. She had always known that; she just hadn't allowed herself to fully accept what that implied.

And it wouldn't have mattered quite so much if she hadn't been so foolish as to go and fall in love with him. But the reality was she had. And this time it was even worse than when she had fallen in love with Arnold Emerson. That time she had not known what the man was really like. She had not realised that he loved money more than her. But with Oliver she knew exactly what sort of man he was, a man who was incapable of fidelity, and she had fallen in love with him anyway.

Unlike Arnold, he had not lied to her. He had let her know from the moment they met exactly what he was like. But her heart had chosen to ignore the facts. Ignore them until Lady Bufford had forced her to face cold, hard reality.

As angry and as upset as she was, she had no right to condemn Oliver for being the man he was. She could only condemn herself for falling in love with him.

And that had never been part of the arrangement.

If their marriage *had* remained one in name only, perhaps she could have forgiven him going to Lady Bufford's bed on their wedding night. Perhaps.

Although the thought that any man could humiliate his wife in such a way was more than she could countenance. It was only one night, for goodness sake. Could he not sleep alone for one night to avoid humiliating his new wife? It would seem not.

She picked up the pile of letters and looked at the embossed envelopes bearing Oliver's family crest, two rampant stags holding a shield.

She threw them back on the desk, causing the pile to scatter. A rampant stag—how appropriate. She shook her head and gave a humourless laugh. That stag was so rampant he couldn't go one night without finding a woman to satisfy his need to rut.

No, she would not read his letters. If she was to protect her heart, she would have nothing to do with him, ever again.

Forcing herself to ignore Oliver's scattered letters she picked up the other pile, the letters she had actually opened, the ones from well-wishers who had seen the play. That was what she should be focusing on. She should be celebrating her success, not dwelling on her humiliation.

Among the letters were invitations from leading theatres inviting her to audition and several offers of parts in forthcoming productions. And, most prized of all, were letters of congratulations from Oscar Wilde and Arthur Sullivan of the famous duo Gilbert and Sullivan.

Yes, that was what she should be focusing on, not those other letters. She cast a disparaging glance at the disordered pile. His latest letters bore the post office stamps from Surrey.

Good. If he was now living in the country, he would not be turning up at the Limelight Theatre. She would not have to see him again. And she never wanted to see him again. Ever.

She continued to stare at the pile. If she was to never see Oliver again, then there was only one solution. She was going to have to formally end their marriage. There was no other way. While they remained married, they were still tied to each other. He would still be part of her life, whether she saw him or not. There was only one solution available. They would have to end this marriage. They would have to divorce.

She sat down in the nearest chair and took in the ramification of this decision.

It was not impossible. People did divorce, after all. It didn't happen very often, and when it did it certainly caused a scandal and was the subject of gossip for many years. People were still talking about the divorce of Lady Mordaunt and Sir Charles Mordaunt and that had happened twenty years ago. But then, that divorce had involved the Prince of Wales, and his letters to Harriet Mordaunt had been published in the *New York Times* in all their titillating detail. Arabella's divorce would not involve such notable people, but it would still be hard to divorce Oliver discreetly.

But what choice did she have? She could not stay married to Oliver. And their marriage had served its intended purpose. It had saved him from getting his just desserts from Lord Bufford and saved the Limelight Theatre from financial ruin.

The success of the play meant the theatre was safe. Even if her father withdrew all his funding or sold off the Limelight it would still survive. No one would lose their jobs.

Yes, it was time to put an end to her marriage.

She picked up a pen and pulled a sheet of paper from the desk drawer. Divorce was the only answer. The ensuing scandal would horrify her father and he quite possibly would never forgive her, but if she did not break completely with Oliver she would never move on. A clean break was essential if she was to put this marriage firmly behind her.

With new determination she dipped her pen in the ink bottle and, before she could debate the matter further she composed a straightforward letter to Oliver, informing him that she would be divorcing him, that their marriage had never been more than one of convenience and it had served its purpose. She also informed him she wanted nothing from him. Would make no claims on his estate, that she would enter into no further communication with him and would appreciate it if he did the same, and she would be consulting with a lawyer immediately.

When she had finished, she ran the blotter over the ink and read what she had written.

It was blunt, to the point, and that was all that was required.

That done, she picked up his letters, took them over to the empty fireplace, struck a match and watched them burn. She should have felt some satisfaction as the pages curled up, turned brown at the edges, then burst into flame, but she didn't.

It was the end. The end of her marriage. The end

of her time with Oliver. There was no denying how happy she had been when she was with him. But there was also no denying how much sorrow she had felt.

No, now that the blinkers were off her eyes and she could see him for who he truly was, she knew that if they remained married all she would feel from now onwards would be sorrow. And that was not something she could tolerate.

Rosie and Nellie had both argued that she should give Oliver a chance to explain. As much as she respected her friends' opinions, she knew she wouldn't do that. She could not trust herself. As soon as she saw him her resolve was certain to falter. One look at that handsome face would cause her to forget her pain, her humiliation, just so she could have him back in her life again.

She turned her back on the still-smouldering letters, pushed the bell for the footman and handed him the letter.

She had made the right decision. There was no going back now.

Chapter Twenty-Two

The lawyer listened politely while Arabella detailed her reasons for wanting to divorce Oliver, then drew in a long, deep breath and stared at her from behind his large mahogany desk stacked with thick legal books and piles of paper.

'I'm afraid, my dear, it's not as simple as that. While your husband could divorce you for adultery, the law does not make the same provisions for the wife. If you're to divorce your husband, then you'll have to prove he's not only committed adultery, but also subjected you to unbearable levels of cruelty.'

Arabella fought to hold back her tears. Surely spending your wedding night in your mistress's bed constituted cruelty, but it seemed the law did not see things this way.

'Another option is an annulment.'

She blinked to clear her eyes and sat up straighter. 'Yes, let's do that then.' That way they could also hopefully avoid a scandal while still putting an end to this farce of a marriage.

'Of course, you'd have to prove that the marriage

was never consummated.' He waited for Arabella to answer.

'Oh, I see,' he said, presumably reacting to the fierce blushing that erupted on Arabella's cheeks. 'And while no one would have trouble believing that Oliver Huntsbury had committed adultery, I doubt that any court would believe he had not consummated his marriage.' He gave a small chuckle before his face resumed its serious, professional look.

'Another option is you could return to your home-land. I believe in some States a divorce is much easier to procure than it is in England.' He chuckled again. 'I've even heard that some of them are making quite a business out of it. South Dakota is getting a repu-tation for people moving there to get a divorce they wouldn't be able to get anywhere else and the hotels are doing a roaring trade.'

Once again his face resumed its serious countenance. 'If you're determined to divorce, then going back to America might be your best option. But really, my dear, I think you should think long and hard about getting a divorce. It rarely goes well for the woman. Consider what happened to Lady Mordaunt. She was sent to an asylum, the courts taking a dim view of women having relations with men other than their husband, particularly as she had done so in daylight hours. I believe the poor woman is still locked away and other women have been shunned by society, even when they're the aggrieved party. Perhaps you should consider doing what so many others have done before you—live as if you're divorced even though on paper you're still married.'

Arabella pulled herself out of the leather chair and

shook hands with the lawyer. He hadn't been much help, but that wasn't his fault, it was these unfair laws that made life so hard for women. But she would not give up. As she walked down the stairs and out on to the busy streets her determination increased with every step she took.

She would do anything that was required to end this marriage. If it meant she had to return to America to get her divorce, then that was exactly what she would do.

But she needed to put all that aside for now. She had a matinee performance to prepare for.

Returning to her dressing room, she went through her deep breathing routine to try to clear her mind and still her nerves. She had to put everything the lawyer had said out of her mind. She had to forget all about Oliver and get in character, something that was becoming harder and harder to do.

The continuing stress was making her nerves so bad that it was affecting her health. She wasn't sleeping properly, was hardly eating and was constantly restless. No wonder she felt so unwell.

And she could not afford to be ill. Now that she was to be a fully independent woman, with no financial support from either a father or a husband, she would need to remain fit and strong if she was to earn her own income.

She continued with her breathing exercises, but they seemed to be having the opposite effect to the one intended. Instead of stilling her nerves, those pesky butterflies in her stomach were becoming more agitated. Her stomach clenched. She felt clammy and nausea swept through her.

This was the worst case of nerves she had ever experienced. She rose quickly from her seat, upsetting her make-up kit, rushed out of the dressing room and ran down the corridor to the bathroom.

Flora was waiting for her when she emerged, carrying a wash bowl and jug of warm water.

'I'm sorry about that,' Arabella said, wiping her mouth. 'I'm not usually this bad, but...you know...'

Flora smiled and handed her a flannel. While Arabella was washing her face Flora gently ran her hand up and down her spine.

'Never mind, Arabella,' she said in a conciliatory voice. 'You're not the first actress who has been with child while on stage and your costume is loose enough to hide your growing belly.'

Arabella stopped, then slowly lowered the flannel from the back of her neck. She stared at Flora and shook her head. 'No, I'm not...it's just... I'm just...'

Flora raised her eyebrows and tilted her head.

Could she be? She had put her mood swings, her fatigue and her tiredness down to the situation with Oliver. She had even decided her courses had stopped because she was so upset and worried about her plans to divorce him. And being sick, well, that was just nerves, wasn't it?

She could not be pregnant, not now.

The flannel dropped to the floor as her hands shot to her face to cover her mouth. This was a disaster. Of course she was pregnant. Pregnant by a man she didn't want to be with, a man she was going to divorce. A man she knew that, despite his faults, would insist on supporting her, would insist on being a father to his child.

She wanted to be free of him, but now she never would be.

It was worse than Oliver had expected. Not only had one of his father's mistresses arrived unannounced at Somerfeld Manor with her child in tow, a child that bore an uncanny similarity to the late Duke, but she had also informed his mother about all the other illegitimate children the errant Duke had fathered.

His mother had been totally bereft. Her illusions about her husband had been well and truly shattered, and Oliver was at a loss as to how he could repair the damage.

All he could do was to stay with his mother, to comfort her, to try to remind her of all the good times they had had as a family, all the things about her husband she had loved.

And his mother's crisis meant he could not leave her. He could not return to London and solve the crisis in his own marriage. He had continued to write to Arabella, to beg her to explain why she had left him, to let him know what he had done wrong and how he could repair any damage he had done.

But she had not replied. When a letter finally did arrive, its contents were most definitely not what he had expected.

Although he had been anxious to read the letter, he had forced himself to remain calm, to not snatch the letter off the footman's tray and rip it open to get at the contents. Instead he had walked to his desk, sat down and, with a calm bearing he had not felt, opened the letter.

But when he had read the contents his feigned calmness had evaporated. He had screwed up the letter, thrown it across the room, had paced up and down, desperately trying to release the explosive energy coursing through his body. In his mind he had argued with her, told her how wrong she was, how she should give him a second chance, until he had finally calmed down and realised that she was right.

It *had* only ever been a marriage of convenience, to get her out of a difficult situation and to save Lady Bufford's reputation, in danger of being destroyed by her bellicose husband.

And hadn't he always told himself that Arabella deserved someone better than him? Well, with their marriage over she had a chance to find that someone.

He had unscrewed the letter and read it again, then written to his own lawyer informing him of the planned divorce and telling him that he would accept whatever blame Arabella's lawyer wanted to throw at him.

He had also urged his lawyer to do everything he could to keep the divorce out of the papers, to protect Arabella's reputation and to make the guilt solely his own, no matter what the cost. He could withstand any scandal a divorce might bring—it wasn't as if he had a good reputation to tarnish. His reputation had lost any lustre it might have had many years ago and society tended to be forgiving of a man, particularly a duke, no matter how he transgressed.

His short-term marriage was to come to an end. He should be grateful to his wife for granting him his freedom, but it was not a sense of gratitude and freedom that filled Oliver's mind as the days passed by. Instead the world seemed to have turned a dull shade of grey.

But there was one ray of hope in an otherwise desolate landscape. During the weeks he had spent at Somerfeld Manor his mother had slowly started to get over the shock of knowing her husband wasn't the man she thought he was. He wouldn't tell her of the forthcoming divorce. She did not need to hear anything that might cause her to suffer a setback. But he knew he would have to eventually. She had asked repeatedly about Arabella and told him how much she was looking forward to seeing her delightful daughter-in-law again. All he could tell her was that Arabella was very busy with the play so was unable to get away—not entirely a lie.

As his mother's strength came back, she had even started to ask questions about the children her husband had fathered. She wanted to know their names, where they lived, what provisions had been made for them and what sort of people they were.

It seemed his mother had more inner strength than he had ever given her credit for.

She also approved of the fact that Oliver was ensuring they were all well looked after and eventually suggested that perhaps they could be invited to the Somerfeld estate, which was their family home after all.

Once this idea had entered her head, she became quite invigorated by the prospect of filling the Somerfeld estate with the sound of children's voices. It was obvious his mother was well on the way to recovery.

He wished he could say the same about himself. His lawyer had received no correspondence about the divorce, so all Oliver could do was wait. In the meantime he had decided to keep himself secreted away at his estate. During the day he took long walks with his mother, around the estate, and in the evenings, instead of partying, he could be found seated in his study, reading through the books that had not been touched for many years. He had no interest in seeing anyone else, no interest in entertaining or being entertained. It would be hard to believe if it wasn't actually happening, but the Duke of Somerfeld was becoming a hermit.

He doubted if he would leave the estate again until he had to go to London for the divorce. He just wished he was able to protect Arabella from any adverse publicity. His lawyer had informed him he would be unable to keep it a secret and there would be nothing he could do once it went to court and was in the public domain.

Oliver knew the newspapers would eat up such scandal, knowing that coverage of a divorce between a duke and an American actress would sell scores of newspapers and keep the readership entertained for many weeks. But as long as he kept a low profile, he would do nothing to add to the scandal and the upset that it might cause Arabella.

Returning from another long walk, he saw a carriage parked in front of the house. No one had been invited and his heart sank as he approached and saw Lord Bufford's crest on the carriage door.

It was the last thing he wanted right now, to deal with that buffoon.

Entering the house, the footman told him that Lady Bufford had arrived and had been seated in the blue drawing room.

Oliver was unsure whether that was better or worse news. Violet's company was also something he could do without right now.

As soon as he entered, she stood up and rushed towards him. 'You cannot, will not, involve me in this divorce,' she said in a garbled rush. 'There's already gossip about what your wife plans to do and I cannot get caught up in such a scandal. My husband would disown me. I'd be ruined. You cannot do this to me, Oliver. I beseech you, please, keep my name out of this.'

Oliver took her arm and gently led her to the nearest chair. 'My divorce has nothing to do with you, Violet. You won't be involved. Why would you even think that you might be?'

She sat down, but her hands continued to clasp and unclasp in an agitated manner. 'Well, I was your lover once, or have you forgotten?'

Oliver took a seat opposite her. 'That was before I was married, adultery has to occur after the marriage. You have nothing to worry about, Violet. Your name won't be mentioned.'

She stood again and paced the room. 'Well, you say that, but can you be so sure your wife won't say that you committed adultery with me?'

Oliver walked over to the mantelpiece. She was being ridiculous. She would not be involved in his divorce, but it was also obvious she needed reassurance. 'Arabella is not like that. And in the unlikely event that her lawyer did try to say we were having an affair, which I'm sure he won't, he would need to produce proof and no such proof exists.'

She turned and faced him, her hands clenched, her lips pinched. 'Well, your wife could say that I told her we were having an affair.' Her clenched hands tightened their grip and she resumed pacing. 'And then there's that stupid powder-room attendant. She heard it all. They could call her as a witness. I'd be ruined.' She sank down into a chair and gripped the sides of her head. 'If this was all made public, my husband would divorce *me*. I'd have nothing. I'd be shunned by society. You have to make sure she doesn't say anything.'

'What are you saying?' Oliver asked, his teeth clenched together. 'What did you say to Arabella? What did the attendant hear?'

'What?' Looking up at him, she saw his expression and gave a small laugh. 'Oh, don't look at me like that. It was just a bit of fun. On the night you were all celebrating at the Savoy. She was looking so smug, and you and her were so cosy, I decided to play a little trick on her. It was all a bit of foolishness at the time, but it's come back to bite me and I have to put it right. You have to put it right. I can't be dragged through the divorce courts.'

'What...did...you...say...to... Arabella?' Oliver asked, slowly enunciating each word.

'Oh, I told her that on your wedding night after you'd deflowered her you came to my bed. I saw her walking in the garden early in the morning after your wedding night and I heard through the servants that you and she had awoken in separate beds, so I knew something had gone wrong and I thought I'd wipe that smug look off her face. But please, Oliver, promise me that nothing that I said to her will come out in court.'

Without answering, Oliver left the room, jumped into Lady Bufford's carriage and ordered the driver to take him to the train station.

Chapter Twenty-Three

Oliver wasted no time. The moment the train pulled into the station, he leapt out, ran down the platform to the waiting cabs and ordered the driver to take him straight to the Limelight Theatre. He knew there was no need to hurry. Arabella would still be on stage and he wouldn't be able to speak to her until after her performance, but still he urged the driver to make haste. His heart was pumping so hard and his body was coiled tight like a spring. He was incapable of keeping still, incapable of slowing down. It was as if by constant motion he could speed up time.

He arrived at the Limelight Theatre and rushed down the alleyway and through the backstage entrance. Then he was forced to wait. He had no choice. But he was finding it impossible to stay still. For what felt like an interminable amount of time he paced backwards and forward, and repeatedly looked at his fob watch, the hands of which seemed to be moving unnaturally slowly.

Once again, he rehearsed what he was going to say. He didn't know if informing her of what Violet

Bufford had told him would make a difference. There might be other reasons why she wanted to divorce him—after all, he was hardly the sort of man a sensible woman would want to remain married to—but he had to try. He had to let her know he would not treat her in such a disrespectful manner.

When he heard the thunderous sound of the audience's final applause, he quickly walked through the backstage area to wait in the wings. To his mounting frustration, he had to endure a seemingly endless round of curtain calls. Once he would have been so proud of the ongoing accolades his wife was receiving, and he was still proud, he just wished the audience would hurry up and finish expressing their appreciation.

Finally, the cast came off stage, all chattering excitedly, all, that is, except his wife, her face inexplicably forlorn. She saw him and stopped in her tracks, her eyes wide, her body rigid, as if a wild animal was cutting off her path.

'Bella,' he said gently, 'I need to talk to you. Please, can you just give me a few minutes of your time?'

She gave him a wary, sideways glance. 'I don't believe we have anything to discuss. And anything you want to say to me can be said through our lawyers.'

'We do need to talk, Bella,' he pleaded. 'I've heard something that changes everything.'

Her shoulders slumped and she released a sigh of exasperation. 'I suppose you were bound to find out eventually, but it makes no difference. I still want a divorce. We'll work out the details later.'

He stepped towards her. 'Please, Bella, hear me

out. If you hear what I have to say, it might change things between us.'

She shook her head. 'No, Oliver. I still want a divorce. But I'm sure you'll want to be involved in our child's life. I won't stop that, but I don't want you involved in my life.'

Oliver stared at his wife as if she was speaking a foreign language. 'Child? What child?'

She tilted her head and stared at him; her gaze still wary. 'Isn't that why you're here, because you've heard that I'm with child?'

He struggled to breathe as he stared at her, trying to take in the implication of what she had just said. She was with child. He was going to be a father, something he had vowed would never happen. It was one of the two vows he had made to himself as a young man, so he could be sure of never hurting anyone the way his father had hurt so many. He had also promised that he would never marry. He'd already broken that vow when he'd married Arabella. Now he had broken the second vow. He was no better than his father after all. But he had tried to be careful, hadn't he? Hadn't he always withdrawn when they made love so that this would not happen?

He closed his eyes and drew in a strained breath. No, he hadn't. Not every time. Selfishly there had been times he had thought only of his own pleasure and had let his desire to be as close as possible to her override any thought of the consequences.

He opened his eyes. And now she was pregnant, pregnant with his child. He was going to be a father. Oliver smiled at the thought.

He was going to be a father.

His smile grew wider. Arabella was having his child. This beautiful, talented woman was going to be the mother of his child.

This was not bad news. Not bad news at all. It was the best news he had ever heard. 'Bella, that's wonderful. You're going to be a wonderful mother and don't worry about your acting career. After all, Lillie Langtry and Sarah Bernhardt both continued acting after they had children. If they can do it, then the fabulously talented Arabella Huntsbury can do it as well.' He knew he was babbling, but he couldn't stop. 'And my mother is going to love being a grandmother. This is the best news.'

She continued to look at him sideways, her expression still wary. 'You didn't know about the child?'

'No, but I couldn't be happier. You've made me a very happy man.'

'So why are you here?'

He tried to stop smiling, but couldn't. They were going to have a child together. He wanted to shout it out so all the world could hear. But that wasn't why he was here. He needed to concentrate. He forced his smiling face to take on a more serious demeanour. 'Violet Bufford visited me at Somerfeld Manor. She was worried that she might get caught up in the divorce proceedings.'

'Oh, I see.' She pushed past him and walked quickly down the corridor, her body rigid.

He rushed after her. 'Bella, we must talk. You must listen to me.'

She increased her walking pace. 'I don't have to listen to you and I certainly don't have to discuss your mistress's worries.'

He gently took her arms to halt her progress. 'Bella, please listen to me.'

She looked down at his hand, her face tight with disapproval. He was about to release her, but changed his mind. He would not let her flee before he had a chance to explain. 'I'm sorry, this is not coming out the way I meant. I rehearsed what I was going to say all the way here, but now I've made a mess of things.'

'Yes, you have,' she said, pulling against his grip.

'Violet Bufford lied to you,' he blurted out before she could pull away. 'She made up that story to hurt you. Of course I *didn't* spend our wedding night in her bed. I spent it lying in my own bed, staring at the door to your room. I didn't sleep. I just tossed and turned all night. All I could think about was you, so close but so unattainable.'

'Lady Bufford lied?' She stopped pulling against his grip and looked up at him.

'Yes, she lied. I most certainly wasn't thinking about her on our wedding night, or any other woman. In fact, I haven't thought of any other woman since I first kissed you in this very building.'

He released her arm and stared at her, the implication of his words hitting him. 'That's also true,' he said, hardly able to believe it himself. 'I haven't thought of another woman since I first saw you. Unbelievable.' He smiled in amazed joy. 'You're the only woman I ever think about. The only woman I want. The only woman I will ever want.' He looked down at her and shook his head. 'Bella, it seems I've fallen in love with you.'

She stared up at him, his own astonishment reflected in her face.

'Of course I've fallen in love with you.' He laughed with relief. 'That explains everything. It explains why I think about you the moment I wake up in the morning and continue to think about you until I fall asleep at night. Why I dream about you every night. It's because I love you.'

'You love me?' She whispered her question, staring up at him wide eyed.

'Yes, I love you,' he repeated, certain that he would never tire of saying those three words. 'When we said our wedding vows, I promised to forsake all others and that's exactly what I've done. I've forsaken all women not just in act, but in thought as well. Bella, you've done what I had once thought would be impossible. You have changed me, reformed me, made me the man I've always wanted to be, but thought I couldn't. Bella, I love you and I want to marry you. Will you marry me?'

'You…what…will I what?'

'I love you and I want to marry you. Bella, will you marry me?'

Her blue eyes still enormous, she shook her head. 'What? What are you talking about? We're already married. It was our divorce we were discussing.'

'But I don't want to divorce you. I want to marry you.'

'But…but…'

He pulled himself together. With the announcement of the baby and the realisation that he was in love he had lost track of what he was meant to be saying and he knew he was rambling. 'Why do you want to divorce me? Is it because you don't trust me? Is it because of Violet Bufford's lies? Because that's all they are, Bella, lies. Violet Bufford is an unhappy woman in an unhappy marriage. She wanted to ruin our happiness and she almost succeeded.'

She stared at him. 'But she said…she was so convincing… I thought—'

'And I can understand why you believed her. I can see why you thought a man like me would do something like that. I can see why you thought I could be so cruel and so selfish.' It was true. Violet Bufford had indeed lied, but Arabella had believed her lies because she knew he was capable of such despicable behaviour. That spoke volumes about the sort of man he was, a man who was certainly not worthy of her love. Perhaps he *was* a fool to think a woman like Arabella could ever love a man like him, even if he did love her entirely, with his mind, body and soul.

She placed her hand gently on his arm. 'You're not a cruel man, or a selfish one, Oliver,' she said quietly. 'You care about people. You're a loving son to your mother. And there's all those women and children you support. You even married me to get me out of a difficult situation with my father. A bad man would not have done that.'

She looked up at him with those soft blue eyes. 'And I realise now that of course Lady Bufford was lying. You would never do anything that cruel. You would never humiliate anyone in the way I thought you had humiliated me. I judged you harshly because I misjudged a man once before, a man I thought I loved, and I had been hurt as a result. I didn't want to be hurt again so I chose to believe Lady Bufford's lies.'

Hope blossomed inside him. 'Does that mean you

are willing to give me another chance, to give us another chance?' He clasped her hand in both of his. 'If you will, then I promise you, I will do everything in my power to be worthy of you. I have enough love for you to make it work and I already love our child, and perhaps if I prove myself you will come to love me the way I love you.'

She bit the edge of her lip. 'You *are* a worthy man, Oliver, you always have been. And, well… I suppose I love you as well,' she said in a quiet voice.

Hope flourished in Oliver's heart, making him feel light and buoyant. He put his hand to his ear as if he was hard of hearing. 'What was that? What did you say? Something about love?'

Her smile grew wider. 'Oh, all right. It's true. Yes, I'm in love with you as well. I think I started falling in love with you the first time you kissed me and that love has continued to grow. Yes, I love you, Oliver Huntsbury.'

It was exactly what Oliver wanted to hear. He picked her up, twirled her around before kissing her. 'And I love you, Arabella, with my heart and soul. I love being with you, laughing with you, talking with you and, of course, making love to you.'

A group of giggling actresses pushed past them and he lowered her slowly to the ground, his hands still around her waist.

'But if you're going to give me a second chance, then let me do this properly.' He dropped to one knee and took her hand in his. 'Arabella, would you do me the honour of becoming my wife? My real wife. I want to marry you, to cherish you and love you until death do us part.'

Arabella giggled. 'Well, I *do* want to marry you, but I'm already married, and I've already promised to stay with *him* until death do us part.'

'Oh, *him*, that man was never good enough for you, but I promise you I will be.'

'You already are, Oliver,' she laughed, pulling him to his feet.

With that he lifted her up and kissed her again, to the resounding applause of the cast who had emerged from their dressing rooms, all eager to see the real-life drama being played out before them.

Epilogue

Arabella took her bow, revelling in the applause of the ecstatic audience. When her run at the Limelight Theatre had finished, she'd taken up the offer to appear in the latest Gilbert and Sullivan production.

Flora had been right, she had been able to act through her confinement, although she doubted that would have happened without the support of her loving husband. Oliver had told her there was no reason why she couldn't have it all, motherhood and an acting career. And when their daughter, Olivia, was born he had been true to his word.

He had not only acted as her theatrical agent, but had also been a doting father, not to mention a wonderful husband and lover.

Arabella bowed again. As much as she was enjoying the success of the play, she was anxious to get back to her family. A family that not only included her husband and child, but stretched the length of the country. Now that Oliver's mother had discovered just how many children her husband had fathered she had been determined to include them all. It meant baby

Olivia was now part of a large extended family, with a multitude of doting uncles and aunts.

Even Arabella's father had joined the family, rather than continuing to seclude himself away in New York, buried in the world of finance.

As soon as Arabella had sent word that she was with child Mr van Haven had left New York and returned to England.

His reaction to her pregnancy had taken her by surprise. She had seen real fear on his face and throughout her pregnancy he had been constantly concerned about her well-being, wanting to call the doctor on an almost daily basis in reaction to a raft of imagined ailments.

Eventually she had asked him what was wrong, why he was behaving so out of character. After much prodding he had told her how her mother's death, as a result of complications following childbirth, had devastated him. Arabella's pregnancy had brought back all those emotions that his wife's death had caused, emotions that he had buried for the last twenty-one years. With tears in his eyes he apologised for the way he had closed down, had never been a true father to her, but he had been so scared of ever exposing himself to love again, and the pain it could cause, that he couldn't even show love to his only daughter. Instead he had focused solely on making more and more money, trying to fill the void left by his wife's death, but all that had done was make him more dead inside, had meant he had missed out on so much.

But he was making up for it now. Just like Oliver's mother, he too had become a doting grandparent. The two grandparents were spending so much time together Oliver and Arabella were beginning to wonder whether wedding bells might be chiming again in the near future.

A stagehand presented Arabella with a large bouquet of flowers as she took her final bow and departed the stage.

If they did marry, it would be the third marriage in the family. Oliver had insisted that they hold another marriage service, one that was a celebration rather than a mere contract. They had held it at the estate, with only his mother and the Duke and Duchess of Knightsbrook in attendance. It might not have been a real wedding, like the official wedding they had held in the church, but it had felt more real and had been the happiest day of Arabella's life. Up until the day she'd given birth, that is. Then she'd had the joy of becoming a mother and, since then, every day had become even more of a joy than the day before.

* * * * *

If you enjoyed this book, why not check out Eva Shepherd's stunning debut

Beguiling the Duke